Praise for Jinxed

"Fast-paced, sizzlingly sexy fun!"
~USA Today bestselling author Karyn Monk

"JINXED is an enjoyable private investigative romance that has the feel of the 1930s Hepburn-Grant madcap comedies. The story line is fun to follow as Jake does not know whether he needs to lock up or kiss Afia. Fans of screwball romantic romps will enjoy the love tale of the socialite and the sleuth."
~Amazon.com #1 Reviewer, Harriet Klausner

10 out of 10! "Every once in a great while, a writer comes along and really breaks new ground. What makes JINXED so different from other detective-dame stories is the totally original 'voice' of author Beth Ciotta. The whole package works. I found myself laughing out loud and falling in love with Afia and Jake and flat out rooting for them to succeed on their own and as a couple. Can't wait to read more from this promising new-to-me author."
~Review by Live2WriteNow at www.reviewcentre.com

Jinxed

by Beth Ciotta

GOLD IMPRINT

Dedication

For Helen Rosburg and Leslie Burbank:
two mavericks who spin dreams into
heart-tripping reality.

March 2004
Published by Medallion Press, Inc.
225 Seabreeze Ave.
Palm Beach, FL 33480

ISBN 0-9743639-4-4

Printed in the United States of America

For more great books visit www.medallionpress.com.

Acknowledgments

My thanks to:

Cynthia Klimback, Julia Templeton, and Mary Stella: cherished friends, amazing critique partners, and persistent warriors. Thank you for your invaluable input and for slaying my personal demons (aka creative insecurities) on a daily basis enabling me to conquer this exciting challenge.

Linnea Sinclair for her overall generosity and insight into the life of a private investigator.

Sebastian Goldstein for his friendship, support, and legal expertise.

Melanie Rice and Duane Leeds: treasured friends and true inspirations. You enrich my world with your humor, heart, and artistic pursuits.

Stephanie Bond, Sandra Chastain, Kathryn Falk, Heather Graham, and Connie Perry for their friendship, guidance, and never-ending support. I am blessed to have you in my life.

Steve Ciotta, my husband and true-life hero. Thank you for supporting my dream, especially when I'm stressing out over plot points, writer's block, and deadlines. You are a generous, inspiring soul, and you fill my heart with joy.

Author's Note

Although this story takes place in Atlantic City, New Jersey (the, gaming playground of the East Coast), please note that the Carnevale Casino, the Bizby, the Sea Serpent, and the Seaside Charity Committee are purely fictional.

Chapter One

"Declined."

"Excuse me?" Afia blinked at the quasi-Euro sales associate, a black-rimmed spectacled, chic-suited man who three minutes before had been all smiles and pleasantries.

"Your privileges have been revoked, Ms. St. John."

The woman standing behind her in line snickered. Afia blushed. Exclusive shops such as *Bernard's* treated their patrons like royalty. So why did she suddenly feel like the rabble? "There must be some mistake."

The associate retained a deadpan expression. "Perhaps you'd like to try another card."

Her business manger, Henry Glick (a financial wizard according to her mother), had asked her to make all of her purchases on one specific credit card until further notice. Something to do with interest rates and consolidation. So seven months ago she'd handed over the bulk of her cards to Mr. Glick, except for the American Express that she'd tucked away for emergencies. As her dignity was at stake just now, she considered this a genuine crisis. Fishing her Gucci wallet out of her matching handbag, Afia handed the sales associate her backup card. He slid her platinum plastic through the gizmo next to the cash register, starting the process all over again, leaving her to ponder the mystery of her "declined" Visa. Obviously, the card was defective. As soon as she got home she'd call Mr. Glick and have him order her a replacement.

The clerk glanced up, with one haughty eyebrow raised, and a trace of a smirk playing at his glossed lips.

Afia's stomach clenched. *Stop looking at me like that. I haven't done anything wrong.* Funny how many times she'd wanted to scream that sentiment in her cursed life. But as always she kept her feelings inside. Calm. Dignified.

The associate sidled over to the phone and placed a call.

Afia tucked silky strands of poker-straight hair behind her diamond-studded ears and willed her pulse steady. *I haven't done anything wrong.*

Casting her a sidelong glance, the associate mumbled a cryptic "uh-huh" and "I see," and then hung up. He returned and passed Afia her American Express. "Declined."

Bernard's four other patrons—plump-lipped, tight-skinned women who looked as though they frequented the same plastic surgeon—conversed in hushed tones. Afia hated being the center of gossip. Mortified, she leaned over the counter and crooked a finger at—she glanced at his nametag—"Douglas. There must be something wrong with your credit card device."

"Our Zon is functioning properly. I'm afraid it's your credit that's in question. Perhaps you'd like to write a check."

"I don't have my checkbook." Mr. Glick oversaw her bank

2

account and paid her bills. She'd been relying on cash and her Visa for months. She'd yet to have a problem. Until now. "Please try again." Panic fluttered in her chest as she re-offered Douglas her Glick-approved Visa. Those strapless, wedge-heeled Chanels sat on the counter waiting to be bagged. The perfect mates to the silk shantung dress she'd just purchased at Saks.

Two minutes later, Douglas re-shelved the wedge-heeled Chanels. On the verge of hyperventilating, Afia fled *Bernard's*. The shoe fiasco had dashed the last of her tremulous composure as she navigated the bustling city sidewalk. She'd survived two high profile weddings and three funerals in seven years. Not to mention the unflattering media surrounding her bizarre personal dramas. Being labeled "The Black Widow" by an unfeeling gossip columnist had been the cruelest blow. Anyone who knew her, knew the insinuation was absurd. Still, her second husband's sudden death had earned her a fair share of suspicious double takes. Her small circle of friends had dwindled to one. She'd managed to cope and found shopping a temporary cure-all for her ever-increasing bouts of depression. But surely, *surely* she hadn't shopped herself into the poorhouse. Each of her husbands had left her a fortune.

Her mind racing with one horrible possibility, she quickened her spike-heeled steps and avoided walking under a workman's ladder only to step on a crack in the pavement. Out of habit she clutched her left wrist and stroked the charm bracelet her dad had given her to counteract ill luck. That's when she felt it. The gap. She quickly fingered the charms, ticking them off in her mind—horseshoe, wishbone, four-leaf clover— stumbling twice in her haste to make it to the car. The third time she went down. Face down on the crowded sidewalks of Fifth Avenue.

Rudy came to her rescue. The muscle-bound chauffeur whisked her up and carried her to his double-parked limousine. "Animal," he said of a snickering passerby and then opened the door and helped her into the back seat.

"I'm all right," she said.

"You're crying," Rudy said. "And you've got a run in your hose."

Afia glanced at her left shin and cried harder. "Darn!"

"I knew this wasn't a good idea. I should've taken you shopping somewhere cheerful and sunny. Like Miami." Rudy slammed her door, took his place behind the wheel, and revved the engine. "What happened in there?"

"They declined me."

"What?"

"Never mind." *Sniffle.* "I just want to go home." Again, she glanced at her charms. Twelve. She counted only twelve. There were supposed to be thirteen, unlucky thirteen acting as reversed bad luck. She was missing her gold moneybag marked with the dollar sign. The charm that represented "wealth." She could have lost it in any one of several stores. Or on the street. Down a grate, in the gutter. *Gone,* her rational mind whispered. It was the only thing that kept her from going back and searching every square inch of Manhattan. This bracelet had been a gift from her dad, her champion, the good-humored buffer between her and her superstitious mother. Losing a charm was like losing a piece of her hero. It also smacked of a bad omen. Hands trembling, she pushed aside a day's worth of shopping bags and searched her leather satchel for tissues and her cellular.

She punched in her business manager's number while Rudy eased his way into the bumper-to-bumper traffic. "Be home, Mr. Glick. Please be home."

Rrrring. Rrrring. "I'm sorry. The number you have dialed has been disconnected. Please—"

She hung up and speed dialed his cell number.

Rrrring. Rrrring. "I'm sorry. The number you have dialed—"

"Henry, how could you!" She strangled the phone wishing it were Henry Glick's skinny, double-crossing neck, and then dropped the cell in her lap. Mental note: Strike Glick off of my Christmas list! Stroking her wounded bracelet, she glanced out the tinted side window, tears blurring her vision and distorting her view of Manhattan. In her hypersensitive state, the sky-scrapers tilted, threatening to crumble and crush her. The relentless traffic melded, threatening to run her over. She missed her Dad. Randy, and Frank. The men in her life who made everything all right. She knew that made her unfashion-ably dependent. Yet how did one fight one's nature? She'd been trying to cope, struggling to maintain proper grace. Losing that lucky charm, a charm she'd had since she was thir-teen years old, had been the final straw. "I can't breathe," she squeaked, suddenly and horribly overwhelmed.

Rudy blared the limo's horn, jerking the wheel left as a taxi veered too close. "Idiot."

Afia sobbed into a handful of tissues.

"Not you, honey. The cabbie." He edged over into the far

lane behind an exhaust-belching bus. "What's going on, Afia?"

She blew her nose and then glanced up, meeting Rudy's concerned blue gaze in the rearview mirror. Dear, sweet Rudy. Her chauffeur. Her best friend. Her only link to sanity this past emotionally charged year. "I'm not sure."

"Just remember, honey, everything happens for a reason. No matter how bad it seems, it could always be worse."

Rudy had been spouting new-age assurances for three weeks now. Ever since he'd discovered the self-help section of Amazon.com. She wished he'd stop. The more he tried to lift her spirits, the more she drifted toward despair. Self-help suggested helping one's self. Relying on one's own judgment. Trusting one's instincts. As her mother was fond of pointing out to Afia, following her instincts generally led her to disaster. Sick to her stomach, she picked up the phone and dialed her no-nonsense godfather.

He answered on the third ring. "Hello?"

"Harmon?"

"Afia? I'm in the middle of a golf game, Peanut. What is it?"

"Oh, Harmon." She hiccupped twice before regaining control. "My credit cards. They . . . they . . ."

"What?"

"Mr. Glick. He . . . he . . ."

"What? What did Henry do? Where are you?"

"Manhattan. Oh, Harmon they . . . they . . ."

"They who? They what? Afia stop sobbing and tell me what's going on."

"They were so cute, the strapless Chanels, and I . . . I couldn't buy them. I was . . ." *hiccup, sniffle,* "declined."

Harmon groaned. "Go ahead," he said to someone else. "I'll meet you at the clubhouse. Afia."

"What?"

"Where are you exactly?"

"In the limo."

"With Rudy?"

She nodded.

"Peanut, I have the feeling you're nodding. That doesn't help."

"Rudy's driving," she croaked.

"Put him on."

She leaned forward, handed the phone to Rudy, and then rooted through her bag for more tissues.

"Yes, sir, Mr. Reece." The metro bus stopped short. Rudy jammed on his brakes.

Afia flew forward, landing on the carpeted floor on all fours. "Darn!"

Rudy glanced over his big shoulder. "Are you hurt?"

She climbed back up into her seat and inspected her right knee. "Another run."

He sighed and then focused back on the traffic. Putting the phone back to his ear, he answered, "She's fine." Again he glanced over his shoulder. "Mr. Reece said buckle up."

She nodded and waved him off, contemplating her stockings. Ruined. Much like her life.

"To get home?" Rudy shrugged. "Two to three hours. I'm gridlocked. Yes, sir. As soon as possible."

He passed the phone back to Afia. "Harmon?" She kicked off her three-hundred-dollar Prada pumps and peeled off her pricey sheer to waist hosiery. "Tell me I'm imagining the worst."

"I have to make some calls. Did Rudy stock the mini-fridge?"

She pried open the door with her big toe. "Laurent Perrier `76."

"Drink up, Peanut. Kick back and don't worry. Rudy will have you home in no time. I'll meet you there."

"You're suggesting I tie one on at two in the afternoon, Harmon. That doesn't coincide with *don't worry*."

"Then don't think about it." *Chirp*.

Chirp. She tossed the phone into her bag, cracked open the Laurent Perrier, and proceeded not to think about it.

For three hours and twenty-five minutes.

By the time they reached South Jersey, she was feeling no pain.

Rudy pulled into the circular drive of her second husband's summer home. Odd, Frank had been gone for almost a year, and she still thought of the sprawling three-story stucco as his home. She'd never warmed to the ultra-modern design. In recent months she'd filled the stark, spacious rooms with nine-teenth-century art and antique furniture. Anything old to offset the cold contemporary feel.

But for all the clutter the house remained hollow and lonely.

Like her.

She glared through the limo's window at the offending architectural monstrosity, tensing when she saw Harmon waiting on the doorstep.

Rudy opened the car door. Refusing his help, she climbed out with four shopping bags looped over her toned, creamy arms, and, on shaky legs, wove her way to the polo-shirted lawyer's side. "Give it to me straight, Harmie. I can take it." She'd spent the last few hours bolstering herself with vintage champagne and Rudy's guru advice. The more she drank, the more he sounded like the Dalai Lama. Who wouldn't take heart under the Dalai Lama's guidance? *Everything happens for a reason. No matter how bad it seems, it could always be worse.* "How much did Glick embezzle?"

Grim-faced, Harmon pulled her into his arms and whispered in her ear.

Rudy was wrong. It couldn't be worse.

"I'll fix this, Peanut."

Afia dropped her bags and clutched her chest, her alcohol-induced bravado obliterated. "I'm *broke*."

"Financially challenged," Harmon countered. "A temporary inconvenience. Wait until your mother hears about this. Henry better pray that it's me who tracks him down."

"Mother's somewhere in Tahiti," she said, half dazed. "On her honeymoon. She left specific instructions not to be disturbed." Weary of widowhood, Giselle had married Bartholomew Tate, a pompous bonbon baron who seemed intent on widening the already canyon-sized gap between mother and daughter. Could Harmon fix that, too?

"She'd want to know."

"She's already put out with me. Absolutely not."

"All right then. You'll stay with Viv and me while we figure this out."

"Thank you, but no." She turned her back on both men. Stepping onto the manicured lawn, she circled the rose bed in a liquor-fogged daze. "I'm *poor*." She'd been born into money. Married money. Now she couldn't afford a bubble bath let alone a day at the spa.

"You're staying with me," Harmon insisted.

She was tempted. Harmon would take care of her. Somehow, some way, he'd make everything all right. Rudy's self-help preaching rang in her ears. *The sooner you stop looking to others to fix your problems, the sooner your problems will disappear.* "I couldn't impose," she heard herself saying.

"I'm your godfather."

"I'm in between roommates," Rudy said.

"You need someone to share the rent," Afia said, still circling. "I can't do that. I don't have any money. Or credit." She swept aside her blunt-cut bangs to massage a dull throb at the center of her forehead. "What about my charities?"

Harmon spread his hands wide. "If you're that concerned—"

"Of course, I'm concerned!"

"You could donate your time instead of money," Rudy suggested.

"She already donates her time," Harmon said, clearly annoyed.

Intoxicated as she was, Afia knew what Rudy meant. Serving on a committee was all well and good but there were other ways to help. Still, the thought of not being able to make her usual monetary contributions made her nauseous. Thanks to Henry Glick she was not only unable to provide for others but she was also unable to provide for herself. "How am I going to pay off my shopping debts?" The furniture, the paintings, the *clothes*.

Rudy shrugged. "You could get a job."

Harmon snorted. "That's just crazy."

Afia frowned, rebellion rumbling in her belly. Or maybe it was the champagne. She threw back her shoulders and on second try successfully crossed her arms over her insignificant chest. "Why is that crazy?" She freed one hand and smacked Rudy's impressive pecs. "That's an excellent idea. I'll get a job." Definitely the champagne.

Harmon gawked. "You haven't worked a day in your life. What would you do?"

Afia nudged Rudy, and together they collected her designer shopping bags. "I have skills," she informed her godfather. "Now come inside and help me figure out what they are. You too, Rudy."

"This could take all night," the older man mumbled, reaching out to steady her as she staggered toward the mansion's front door.

She shrugged off Harmon's help along with the hurt of his lack of faith. Something had snapped inside of her on the tense ride home. She'd spent her entire life being sheltered and maneuvered. Being told that others knew what was best for her. She'd believed them, too. Right up until today. When a man she'd trusted implicitly because her mother had told her to, stole her every cent.

Her life was out of control because she had no control in her life. At least that's what Rudy had said midway down the Garden State Parkway. "I'm going to track down Henry Glick and get my money back," she declared as she struggled to punch the security code into the keypad. "Starting tomorrow I'm taking responsibility for my life."

The door swung open. Miscalculating the foyer steps, she

tripped and tumbled flat out on the polished Italian marble. Heart pounding with determination, Afia pushed herself up on her elbows, blew her bangs off of her forehead, and hiccupped. "Tomorrow I'm getting a job."

Chapter Two

"Jake Leeds to see Harmon Reece."

The prim-suited secretary scanned her appointment book and then Jake. Her hazel gaze hovered below his silver belt buckle a full five seconds before drifting up and over his shoulders, settling at last on his face. She smiled. "Mr. Reece will be right with you. Can I get you anything? Coffee? Tea?"

Me? Jake read her playful grin and flashed a one-dimpled smile. "No, thank you, Miss . . ."

"Givens. Marla Givens."

"Miss Givens."

"Marla."

Marla had one of those throaty voices, the kind that caused a man to sit up and take notice. The fact that she dressed like a librarian only heightened the allure. "No thank you, Marla."

Too anxious to play a witty game of innuendos, he excused

himself with a wink and then turned and feigned interest in the seascape photographs lining the law firm's walls. Normally, he would've taken advantage of Marla's interest, charmed her, and asked her out on a date. She was a looker, regardless of her buttoned-to-the-neck blouse and mid-shin-length skirt, and he could use a contact here in the office. But there was nothing normal about this moment.

Harmon usually doled out assignments over lunch and scotch. Being summoned to the offices of Reece, Mitchell and Cooper tweaked his suspicions. He sensed a juicy case with a fat fee.

Perfect timing.

"Mr. Reece will see you now."

Jake thanked the dreamy-eyed woman with a practiced smile then strode to the ornate mahogany door displaying Harmon's engraved nameplate. Sliding into corporate-private-eye-mode, he tugged at the cuffs of his single-breasted dove-gray jacket and straightened his gray and burgundy striped tie. He would have preferred a mock tee and leather blazer to this monkey suit, but when in Rome . . . He knocked.

"Come in."

He entered, arm extended. "Harmon."

"Jake." The esteemed lawyer rose, shook the proffered hand, and then motioned him into a rustic brown leather chair.

"How's Joni?"

He froze midway to relaxing against the high-backed seat. Harmon's interest in his sister surprised him. "Happily married and seven months pregnant."

"That's nice." Harmon reclaimed his seat behind his massive antique desk. For all the space, only necessities occupied the polished desktop. Laptop. Phone. Lamp. A blotter, free of scribbles and doodles. Nice and neat. Just like Harmon. "Last time we spoke you still hadn't replaced her."

Still wondering at the man's angle, Jake stretched out his long legs and crossed them at the ankle. "I've been through four temps, each one worse than the one before. I'm beginning to think Joni was one of a kind." His kid sister had been his secretary and undercover sidekick rolled into one. His partner at Leeds Investigations for the last three years. Until an abnormal ultra-sound had forced her to bed rest. Although the crisis had passed, she was still under orders to take it easy.

His expression intense, Harmon rested his elbows on the desk and steepled his fingers.

Here it comes. Jake used to care more about the case than the cash, but not these days.

"I know another one-of-a-kind," the lawyer said. "Afia St. John."

"Your goddaughter?"

Harmon nodded. "She's looking for a job, and I want you to hire her."

"Why? She's rich." Compliments of her daddy and two husbands, one a legal eagle, the other the president of a pharmaceutical company.

"Not any more. Between you and me, and I mean it Jake, I don't want to read about it in the papers tomorrow, she was screwed over by her business manager."

"How much?"

"All of it."

"That's—"

"A small fortune."

Jake whistled. "Sonuvabitch skip the country?"

"Looks that way."

"Contacted the cops?"

"No."

Intrigued, he unfolded his legs and leaned forward, forearms braced on his thighs. "No cops. No press."

Harmon nodded.

"Any leads?"

"A couple."

Jake waited for details. Waited for Harmon to put him on the case.

"I'm worried about her," the older man said. He spread his hands flat on the ivory blotter. "She won't take any money from me, and she won't let me contact her mother. Thanks to the damned creditors Afia's living with a friend."

Jake shifted in his seat. He knew all about creditors.

"She's displaying an independent streak that has me baffled and, quite frankly, worried. I think she's having a nervous breakdown."

"Just because she wants to get a job? Seems the reasonable thing to do when you have no money."

"She has money," he said, toying with a sterling silver pen. "It's just in another man's hands. Something I'm in the process of rectifying."

Why the hell was Harmon beating around the bush? "That's why you sent for me," Jake said, helping him out. "You want me to track the guy."

Harmon shook his balding head. "I hired someone else to do that."

Jake waited.

"Kilmore."

Ah. Oscar Kilmore. Philadelphia's finest. Big-time agency. State-of-the-art equipment. A secretary *and* a field associate. A pain in Jake's ass. "So why am I here?"

"I told you. I want you to hire Afia. You need an assistant. She needs—*wants*—a job."

"So she asked her influential godfather to arrange one." Typical.

"I wish that were the case. As I told you, she won't accept my help. Not on any level. She's been acting on her own, hired and fired from two jobs in three weeks."

Jake drummed his fingers on the arms of the chair jonesing for a cigarette. "And you want me to take her on."

"I would deem it a personal favor. I have to leave town for a few days on business. I need to know she's safe."

Still smarting over Kilmore, Jake pushed out of the leather high-back. "Get someone else. I'm doing just fine with an answering machine." He didn't need this.

"I'll pay you."

Or maybe he did. Temples pulsing, he studied the toes of his Doc Martins and took a deep breath. What had possessed him to take out that mortgage? Why did his kid sister have to marry a free-lance musician? No health benefits. Unreliable income. Christ. His gaze flicked to Harmon. "How exactly would that work?"

"I'll double your corporate fee and pay her salary."

Jake loosened his tie. "Damn."

Harmon shrugged. "She's important to me. Her father and I were like brothers. I promised I'd take care of her if anything ever happened to him. I screwed up when I didn't take a firmer hand after her second husband died. I allowed her mother to bully her into hiring Henry Glick as her business manager. Financial wizard, my ass. That's what I get for trusting Giselle's instincts." He sighed. "What's done is now left for me to undo. All I ask is that you keep Afia busy. Keep her out of trouble until her mother returns from her honeymoon."

"Which will be . . ."

"Two weeks. Meanwhile I have Kilmore on the case."

"So you said." Jake's pride stung. All the same, he couldn't dismiss that kind of money. Couldn't get his mind off of Joni and her escalating medical bills. "I'm a private investigator, Harmon, not a babysitter."

"And as a P.I.," the man reasoned, "you sometimes protect as well as detect. Yes?"

"Your point?"

"I'm hiring you to protect Afia."

"From who?"

"Herself. She's a disaster waiting to happen."

"Waiting to happen?" Newspaper articles whizzed through his mind like reels of microfiche. "She's the one who accompanied Judge St. John on that fateful safari."

"As if she had any control over a rabid rhino."

"Gave her first husband a heart attack."

Harmon poked his tongue in his cheek. "But what a way to go."

"And that second guy—"

"Dumb luck."

"And now this. Ripped off by her business manager." Jake shook his head. "The woman's jinxed."

"Listen, just because she was born on Friday the thirteenth—"

"You're joking."

"—that doesn't mean she's jinxed. I don't care what Giselle says."

"Her mother's superstitious?"

"Worse. Paraskevidekatriaphobic."

"Fear of . . ."

"Friday the thirteenth."

"I'll be damned."

"Actually, if one puts stock in folklore that would be Afia." Harmon raised one wiry, silver brow. "So will you do it?"

Eyes narrowed, Jake braced his hands on the desk and leaned in. "Why me?"

"I trust you."

"Uh-huh." This assignment had fiasco written all over it. Shoving off the desk, he made a last-ditch suggestion. "If you really think she needs protection, get Colin Murphy. He specializes in bodyguard services."

"I don't want Murphy. I want you." Harmon blew out an impatient breath. "Are you in the middle of one of your special cases?"

"No."

"Then what's the problem?"

Other than having the insane urge to invest in a boatload of rabbits' feet and four-leaf clovers, he couldn't say exactly.

The older man opened his top drawer and withdrew his checkbook. "Obviously, Afia is to know nothing of our arrangement. As far as she's concerned, we don't know each other."

"How will she know about *the job*?"

"Leave that to me." He signed his name at the bottom, folded the check, and passed it to Jake. "A substantial retainer."

Swallowing his pride, Jake pocketed the money. "Tell her to be at my office Monday morning, ten a.m. sharp." *What the hell?* he thought. How inept could Afia St. John be?

Chapter Three

"Are you computer literate?"

"I know the basics."

"Can you type?"

"If I look at the keys."

"File?"

Afia fidgeted in her seat, uncomfortable with her prospective employer's clipped tone. "I'm sure if you explained your system . . ."

"You can answer the phone, right?"

"Of course."

"Jot down messages?"

"Yes." She sighed. "Mr. Leeds—"

"Call me Jake." He opened his top right drawer. Closed it. "What about coffee?"

"No, thank you, Jake. I'm already over my limit this morning."

His keen emerald gaze shifted from the drawer to her bouncing legs.

She willed them steady and offered a weak smile.

"Caffeine gives me the jitters." *And so do you.* She was accustomed to men falling all over her. She'd been blessed with good looks, exquisite taste, and old money. Qualities that appealed to 99% of the male population. Apparently, Jake Leeds was in the one-percent minority. He showed no signs of adoration. In fact, he'd seemed vaguely annoyed with her from the moment she'd walked into his unaesthetic reception area, though she couldn't imagine why. She'd been on time. She'd dressed appropriately. A carnation pink Prada shift with coordinating sling backs. Professional, yet cheery. Still, he kept studying her with that disturbing, disapproving gaze.

I haven't done anything wrong.

He'd probably read about her in the papers. Although she'd bet her Gucci sunglasses he skipped the gossip columns, he no doubt skimmed Region and Lifestyles. Maybe he'd read her name in one of her two wedding announcements. Or in one of the three obituaries. Or maybe he'd caught the article on Frank's golfing accident. Sports section, front page. An eleven-month-old headline, but bizarre tales lingered in one's memory. No doubt Jake Leeds was wondering why on earth he should hire Atlantic County's own Urban Legend.

Afia's stomach twisted. She not only needed this job, she *wanted* this job. She couldn't afford to hire a private investigator to track down Henry Glick. But if she worked for one . . . She resisted the urge to stroke her charm bracelet. Rudy had suggested creative visualization over a sentimental talisman. Since she was striving to better control her fate, she visualized herself sitting behind that hideous beige metal receptionist desk, utilizing the skills she'd learned from a cranky P.I. to locate a shifty thief.

"I meant can you make it?"

"Excuse me?"

"Coffee."

Her cheeks warmed. "Oh." She wasn't sure, but she thought he cracked a hint of a smile. Or was it a smirk? Either way, at least it made the stony-faced Mr. Leeds more human. His boxer-build and dangerous aura superseded his boyishly handsome face. He was, in a word, intimidating. "I make excellent cappuccino."

"What about plain old coffee?"

"Percolated?"

"Automatic. Ten-year old Mr. Coffee."

"I can do that."

"Great. You're hired."

"I am?" His war-zone desktop suggested that he was desperate. Scattered files, phone books, and roadmaps. A mound of receipts. Stacks of CDs and abandoned coffee cups. How could he function effectively in such chaos?

He scooped up a small stack of manila folders. "You can start with these. Staple the data sheets into the folders and then file them alphabetically by last name." That pesky smile or smirk or whatever made another brief appearance. "That's my system."

"You want me to start today? Right now?"

"Is that a problem?"

"No!" She cleared her throat. "I mean, no." *I just can't believe it.* "I just need a minute. I left my . . ." she fluttered a hand toward the outer door. "The car, it's . . ."

"Go ahead," he said, still holding onto the folders.

She reached out to relieve him of the files, and their fingers brushed. An innocent touch that made her blush and set her heart fluttering. Unsettled, she jerked back, tipping over her brown vinyl chair. The folders slid out of her grasp. Papers scattered to the four corners.

Jake stood and rounded his desk.

She cringed at his mumbled curse, relatively certain she hadn't heard "fudge." Two seconds into her new job and she was already ticking off her employer. A new record. At this rate, he'd fire her before day's end.

No. She wouldn't let that happen. She'd endured repeated humiliation these past three weeks thanks to heartless creditors and impatient employers. She may not have a talent for juggling numbers or a burgeoning food tray, but filing and making coffee? This she could handle.

This screamed of disaster. Jake eyed Afia St. John wondering who should get his head examined first. Him or Harmon? Jinxed? Unlucky? Inept? Talk about an understatement.

He bent over.

She bent over.

Their heads knocked.

Jake straightened with a curse.

"I'm sorry. I . . ."

He grimaced at the tears shining in her wide brown eyes. Don't you *dare* cry, lady. If she cried he'd have to comfort her. Which might entail holding her in his arms. Which would definitely entail risking what was left of his control. He was a private investigator, a master at concealing his emotions, an expert on practiced behavior, but he was also a man. *She* was a goddess. An accident-prone goddess, but nonetheless, a living, breathing angel on earth. He'd known she was pretty. He'd seen pictures. Last year alone she'd made the region section and the sports page. But, damn, in person she was captivating. A five-foot-two, doe-eyed, glossy-haired waif with impeccable taste in clothing. A twice-widowed beauty with questionable job skills and piss-poor business sense.

"I'll get them," she said. "My fault."

She kneeled, her form-fitting dress hiking up to reveal shapely thighs, her head level with his . . . Christ. He stooped down to hide an untimely erection. "I've changed my mind," he said.

Hands full of ill-sorted data sheets, she looked him square in the eye.

Oomph. A punch in the gut. He had a very hard time reconciling this vulnerable woman with her media nickname. "Black Widow?" More like "Lost Puppy."

"You're firing me?"

"Look, I . . ."

She scrambled to her feet, affording him a brief, heart-tripping peek up her skirt.

Jake rose, damning Harmon and his misplaced trust. Well, not misplaced, but certainly inconvenient. A man would have to be dead not to be attracted to Afia St. John. Although two men who *had* been attracted to her *were* dead. Good thing he wasn't superstitious, otherwise he'd have to show Ms. St. John the door, screw the money. Bolstering himself, he zeroed in on the trembling woman, prepared for waterworks. She surprised him with fire.

"You can't dismiss me," she said in rush. She glanced down at his appointment book and the blinking light on his message machine. "You're overwhelmed. I can help."

Jake eyed the scattered case files. "This is helping?"

"I have excellent people skills," she continued. "I'm courteous and . . . and I'm a good listener. Your clients will love me." She glanced around the room, brow creased as though she were in pain. "I'm also organized and have a flair for decorating."

"Forget it."

"But—"

"No decorating."

Hope sparked in luminous sable eyes. "What about the good with people part?"

"I'm fine with the good with people part."

She smiled, a thankful smile that twisted his gut into a knot. Well, hell. Normally an unforgiving judge of character, he cursed his bleeding-heart reaction. Beautiful, pampered, born and married into money—she was a walking cliché. It was absurd to feel anything for her other than blatant lust.

"So I'm not fired?"

"You were never fired." He bent over to gather the rest of his files.

"But, I thought—"

"You jumped to conclusions. We'll have to work on that. I was merely about to suggest that we postpone your start time until you go home and change."

He felt more than saw her tense. "What's wrong with what

I'm wearing?"

Nothing. "Everything." He scanned her petite body—from strappy pointy-toed heels to belted waist to scooped neckline— while rising to place the papers on his desk. Classy. Sexy as hell. Skinny for his taste, but that face . . . huge soulful eyes, lush pink lips . . . Hell. "Unless otherwise notified," he said, craving a cold shower, "dress to blend. That means no bright colors. No short skirts." He pointed to her dainty pink shoes. "How the hell do you expect to run in three-inch heels?"

"I'll be running?"

"You never know. And do something with your hair."

She smoothed a delicate hand over her loose, sable locks looking as though he'd just insulted her to the quick. "Like what?"

Like shave it off. But imagining her bald didn't diminish his desire. "Try a ponytail."

"Anything else?"

"Nix the perfume." The light, spicy scent would get a rise out of a Eunuch.

"Anything *else*?"

"Lose the limo."

* * *

Afia descended the narrow stairs of the four-story walkup, dazed and intrigued. No one had ever criticized her sense of fashion. According to her mother, her good looks and unique style were the two things she had going for her. Something high-profile men would appreciate. Men like Randy and Frank. Indeed, her adoring husbands had positioned her on a lofty pedestal. Young, pretty, and eager to please, aside from her occasional brushes with misfortune, she'd been the perfect trophy wife.

Her deceased husbands, both driven, successful men, had preferred she not work as it enabled her to concentrate on their needs. Serving on the Seaside Charity Committee, they'd said, was work enough, and politically advantageous. They'd given her *carte blanche* when it came to shopping. Both liked that she turned heads. Not that it was a conscious act on her part. She just happened to enjoy designer fashion, a bonus when one circulated in a world of dinner parties and black-tie affairs. Her wardrobe, just about the only thing that hadn't been repossessed, consisted mainly of silk suits, chiffon blouses, and beaded evening gowns.

Dress to blend? Jeans, T-shirts and sneakers? Did the prickly P.I. have any idea of what he was asking? And his last request . . . *lose the limo.* How did he know she'd come by limousine? Unless he'd been looking out his fourth-story window when she'd arrived. But then, even if he didn't know who she was *specifically,* he'd assumed that she was privileged. Wouldn't he wonder why she was applying for a job as a glorified receptionist? Wouldn't he ask? The more she thought about it the greater her confusion. What had just happened?

She hit the last flight of stairs, brow scrunched.

Rudy waited at the bottom. He closed the book he'd been reading (no doubt a guide to some sort of enlightenment), smoothed his onyx suit jacket, and smiled. "How'd it go?"

"He hired me."

"Great."

"Strange."

"Why?"

She paused on the second to the last step, putting herself eye to eye with her six-foot-three friend. "I'm not qualified." Despite her bluster not two minutes before, her confidence waned. Yes, she was good with people, but she was a self-taught typist and clueless about computer programs beyond Microsoft Word. Wouldn't he need her to surf the Internet? Hack into corporate and private systems? Isn't that how a modern-day P.I. solved cases?

"But he hired you."

"You see my point."

"Not really. You wanted a job. You got one. Working for a dick no less."

Afia narrowed her eyes. "What have you heard?"

"Nothing."

"But you called him—"

"Haven't you ever seen a Humphrey Bogart movie?"

She glanced up the stairwell then back to Rudy. "Are you sure he doesn't owe you a favor?"

"I told you, I don't even know him. I overheard a couple of the guys talking down at the club—"

"You said you were giving up clubbing."

"I slipped. Anyway, they were going through the want ads and—"

"I don't remember seeing—"

"So what's your schedule? Monday through Friday? Nine to Five?"

"He didn't say."

"Benefits? Salary?"

"They didn't come up."

"Afia, honey. You have to ask these things."

"I had every intention, but he rattled me."

"Rattled you?"

"I don't think he likes me."

Rudy tweaked her nose. "Nonsense. What's not to like?"

"He frowned through the entire interview. Not that it was much of an interview."

Her friend waved off her concerns. "He's lucky to have you. When do you start?"

"As soon as I change my clothes."

"What's wrong with what you're wearing?"

"His exact words: dress to blend."

"With what?"

She indicated the surroundings of the Bizby, a building that looked as if it hadn't been redecorated since 1965.

Rudy looked around at the faded red and brown linoleum, the peeling paint of the pea green walls, and shuddered.

She grimaced. "I know."

"Well, what was he wearing?"

"Jeans. Dark blue. Loose fitting. A taupe T-shirt. Tight-fitting."

Rudy's mouth twitched. "Nice. What about his shoes?"

"Work boots. Brown."

"Sexy."

Afia rolled her eyes, but she'd thought the same thing.

Rudy took her elbow and led her out onto the buckled side-walk.

30

Two platinum-blond, frizzy-haired women wearing cut-off jeans and oversized T-shirts exited the next-door Laundromat, stopping directly in their path. One snapped her gum. The other whistled. They both repositioned their plastic clothesbaskets on generous hips and openly gawked. Afia wasn't sure if they stared because they recognized her, thought she looked out of place, or because Rudy looked like a cross between an F.B.I. agent and a goateed body builder. Either way their regard made her uncomfortable. Blushing, she dipped her head in greeting as Rudy whisked her along.

"So?" he asked as they neared the limo.

"So what?"

"Is he cute?"

Handsome, maybe. Charismatic, absolutely. But cute? She shrugged. "I didn't notice."

Rudy laughed. "That means he's young and straight."

"How do you figure?"

He unlocked the back door. "You're only attracted to gay men or men twice your age."

Afia settled in and opened her purse in search of an antibacterial towelette. Mental note: Dust the office. "That's ridiculous."

"Both of your husbands were old enough to be your father. In fact they were both friends of your father."

"You make them sound ancient. Randy was forty-four when we married. Frank, fifty. That's not old."

"Not for a forty-year-old woman, no. You were twenty-two when you married Randy. Twenty-six when you hooked up with Frank."

She finished cleaning her hands and tossed the soiled wipe in the litterbag. "So?"

Rudy closed the door, rounded the limo, and then slid in behind the wheel. He glanced over his shoulder. "When's the last time you were attracted to a man no more than five years your senior?"

"Jeff Morton."

"Gay."

"Rickey Freeman."

"Gay."

"Carlos—"

"Been there. Done him."

"Your point?"

He faced front, revved the engine. "Either you connect with men you have no chance of hooking up with, or you hook up with men you have no chance of connecting with."

Afia resisted the childish urge to cover her ears. She did not want to hear this. "So now you're reading psychology books?"

"You know what your problem is?"

"I'm sure you're going to tell me."

"Fear of intimacy."

"Oh, please."

"I can explain."

"Maybe in our next session, Dr. Gallow. I need to change my clothes and get back here before Jake changes his mind." Good thing Rudy's apartment was only ten minutes away. Although finding an appropriate outfit would take time since she was living out of boxes. The last few weeks had been an emotional blur, the creditors proving as brutal as Henry Glick.

After the IRS had confiscated Frank's house, she'd had no choice but to move in with Harmon or Rudy. Rudy had been the easier choice even with all of his new age preaching. Harmon, though well-intentioned and loving, represented a lifestyle she was trying to shed like old, ill-fitting skin. She wanted to learn how to make it on her own.

"So what's he look like?"

"Jake? Straw-blond hair. Short. Spiky. Longish side-burns. Remember my emerald ring?"

"Mmm."

"Eyes a shade deeper. Crescent moon scar on his right cheekbone. Square jaw. Full lips."

Rudy laughed. "Not that you noticed."

Afia blushed. She hadn't realized she'd been looking that hard.

"Tall? Lean? A real hard-body?"

Her head snapped up. "You *do* know him."

"No." Rudy pointed up ahead. "Straw-blond hair. Short. Spiky."

Afia scooted forward and peered through the windshield. Sexy work boots planted slightly apart, Jake Leeds leaned back against the brick façade of the Bizby and lit a cigarette. Mental note: Remind him smoking is bad for his health. Tapered torso, sculpted biceps, he looked rugged and dangerous, and yet not one of several pedestrians gave him a second look. *Dress to blend.*

Rudy gave a low whistle.

Afia's lip twitched. "Down boy. Not your type."

"So he is straight." Rudy pulled out onto Atlantic Avenue.

Afia shifted her gaze to the lowered side window. Straight *and* sexy. Good Lord.

"And definitely under forty, honey. Not your type either."

The private investigator's disturbing green gaze locked with hers. He blew out a stream of smoke, gestured to his watch, and mouthed, "One hour."

Sixty-minutes to transform herself into an anonymous, low-profile woman. Her heart thudded in answer to the challenge. Or maybe it was because of the one-dimpled smirk he quirked just as Rudy made a right turn. "No," Afia whispered, mesmerized by the intensity of the enigmatic P.I. "Not my type at all."

Chapter Four

"I've never done anything like this before."

Hoping to put his potential client at ease, Jake leaned back in his chair, adopting a casual air. "How can I help you, Ms. Brannigan?" The slender, five-foot-eight woman with the tanning bed glow hadn't made an appointment. She was a walk-in, suggesting she was either impulsive or paranoid. Given the way she kept looking over her shoulder, his money was on the latter.

"I think my fiancé is cheating on me."

Angela Brannigan was a well-dressed, spike-heeled, curvy stunner with killer legs. Mid-to-late thirties. Eyes the color of iced cappuccino. Between her pouty lips and the honey-blond hair flowing over her shoulders in seductive waves, she reminded him a little of Kim Basinger in *L.A. Confidential*. She reeked of cool sophistication and hot sex. If her suspicions were true then her fiancé was an ass.

"I hope I'm wrong. I *desperately* want to be wrong, but if Anthony's . . ." In an agitated manner, she twisted her engagement ring, a three-carat rock that suggested *Anthony* was either loaded or in hock. "I need to know, Mr. Leeds. When I marry it will be forever. I . . . I don't want to make a mistake."

Precisely why he was thirty-three and still single. It wasn't the life-long commitment that had him dragging his feet, but the fear of failure. His parents' rocky marriage combined with the domestic investigations he'd conducted, on and off the force, had branded him a cautious cynic. To his way of thinking, if she had any doubts as to her future husband's fidelity, this pro-active measure was not only logical, but also smart.

"I found lipstick . . ." She fingered the collar of her dress. "It's so clichéd . . . and, of course, he had a reasonable explanation, but . . ." Her breath hitched.

"Do you suspect any woman in particular?"

"No," she croaked. "It could be a co-worker or a customer. It could be the woman who tailors his suits for all I know. He's a very charismatic man."

A ladies' man. Jake snagged a box of tissues from his bottom drawer, rounded the desk, and had a Kleenex in her hand by the time the first tear rolled. Wronged women and kids. His ultimate weakness.

The timing sucked.

Harmon had hired him to keep Afia out of trouble. Although she might wonder if he didn't conduct some sort of investigation while she was in his "employ." In addition, if Anthony *was* a faithless pig, he sure as hell didn't want to be the one responsible for a doomed marriage. "If your fiancé is playing around, Ms. Brannigan, depending upon how careful he is, it could take a couple of weeks to get audio/visual. I'm assuming you do want evidence."

She blew her nose into the tissue and nodded. "I don't care how long it takes. I need to know for sure one way or the other." She pulled a mirrored compact out of her clutch purse and checked her makeup, which, despite the tears, hadn't smudged.

"Could be costly," he said, folding his arms over his chest. "Between the retainer, expenses, and my hourly fee—"

"Money isn't an issue."

Why couldn't this woman have walked into his office a couple of days ago? *Before* his meeting with Harmon. Now he had two plumb assignments and an unqualified assistant—a destitute socialite who still tooled around in a limo—with questionable work ethics. He'd asked Afia to return in one hour. She was now—he glanced at his watch—forty minutes late.

On cue the outer office door slammed.

Ms. Brannigan whirled in her seat. The compact flew out of her hands, ricocheted off the center file cabinet, and skittered across the hardwood floor. "Who's that?"

Afia blew into his office looking harried and pretty as hell. "My assistant." He'd been wrong about the ponytail. Instead of making her less attractive it only accentuated her pixie features. Pert nose, high cheekbones, huge eyes fringed with thick, dark lashes. Her glossy straight bangs grazed perfectly arched eyebrows. A foot taller and she could've been one of those waif-like, anorexic models splashed all over MTV. Even though she'd dressed down in red-leather sports shoes, slim-fitting black pants, and a tailored crimson blouse, she still looked dressed up. Ms. Brannigan, stunning as she was in her floral-print halter dress, paled in comparison. Then it struck him. It had nothing to do with outer beauty. Afia St. John radiated an innocence that seduced a man into a stupor.

Jake frowned.

His client panicked. "If this gets back to Anthony—"

"It won't." He nabbed the folders from his desk and crossed the room, chin lowered, gaze intent on Afia. "This office prides itself on maintaining confidentiality." Hopefully, she'd get the point and make a discreet exit.

She hovered on the threshold, one hand on the doorknob, her sable-brown gaze bouncing back and forth between him and the leggy, teary-eyed blond. Then she spotted the shattered mirrored compact and winced. "Someone's cursed."

Ms. Brannigan burst into tears.

Jake shoved the folders into Afia's hands. "Alphabetically by last name. Thanks, *Jinx*." Grasping her shoulders—damn, they were bony—he spun her around, nudged her into the reception area, and shut the door. So much for discreet.

* * *

So much for making a good impression.

Afia had tried on four different outfits before settling on her low-riding rayon pants and knock-around CK shirt. She was determined to please the cranky P.I. from her functional pony-tail to her Dooney & Bourke sport utility shoes. The only rea-son she was late was because she'd asked Rudy to stop by the daycare center. She'd promised to deliver hats and scarves for "dress-up day." A day she was going to miss because of her new job. Mrs. Kelly had detained her further, trying to ascertain when she could volunteer a few hours. An impossible task since she didn't know her work schedule. Something she'd promised to rectify as soon as she got back to the office.

Then she'd asked Rudy to drop her two blocks from the Bizby. She couldn't *lose* the limo as it belonged to Rudy and, even though she could no longer afford his services, he insisted on driving her when his schedule allowed. He also insisted on escorting her to the front door of the timeworn walk-up, worrying that she'd run into an unscrupulous character along the way. He'd sworn it wasn't because he thought she attracted trouble. He would have done the same for any female, which she tended to believe since Rudy was an innate protector and true gentleman.

Unfortunately, it had taken him ten minutes to find a parking space.

She'd jogged two blocks and run up four flights of stairs, barging into Jake's office with an apology on her lips and the intent of organizing his unkempt desk in record time.

Instead, she stood on the buckled carpet of the cramped reception area, holding folders that he'd told her to file, although how could she when the filing cabinet was in his office? She spun on her rubber souls and stared at the door Jake Leeds had essentially slammed in her face.

Was there no end to this man's hostility? Rudy would tell her to confront the jerk. *"Aren't you weary of being a doormat?"* He'd surprised her with that question after she'd told him she'd agreed to resign from the Seashore Charity

Committee. Although Harmon had managed to keep her latest fiasco out of the newspapers, he hadn't been able to stop her neighbors' wagging tongues. Word of her misfortune had reached the president and vice-president of the SCC board the day after she'd lost Frank's house. She didn't know which had shocked Dora Simmons and Frances Beck more: that she was broke, or that she was living with her ex-chauffeur.

Doormat.

Is that how the world viewed someone who chose not to make waves?

Clutching the folders to her chest, she padded to what she assumed was her desk, thinking back on her interview with Jake. He'd cussed when she'd dropped the files, insulted her clothes and hair, and had ordered her to acquire another mode of transportation. He'd walked all over her, and she hadn't said boo.

Groaning, she plopped down on a black-cushioned swivel chair, placed the folders on what had to be her desk, and idly fingered her twelve charms while scrambling for a positive slant.

Better a doormat than a jerk.

The least he could have done was introduce her to that distraught woman before tossing her out. Perhaps she could have offered comfort: a sympathetic ear, a cup of tea . . . her charm bracelet. Blondie was in for seven years of bad luck.

Unless it had been Jake who'd broken the mirror.

She almost smiled at the thought. It would serve him right for making fun of her.

Jinx.

He definitely knew who she was. Afia St. John-Harper-Davis, the Jersey socialite who'd lost a father and two husbands in separate, yet equally bizarre, accidents. AKA "The Black Widow."

It occurred to her then that Jake wasn't superstitious. Nor did he put stock in gossip, believing that she'd offed (was that appropriate detective lingo?) the men in her life for financial gain. Otherwise this morning he would have shown her the door and ushered in the next applicant.

Unless there were no other applicants. Maybe he'd scared them all away.

She commiserated. Three weeks ago he would have scared her away too. She wouldn't have survived ten minutes with the intimidating man, let alone an entire interview. But things were different. *She* was different. She wanted her money back and, more importantly, her dignity. Jake could be as surly as he wanted as long as he taught her a few tricks of the trade.

Like tracking a missing person.

That, she decided, was that. "He needs a hand," she said noting the phone's blinking message light. "I need a dick."

"Don't we all."

Afia started as a pregnant woman shuffled over the threshold. She hadn't even heard the door click open.

"It's been a month, and I'm horny as hell." The husky-voiced blond grinned, revealing a deep dimple in her left cheek. "The downside of getting knocked-up. Where's Jake?"

Afia eyed the candid woman with interest. Generic capri jeans, a pale blue maternity blouse, and navy-blue boat shoes. Golden skin buffed to a natural glow. Shoulder-length hair tied in a low ponytail, topped with a NY Yankees baseball cap. She lacked style and polish, and yet Afia was transfixed. The woman had entered the room as though she owned the building.

Or the boss.

She squirmed in her seat, wondering if this woman was Jake's other half. For some reason the notion bothered her. Maybe because he was behind closed doors with another attractive blond. "Umm . . ." she pointed to his office. "He's with a client."

Blond number two glanced at Jake's private door. "Man? Woman? What's the name?"

Flip to intense in two seconds flat. Afia cleared her throat, hoping mother-to-be wasn't violent . . . or hormonal. "I'm not at liberty to say." Not to mention, she didn't know.

Instead of striking out, the stranger laughed. "You just might last longer than the others." She thrust out her hand in greeting. "Joni McNichols."

What others, Afia wanted to ask, but instead stood and clasped Joni's hand. "Afia St. John."

One eyebrow rose. "Oh. I'm sorry, I just assumed . . ." She frowned. "Damn, I'm slipping. I thought you were Jake's new assistant."

"I am."

"Really." She pursed her naturally rosy lips. "Hmm."

Afia could see the woman's wheels turning. Stroking her bracelet, she braced herself for a deluge of questions. None came. Feeling awkward, she swept her hand toward a brown pleather couch that was in dire need of being replaced or reupholstered. "Would you like to take a seat while you're waiting?"

"Mmm. No. What I mean is, I can't wait." She rested her hand on her extended belly. "I have an appointment with my obstetrician."

Afia experienced a pang of envy. When she'd asked Randy about children, he'd said, *"What's the rush? We have time."* He'd been wrong.

Frank hadn't been adverse to a family but seemed incapable of delivering the goods.

"I just stopped by to give him these coupons." Joni pulled a crumpled envelope out of her canvas backpack and handed it to Afia. "Will you see that he gets them?"

Nodding, she tried to imagine Jake pushing a cart down the aisle of the local grocery store, stocking up on milk, bread, and disposable diapers. Instead, she envisioned him pumping iron in a gritty gym. Bulging biceps and rippling abs. His skin glistening with sweat. She imagined coming up behind him, smoothing her hands over his broad shoulders, kissing the nape of his neck and . . .

O-ma-god.

She blew her bangs off of her forehead, stunned by her prurient thoughts. Fantasizing about a man in the presence of his wife, girlfriend, or whatever. Celibacy was taking its toll.

"Also tell him dinner's at six-thirty and to bring ice cream."

Flustered, Afia sank in the chair and scanned the desktop for a notepad.

Left hand supporting her lower back, Joni hedged around and opened the top right drawer. "Memo pads, pencils, pens, stamps, paper clips, and extra staples." She placed a pad and pencil on the desk. "Always print. Jake hates deciphering flowery script, and always take down as many details as possible."

"What flavor?" Afia asked, concentrating on her penmanship.

Joni laughed. "Not bad," she said, while moving toward the door.

Afia jerked up her head. "Wait! Do you need ... can I ... help?" She fluttered a hand toward the hall. What if she lost her balance navigating those steep stairs?

"I may have balls, as Jake is fond of saying, but I'm not crazy." She flashed her sole dimple. "I'm taking the elevator. Later." Slinging her backpack over her shoulders, she exited and shut the door.

Afia stared after the woman unsure as to what shocked her more—Joni's language or the news that the Bizby had an elevator.

She'd have to ask Jake about that mysterious elevator. She'd have to ask him about a lot of things. Like her hours, her salary. Maybe when she handed over the coupons and dinner message, he'd fill her in on his relationship to Joni McNichols. She hadn't noticed a wedding band, but that didn't mean anything. She wasn't sure why she was obsessing over whether or not they were a couple. If they weren't he was probably hooked up with someone else. Not that she cared. He wasn't her type. Worse, he was her boss.

An office affair. Like she needed another disaster in her life.

She rolled back her shoulders and started arranging the folders alphabetically by last name. Next she'd transcribe the messages on the answering machine and then organize her desk drawers and the supply closet, if there was one. She'd also brought a tote bag of cleaning supplies. Hopefully, Blondie would depart soon giving her access to Jake's office. The sooner she whipped this place into order, the sooner she could talk him into teaching her the trade.

The sooner she'd catch a thief.

Instead of crossing her fingers, she followed Rudy's advice and chanted two of the affirmations he'd gleaned from his current read, *Creative Visualization.*

"Infinite riches are now freely flowing into my life.

"The more I have, the more I have to give."

She glanced at Jake's door. "Blondie will hit the road."

She suppressed a gasp when the door actually swung open and Jake ushered the curvaceous woman across the reception area to the outer door. Mental note: Affirmations are powerful.

He shot Afia a look that promised a lecture before escorting Blondie, who hadn't so much as glanced her way, out into the hall.

Afia chanted an oldie but goodie, "I haven't done anything wrong," quickly followed by "I will not be intimidated." Still, her heart raced as she scooped up the folders and hurried into his office. Work quickly, she told herself. Show him you're efficient. Maybe he'll be so impressed that he'll forget that you were forty minutes late and nix the finger-wagging session.

She stood in the center of his office breathing in the lingering scent of Opium. Blondie's scent. She crinkled her nose and frowned. Something about that woman bothered her, and she refused to believe that it had anything to do with the fact that she was California, albeit artificially, gorgeous. The epitome of most men's fantasies. She wondered if Jake typified "most men."

Focus, Afia. Focus.

She curled her fingers around the folders, rocked back on her rubber heels, and considered her uninspired surroundings.

Three locking file cabinets lined the west wall. Nothing fancy. Basic steel. Boring beige. Then again, everything about Leeds Investigations, aside from its owner, was basic and boring. The two-room business lacked style and color. The furnishings and sparse accessories were neither masculine nor feminine. Kind of like Rudy's new roommate, Jean-Pierre. Although Jean-Pierre had flair. She noted the stark beige walls, scarred hardwood floor, the two brown-vinyl chairs opposite the pressed-wood desk that boasted a laptop computer, multi-lined phone, and non-descript table lamp.

Jake's office could definitely use some flair.

No decorating.

Sighing, she determined the appropriate cabinet, filed all of the folders, alphabetically by last name, and then moved to his desk. What a mess. She sorted through a mountain of bills and receipts, trying to decide whether to separate by month or category.

"What are you doing?"

She jerked and spun. Receipts sailed out of her hand and fluttered to the floor. *Oh, no.*

Jake clenched his jaw, dragged his fingers though his hair. "Leave them," he said, when she crouched to gather the papers.

"But—"

"We're going out."

"Now?"

"Now." He swung open the door to a tiny closet and snagged a short-sleeve, button-down shirt off of a wire hanger. Of course, he would have wire hangers. Everything in this office was bargain basement issue. Not that there was anything horrid about a bargain. She was learning to appreciate coupons and sales and, thanks to Rudy, the wonders of E-bay. But plastic hangers were inexpensive and didn't leave indentations in the shoulders of one's shirts and sweaters. She imagined his closet at home and shivered.

"You okay."

"Yes, of course.

He slipped the dark-brown shirt over his taupe tee while crossing to his desk. "You look a little flushed."

"I'm fine." *Liar.* She was fantasizing about re-organizing his bedroom close and, worse, his underwear drawer. Fantasizing about him walking around in a pair of Calvin Klein briefs.

"You like wieners?"

"What?"

"Hot dogs."

Her cheeks burned. "I guess."

"You don't know?"

"I haven't had one in years."

"Figures," he mumbled while bending over to open his bottom desk drawer.

Afia frowned. Fantasizing about a jerk. Definitely losing it. She watched in wide-eyed horror as he withdrew a holstered gun and strapped it to the right side of his belt. "Is that legal?"

He buttoned up the bottom half of the boxy shirt effectively concealing the weapon. "Not any more." He opened his top drawer, pulled out a pack of cigarettes and tucked it in his left breast pocket.

"Smoking is bad for your health."

He tugged on a taupe baseball cap. "So is poking your nose into other people's business."

She snorted. "This from a licensed snoop."

His lip twitched, and her heart skipped. She wondered how she'd react if he actually smiled. Her bones would probably melt. The notion was nearly as frightening as his gun. Being attracted to this man was not an option. She'd only been widowed a year. He was a bossy jerk and quite possibly married.

Which reminded her . . .

"Joni dropped by."

"She okay?"

Her stomach knotted at the concern glittering in his eyes. Married or not, he obviously cared a great deal about Joni McNichols. "One might call her feisty," she quickly assured him.

"That's my Joni."

He smiled then, a genuine, affectionate smile that affected parts other than her bones.

Mesmerized by his full lips, her mind skipped merrily down fantasy lane.

"What did she want?"

She blinked, met his questioning green gaze, and blushed. "Excuse me?"

48

Jinxed

"Joni." He held her gaze a brief, cleavage-damp moment before breaking off and snatching up a pair of aviator sunglasses. "What'd she want?"

"Oh. She dropped off some coupons and said to tell you dinner is at six-thirty and to bring ice cream."

"What flavor?"

"I . . . um . . ." Darn!

"Never mind." He nudged her into the reception area. "Can't make dinner anyway. I'll be working."

"At six-thirty?"

"This isn't a nine to five."

"Does that include me?" She didn't mind working late. The more time she spent with Jake, the greater her chances of tracking down a crooked accountant. Only, she'd hoped to squeeze in a few hours at the daycare center. It bothered her that she could no longer make her monthly donation, although, as Rudy had pointed out, time was also valuable. Unfortunately, she'd spent every minute of the last few weeks dealing with the fallout of Henry Glick's betrayal.

"Depends on the case and whether or not I need assistance in the field," he said. "We'll talk about it over lunch."

"Lunch?"

He glanced over his shoulder toward the scattered receipts. "I have to be somewhere, and I figure it's safer than leaving you here unsupervised."

She refused to take offense. Her body hummed at the prospect of being an active participant in a case. A chance to learn some actual investigative techniques. Could it be her luck was changing for the better? "Just a minute." She hurried over

49

to her desk, snatched up her Chanel handbag, and then turned
back to find him staring down at her with an intense frown.
Her stomach churned. "What?"

"We've got to do something about that hair."

So much for not taking offense.

Chapter Five

Steering one-handed, Angela Falcone-Brannigan popped two antacid tablets and gunned her silver Jaguar through a yellow light. She needed a drink, but she'd be damned if she'd step one heel in a local lounge and risk running into a friend of her dad's or a co-worker of Tony's. She'd have to hold out until she got home. Home was fifty minutes away, that's if she drove seventy on the Atlantic City Expressway.

She'd drive eighty.

Damn Tony for putting her in this position. Everything had been perfect. *They* were perfect. They shared the same interests, favored the same music and wines, and Caribbean getaways. They had similar taste in clothing for chrissake. He was gorgeous and an extremely considerate lover compared to her first husband and the string of insatiable pigs she'd dated in between. Anthony Rivelli was everything she wanted, but more importantly everything her dad wanted. Educated, sociable, and wealthy. A prominent figure in an Atlantic City casino.

Italian.

She refused to lose him to another woman. Of course, when confronted he'd pleaded innocent. He'd explained the lipstick, a wholly reasonable explanation, and she would have believed him if not for the sliver of doubt stabbing at her ulcerated stomach. Suddenly, she found herself second-guessing everything she'd taken in stride during their whirlwind courtship, such as his habit of spending several nights a week at his condo down at the shore, rather than commuting to his home in Cherry Hill. Considering he put in more than seventy hours a week as the vice president of the newly erected Carnevale Casino, that annoying penchant hadn't seemed suspicious. Until now.

Needing answers and not wanting to risk discovery by hiring a detective anywhere in the vicinity of her hometown, she'd thumbed through the yellow pages of an Atlantic City directory and decided on Leeds Investigations. Since the listing told her shit about the agency's qualifications, she'd opted for a personal visit. Jake Leeds, she'd ascertained in one minute flat, was her man— intelligent, confident, and an obvious sucker for a female in distress. If Anthony was seeing another woman, Leeds would nail the cheating bastard.

What then?

She couldn't think about what then just now. It made her want to puke.

She popped another antacid and sailed through the EZ-Pass lane of the tollbooth, craving a double martini and a scalding hot bath. She wanted to wash away the sleaze of Atlantic City and that P.I.'s crummy office. She wanted to forget the snotty appraisal of his young, obnoxiously pretty assistant, and the fact that she was fast nearing forty. She wanted to put an end to Tony's affair, before her dad found out and put an end to Tony.

* * *

Utilizing Afia as a field assistant was probably a mistake, but preferable to the alternative. Left to her own devices, she'd organize his office into mayhem. He had a system. Bills, receipts, expense reports, arranged in an order that made sense to him. At least they used to be arranged. They currently littered his hardwood floor. First his files, then his receipts. Either her mother was right and she was jinxed, or she was your run-of-the-mill klutz.

He feared the former, as there was nothing run-of-the-mill about Afia St. John. When he'd escorted Ms. Brannigan from his office, he'd expected to find Ms. Socialite filing her nails or skimming a fashion magazine, not diligently sorting folders.

The shiny red plastic tote filled with sponges, paper towels, latex gloves, and assorted cleansers had whipped him into a tailspin. He'd tried picturing her on her hands and knees, scrubbing floors and toilets. The "hands and knees" part came easily, but scrubbing bubbles and bathrooms led to thoughts of bathtubs and scented soaps. Instead of concentrating on Ms. Brannigan's parting words as she'd descended the stairs, he'd digressed into a fantasy involving a bubble bath, a bottle of champagne, and an extremely naked Afia.

"What do you think?"

I think I need my head examined. "Too tight."

"But it's a medium and I'm a small."

"Go for a large." *Preferably something that hangs to your knees.* As thin as she was you'd expect a bony ass. No such luck. She had a great ass and a subtle sway that would garner the attention of every man on the famous seaside boardwalk.

"I won't have a shape."

"Good."

Afia looked at him quizzically, as if trying to process a foreign concept. God forbid she not turn heads. Well, to hell with her ego. If she was going to work surveillance, she needed to be invisible. Tall order for a woman who'd probably been the center of attention since birth.

"You're concerned people will recognize me, that I'll draw attention to us."

"Something like that."

"I understand."

"Good." He tried not to analyze the sad note in her tone. She was depressed because she'd lost her fortune. Bottom line. Three weeks ago she'd shopped in exclusive boutiques, shelling out hundreds of dollars for obscenely overpriced merchandise. Today he'd ushered her into a cheesy souvenir shop. He kept waiting for her to complain. Anything to keep her in the rich bitch category. Anything to make her less attractive. He crossed his arms over his chest and watched as she methodically sorted through a rack of five-dollar T-shirts, passing over lewd cartoon graphics and tacky quotes in favor of small, subtle logos.

Come on, baby. One catty jab.

"I didn't do it, just in case you were wondering."

"Do what?"

"Off my husbands."

"Off?" He would've laughed if she hadn't sounded so earnest.

"Don't detectives use that term?"

"Not this detective."

She worked her way around the rack, avoiding eye contact.

"I'm not a 'Black Widow.' "

"Nice to know."

"Although it is true that I inherited a substantial amount money from both of my husbands."

He held silent wondering where she was going with this. Amazing how much information he gathered by keeping his mouth shut.

"Aren't you curious?"

About whether your first husband had an unusually weak heart or if you're that amazing in bed? Hell, yes. "About?"

"About why someone as wealthy as me would need to work. You do know who I am, don't you?"

He found it interesting that she'd lowered her voice to a near whisper. Famous and infamous were two different things, and from her downcast gaze he suspected she considered herself the latter. "I know who you are. That is I'm aware of your tabloid history. And lots of wealthy people work."

"Yes, but not as a private investigator's assistant." She looked up then. "May I ask how much I'll be earning?"

"Four hundred and fifty."

"Per week?" She smiled, no doubt planning a weekend shopping spree. But then her appealing mouth slacked into a worried frown. "Considering the job, that seems high."

Damned high. But that's what Harmon wanted her to have. He ignored her observation and gestured to the rack. "You want to pick up the pace?" According to Ms. Brannigan, her fiancé spent his lunch hour on the boardwalk soaking up the sun. He knew where and when to catch a glimpse of Anthony Rivelli. The latest addition to Atlantic City's glitzy boardwalk casinos was near, but so was the time.

"I was bored."

"Pardon?"

"With my life. So I decided to get a job." Her cheeks flushed as she concentrated back on the shirts.

She was either too embarrassed to tell him she'd been duped by her accountant, or too proud. He was having a very hard time getting a handle on this woman. Intriguing and irksome at the same time.

"If you want me to disappear, maybe I should get an extra-large," she said, changing subjects. "And maybe I should go with blue." She pulled a sky-blue T-shirt from the crammed circular rack and held it up in front of her. "I look hideous in blue."

He disagreed. She'd make gray look good. He lifted a teasing eyebrow. "Yes, but then people will stare and point and say, *my God, what was she thinking?*"

She smiled, and his gut twisted, dammit. One second stretched into five, and his palms grew moist. He felt like the high school chess geek gawking at the homecoming queen. Christ. It's not like he didn't get enough sex.

Her smile faltered, and something akin to panic flashed in her baby browns. "I'll go with a large. Black. Very unassuming."

"Good idea."

"I'll just be a moment."

He watched her walk toward the dressing room, cute butt and waist-length ponytail swaying, albeit subtly, in a fashion that gave him an instant woody. "About that hair . . ."

She stopped in her tracks, the black T-shirt dangling from her right balled fist. "I'm not cutting it," she said without turning.

Touchy about her hair, was she? The investigator in him wondered why. He wondered a lot of things about Afia St. John. Then he reminded himself that curiosity killed the cat. Or in her case the men in her life. He tucked his thumbs in his jeans pockets and glanced at a bin of gambling paraphernalia, resisting the absurd urge to snatch up a lucky seven key chain. "I was thinking about a hat."

"Oh." She turned, the relief in her eyes hiking his interest another notch. "I love hats. I have . . . had quite a few." She motioned to the front of the store. "I think I saw a hat rack when we came in."

"Remember, Jinx," he said as she walked past, "we're not going to the Easter parade."

"As if I'd pick a Jackie O pillbox to wear with a 100% cotton T-shirt," she grumbled.

He grinned at the bite in her tone. Better a ticked cat than a lost puppy. That underlying sadness, her vulnerability, was a major part of her appeal. Made a man want to take her into his arms and promise to make everything better. Was she always like this? Or was it simply a result of her current dilemma?

Widowed, homeless, and broke. Hell, that would be enough to depress the staunchest soul. Except she wasn't living on the streets. She was living with a friend. And she wasn't penniless. She had a job. For the next two weeks anyhow. After that . . . After that mommy would be home from Tahiti and she, or her insanely rich husband, or Harmon, would make everything better.

Or maybe she'd exert that independent streak Harmon had mentioned and insist on calling her own shots. Maybe he didn't get a bad vibe on Afia, because she wasn't really all that bad. Spoiled, but not rotten. She was a puzzle all right. Damn if he didn't love a good mystery.

✳ ✳ ✳

"King? Grisham?"

"Gawain. Shakti Gawain." Rudy closed his copy of *Creative Visualization,* a paperback that was a third of the size of any Stephen King or John Grisham novel he'd ever seen, and set it aside as Harmon Reece took the seat across from him in one of Ventnor's trendiest restaurants.

"Never heard of him."

"Her," Rudy corrected, and he wasn't surprised. Harmon was hardly what he'd call enlightened. Unlike Afia's wacko mother, who believed in every superstition known to man, Harmon believed in what he could see, smell, hear, and touch. Hard evidence. He'd never dream of meditating or chanting affirmations before entering the courtroom, of visualizing a positive outcome. Men like Harmon achieved their goals through sheer arrogance. He never doubted his actions.

Rudy almost envied him.

Harmon signaled a waitress and ordered a scotch on the rocks. He eyed Rudy's glass of seltzer. "Something stronger?"

"No, thank you. I have a pick-up scheduled at the airport in one hour."

The waitress passed them menus, recited the specials, and then slipped away.

Harmon loosened his tie. "But you'll be back in time to drive Afia home. Or rather to *your* place."

Rudy suppressed a smile. Harmon hated not having Afia under his roof, or more to the point, under his watchful eye. Unfortunately, he expected her "friend" to be his eyes and ears. "Plenty of time," he said, his good humor fading. "But there's a catch. Your dick ordered her to get rid of the limo."

Harmon raised an eyebrow and then turned his attention to the menu's parchment pages. "So pick her up in your regular car."

"That would be my motorcycle."

The man frowned, flipped to the next page. "I'll provide you with a car. Something unobtrusive since I'm assuming that was Jake's problem. A limousine attracts attention. One of the reasons I wanted him to take charge of Afia. He'll keep her low-key while this mess blows over."

Rudy skimmed the entrees, ignoring the part about Jake "taking charge," as if Afia needed another person pulling her strings. It's exactly what she didn't need. She needed to stand on her own two feet. She needed support not domination. He'd watched her struggle with guilt, loneliness, and confusion in the eleven months since Frank's death. Mostly due to her mother who'd somehow convinced Afia that she was jinxed and had nothing to offer the world outside of her looks. His gentle friend had no idea who she was or what she was capable of, because she'd spent her entire life morphing into other people's ideals. Good-hearted to a fault, Afia worried about pleasing everyone except herself. When she'd expressed the desire to wring Henry Glick's traitorous neck, he'd cheered.

Deciding on the pan-seared scallops, Rudy abandoned the menu and stroked his goatee. "Do you really think you'll get her money back, Mr. Reece."

"It is my sincere intention."

In other words, yes. He waited until the waitress served Harmon his scotch and then returned to another point of concern. "Afia knows I can't afford a new car. If I suddenly show up with one she'll ask questions. She's not as ditzy as you think."

Harmon sipped his drink then met his gaze. "Ditzy is not a term I have ever used to describe my goddaughter. She is, however, gullible."

"Trusting." Rudy's gut clenched. "I don't feel right about this whole arrangement, Mr. Reece. I can't betray Afia's confidence by reporting to you her every thought and move."

"I don't need details. I just want to know that she's safe."

Rudy softened at the genuine concern in the older man's eyes. "I won't let anything bad happen to her."

"I know. And neither will Jake. I'll be out of town for the next few days on business. It'll be easier now that I know Afia's in good hands. Jake's got her days. You've got her nights. I'm comfortable with that."

What if Jake gets one of her nights? he wanted to ask, but wisely bit his tongue. Assuming the man was good-hearted, he'd dance with joy and sing *Everything's Coming Up Roses* if Afia got down and dirty with the sexy P.I. As far as he knew she'd never had a one-night-stand. Creative, erotic sex? Might be therapeutic just now. Though Afia was fairly tight-lipped about her bedroom antics, he was fairly certain she'd never experienced anything other than the missionary or a slight variation thereof. He tried picturing Randy or Frank bending her over the kitchen table and shuddered.

Now Jake . . . Hell, he could picture emerald-eyes doing a lot of things. Not with him, of course. That tasty morsel registered off his gay-dar. But with Afia . . . He visualized his friend and the P.I. doing the hetero-nasty and smiled. As for himself . . . his days of flinging were over. He rested his hand on his book, silently chanting, *I am open and ready for a serious, long-term relationship.*

Harmon signaled the waitress that they were ready to order and then eyed Rudy over his drink. "So Afia tells me you have a new roommate. Tell me about him."

Chapter Six

He was trying to kill her. Death by junk food. She'd consumed a jumbo hotdog smothered with mustard and relish because, according to Jake, that was the only way to eat a hotdog, a small bucket of salted French fries, and now he expected her to eat frozen chocolate custard. Afia tugged down the brim of her new baseball cap, pushed her black Gucci sunglasses back up her sweat-beaded nose, and tried not to think about how refreshing, and delicious, that screaming-fat dessert would taste. "I couldn't possibly."

Jake thrust the cone into her hand, his eyes a mystery behind those mirrored aviators. "If you're worried about the calories, don't."

She smirked. "Easy for you to say. You don't need to fit into a size three."

"Neither do you."

She didn't argue. She wasn't about to explain her obsession with maintaining a svelte figure, especially not within earshot of the myriads of tourists and casino workers crowding the beachside boardwalk. Not that she had an eating disorder or anything similarly tabloid worthy, but she had been counting calories and pounding the treadmill since she was sixteen. If she so much as gained five pounds, her mother would notice. She'd raise a judgmental eyebrow, saying, *"You know I don't mean to be cruel, Afia, but high-profile men prefer showcase wives. Have you ever seen Donald Trump with a blimp?"*

Except Afia didn't want Donald Trump or any other high-profile man for that matter. She'd had two, and though she'd felt sincere affection for Randy and Frank, there had been no pulse-pounding passion. No spark. Next time around she wanted fireworks. Unpredictable, heart-stuttering pyrotechnics.

Jake sat down beside her on the wood-slatted bench, and a roman candle rocketed through her blood stream. The man sizzled with an inner intensity that made the backs of her knees sweat.

She resisted the urge to fan herself, although she could easily blame her burning cheeks on the noonday sun. Chocolate custard melted and dripped over her knuckles. She had two choices: start licking or toss the cone in the nearest trash receptacle. She glanced sideways at Jake—lounging comfortably against the park bench as if he hadn't a care in the world—and surreptitiously admired his mouth-watering profile. Square jaw, strong chin, and an interesting nose that looked as if it may have been broken once or twice. But mostly she focused on his full, tempting lips. She imagined kissing that sinfully sexy mouth, and her insides melted along with another ripple of custard.

She thought about Jake's mysterious client. Next to that curvy siren, Afia felt as desirable as an anorexic nun. Maybe if she gained a few pounds in the right places, she'd gain the interest of a man like Jake. Not Jake specifically, of course, but someone like him. Someone who sizzled.

Ignoring her mother's phantom nagging, she attacked the calorie-infested cone with gusto. Rebellion never tasted so good.

Behind her, waves crashed against the public beach, sunbathers worshiped the June sun, and children screeched with joy as they splashed and bodysurfed in the vast Atlantic. A southern breeze blew in the tantalizing scents of funnel cakes, corn dogs, and French fries, catapulting Afia back to her childhood. To the cherished times her dad had brought her to the Steel Pier, a historic amusement venue boasting carnival rides, psychics, and forbidden food. A self-confessed adrenaline junkie, Judge Bradley St. John had introduced his young daughter to the thrills of roller coasters and sky wheels—the higher, the faster, the better. In between, they'd played darts, shot air rifles and had pigged out on cotton candy and cheese fries. She'd never felt so *alive*.

Unfortunately, her mother had worried incessantly that, given Afia's luck, one of the rides would go haywire and they'd end up the victims of some horrific accident. Bad enough that she was being exposed to carnies, gypsies, and midway food. Eventually, her dad had buckled under the weighty lectures, and thereafter, when he'd managed to tear himself away from his courtroom, had taken his young daughter to the latest G-rated movie. It occurred to Afia that were the film censors to rate her life, misfortune and all, she'd barely register PG. The realization proved oddly depressing.

She swirled her tongue around the frozen custard lapping up taboo calories. "Why aren't you having dessert?" she asked Jake in between licks.

"My dessert's in my shirt pocket, but since the wind would blow the smoke in your face, I'll have it later."

Why have the lung-blackening cigarette at all, she wanted to ask, but knew he'd take exception. "That's very thoughtful of you."

His dimple flared. "I'm a thoughtful kind of guy."

He was joking with her again. At least she thought he was joking. Her head ached, and she wasn't sure if it was from eating the frozen custard too fast or from trying to get a fix on Jake. She'd never been around a man like him. So blunt. So . . . what would Rudy call him? *Alpha-male.* And yet underneath that gruff exterior lurked a sensitive soul. She'd seen it in his eyes when he'd dealt with his weepy client, and when he'd asked about Joni's welfare. And even though she clearly wasn't qualified to be a private investigator's assistant, he'd given her the job she so desperately wanted. Was that it? Had he seen the desperation in her eyes? Did the intimidating Mr. Leeds have a weakness for damsels in distress? Her back went up at the notion that he'd hired her because he felt sorry for her. The last thing she needed was yet another man coming to her rescue.

"Your life is out of control because you have no control in your life."

Suddenly all she wanted was to get back to the office.

"You can answer the phone, right? Make coffee?"

Thinking back, Jake's comments had been as insulting as Harmon's incredulous expression when she'd announced her intention to get a job. As if she were a fluff-brained idiot. Although that's exactly what the manager of the casino boutique had called her when she'd been unable to master the computerized cash register. Not that the buttoned-up, pinch-lipped woman had taken the time to properly train her. One quick overview and she was expected to understand. Questions annoyed the standoffish manager, and when Afia unintentionally ticked off a casino high-roller by asking for identification before accepting a check, she'd been terminated on the spot. She'd taken the humiliation in stride, much like her heated dismissal from the hectic themed restaurant.

She hadn't deserved to lose either job. She certainly hadn't earned the insults. Rudy was right. She should have spoken up in her defense because obviously her indignation had been festering. Just now her stomach churned like an active volcano, and she didn't think it was because of the mass quantities of junk food. Although that was a possibility.

"It was very kind of you to buy me lunch," she said, her voice as cool as her devoured custard, "but you mentioned you had someplace to be, and I'd hate to keep you from work." She pulled a moist towelette from her purse, squared her shoulders, and wiped her sticky hands.

"I'm exactly where I need to be, and believe it or not, I am working."

His expression was unreadable and because of those darned sunglasses, she couldn't tell if he was looking at her, the

Carnevale Casino, or the flock of seagulls attacking an abandoned bag of popcorn. "You don't look like you're working." He looked like any one of the surrounding tourists, relaxed and enjoying a humid-free day on the boardwalk.

The corners of his mouth curled into an arrogant grin. "That's because I'm good."

I'll bet. Her cheeks burned. She scrubbed her hands harder as if it would cleanse her dirty thoughts. Darn him for being so charismatic. Darn *her* for being susceptible. As Rudy had pointed out, this wasn't like her at all. Lusting after a straight, under-forty, blue-collar male. *Lust.* The word was almost as foreign to her as poor. Yes, she wanted to break old patterns, but not with a married man. Not with her boss. Her anxiety simmered toward boil. "So what exactly are you doing?"

"Observing Anthony Rivelli."

"Who's Anthony Rivelli?"

"The man I'm observing."

She swallowed an exasperated huff. "Do I look like a fluff-brained idiot?"

He angled his chin at that, and she cursed herself for broadcasting her insecurity. "He's over your right shoulder," he said. "Leaning against the boardwalk railing, having a smoke with a couple of co-workers."

She started to turn, but Jake lazed forward and grasped her chin. Her skin tingled as he brushed his thumb over her lower lip. Propriety dictated she jerk back, but her brain short-circuited. "What are you doing?"

"Wiping custard from the corner of your mouth, and," he leaned closer, lowering his voice to a husky drawl that lulled her into a glassy-eyed stupor, "stopping us from getting burned."

Burned? She was already singed to the bone. His touch worked like tinder to a starving fire. His masculine scent swirled around her, spicy and wildly erotic. Salsa music pulsed from a nearby pavilion, igniting a vivid image of her and Jake engaged in the horizontal Lambada. *Oh, God.*

"If you turn around, he might catch you staring. I don't want Rivelli to know he's being watched. Hence the term covert surveillance."

Her mouth formed an O, but nothing came out.

"So far, if he's glanced this way, all he's seen are two lovers on holiday." He brushed her lips with a cashmere-soft kiss then plucked the soiled towelette from her hand and rose to toss it in the nearby trashcan.

Afia blinked at him from behind her sunglasses, while pressing her fingertips to her smoldering lips. He'd barely skimmed her flesh, and yet he'd left a trail of fire. Her heart pounded as a fierce yearning spiked from her brain to her nether region. Lust was potent and completely unnerving. She didn't know whether to giggle, sigh, or dive into the chilly ocean. She dropped her hands into her lap and fingered her wishbone charm. *This one,* she could hear her dad saying, *means wishes come true. Be careful what you wish for, Peanut.*

She *wished* that Jake's lips had lingered a little longer. She *wished* that he was single and that fleeting kiss had been an actual come on. But then she surveyed his casual attire, *her* casual attire, and the two souvenir plastic shopping bags resting near her feet. She conjured the image of them sitting side-by-side, gorging on junk food, and basking in the sun—*two lovers on holiday*—and she knew the truth.

He was playing a part. The kiss, if one could call it an actual kiss, hadn't been personal. She should be thrilled, relieved at the very least, since he was quite possibly married, and she was most definitely not an adulteress. But instead, her spirits sank like a stone.

This is crazy, she told herself when he sat back down. *You're the one who wanted to learn the tricks of the trade. Get with the program. Stop panting after Jake and start hunting down Glick.* "So are you telling me that we're on a stake-out?" she asked, struggling to feign nonchalance. "Is that why you wanted me to look like Joe Schmo?"

He angled his big body toward her, stretched out his right arm and rested it behind her on the bench. "More like Jane Doe, but yeah."

"Dress to blend."

"Bingo."

She tensed when he stroked the length of her ponytail, idly twirling long strands around his fingers. Was this a test? Was he seeing how far he could push her before she turned skittish? Wondering if she'd prove as inept in the field as she'd been in the office, thereby giving him sufficient grounds to fire her? Needing all the good fortune she could conjure, she squeezed her charms and chanted a string of silent affirmations.

I will keep this job. I will get back my money. I will give as good as I get.

Keeping her back to Anthony Rivelli, she inched closer to the poker-faced P.I. and toyed with the third button of his shirt.

Unlike her stint with the computerized cash register, she knew exactly what she was doing. She'd taken a high school drama class. She could play the enamored girlfriend. "Is Mr. Rivelli connected to the blond woman with the silk chiffon sundress?"

"You're sure it was silk chiffon? Specifically?"

She nodded. "I have an eye for fabrics and designers. She was also wearing Jimmy Choo shoes, which means she has money. She spends a lot of it fighting off time."

"Meaning?"

"She's had work done."

His lips twitched. "You mean her breasts. I noticed."

"Figures," she said, tossing back his earlier sarcasm. Although any red-blooded male would have admired the ultra-perfect 38-Cs. "She spends too much time in the sun, or tanning salon, and then counteracts the negative effects with Botox injections."

"How can you tell?"

Afia slid her sunglasses to the tip of her nose and then pointed to her forehead and the space between her eyebrows. "No wrinkles. She was frowning, intensely. There should have been wrinkles."

"Anything else?"

"She's not a real blond."

He laughed. "Maybe my sister isn't a one-of-a-kind after all."

She scrunched the very brow she'd been pointing at. "Your sister?"

"Joni."

"Joni McNichols is your sister?"

Jake motioned her to lower her voice. "Who did you think she was?"

"Your wife . . . or someone."

His dimple deepened and suddenly she saw the resemblance. "Joni will get a kick out of that one."

"So is there a wife . . . or someone?" She couldn't believe she'd asked such a personal question. She barely knew the man. But he'd kissed her and she'd tingled, and she simply had to know.

"There are a few someones. Just no one in particular."

In other words he slept around. She'd bet her charm bracelet *his* life wasn't rated PG.

He dipped his chin and looked at her over the top of his sunglasses. "You do know that we're just role-playing here."

She forced herself not to flinch. "Of course." She would hold her own with this man if it killed her. Utilizing her rusty acting skills, she affected her best smitten-kitten persona. She skimmed her palm down his shirt, marveling at the hard muscles beneath, trying not to wonder what he looked like naked, which was no doubt *amazing*, and then rested her hand on his thigh. "So why are we watching Anthony Rivelli?" she asked in a throaty whisper.

He eyed her for a moment and then turned away and plucked a small sack of peanuts from one of the souvenir bags. "Because his fiancée, Angela Brannigan, thinks he's seeing another woman."

"Oh." She wondered if Angela had sufficient grounds, or if she was just unreasonably jealous. Like Dora and Frances who'd bullied Afia off of the charity committee just because their wandering husbands' eyes had lately strayed over to her. With Randy and Frank gone, those poor paranoid women assumed, though wrongly so, that she'd be on the hunt for wealthy husband number three. Her latest scandal had given them the fuel they needed to jettison Afia out of their social circle thereby banishing temptation. "Does she have any proof?"

"That's why she hired me." He popped a peanut in his mouth. "To *get* proof."

Afia's mind skipped to another sneaky snake. She leaned closer, her hand edging farther up Jake's thigh. "So how hard is it?"

He lapsed into a spasm of choked coughs. "What?"

Afia reached around and whacked him on the back. "How hard is it to track someone?"

"Oh, for Christ's . . . why?"

"Just curious."

"You can stop pounding on me. I'll live." He eyed her over the rims of his sunglasses. "I hope."

Her stomach turned. "Don't joke like that." *I haven't done anything wrong.*

He chucked the peanut sack into the souvenir bag. "Who do you want to track?"

"No one."

"Leave the snooping to the professionals, Afia.

"Maybe I'd like to become a professional."

"You don't have what it takes. Ah, shit." He tugged at the brim of his cap. "Here comes Rivelli."

"You haven't worked a day in your life."

"You're a fluff-brained idiot."

Afia's breath quickened as a surge of anger spiked her heart rate. *Harness your feelings, swallow the hurt.* Outbursts, according to her mother, were undignified. And by nature Afia abhorred confrontation.

"You don't have what it takes."

Her heart thundered in her ears. How did *he* know what she was capable of? She didn't even know herself until she unconsciously positioned herself in his lap, shielding him from Rivelli's view.

Spurred on by frustration and the driving, salsa beat, she shed her smitten-kitten routine and adopted the role of the brazen vixen. She wrapped her arms around Jake's neck and devoured that sinfully, sexy mouth. She nipped and suckled his lower lip, teasing the seam of his mouth with her tongue. He groaned, or maybe it was an exasperated grunt. She couldn't tell. She didn't care. When he opened his mouth and took possession of her tongue, an extravaganza of fireworks exploded behind her closed lids.

He tasted of spicy mustard, smoke, and sin.

She wanted to drown in his decadence. This kiss sizzled. This kiss was rated R.

It was all she could do not to totally combust when he cupped her bottom and pulled her snug against his crotch. This morning she'd thought him immune to her physical blessings. Oh, no. He absolutely, without a doubt, wanted her. He wanted her in a *huge* way, and considering the torture he'd put her through thus far, it did wonders for her fragile self-esteem.

"Get a room," a passing woman grumbled, piercing a hole in Afia's euphoric bubble.

Beth Ciotta

Oh, God. She'd made a spectacle of herself. Drawn attention when she'd meant to divert it. She'd lost control. Cheeks burning, she placed her palms on Jake's chest and eased back. *Don't panic.* "Is Rivelli gone?" A business-related question. Good. Showed she could focus. Too bad her voice cracked.

Jake peeked around her shoulder. It took him a full second to respond, and when he did his own voice sounded scratchy. "Yeah."

Was it possible that he'd witnessed fireworks as well? Nerves jangling, she hooked a finger over his sunglasses and slid them down his nose until their eyes locked.

His smoldering gaze ignited a fire that burned a path to her inner thighs.

Her mouth went dry. A trickle of sweat rolled down between her breasts.

Sizzle.

She had two choices: Break the mood or pick up where they'd left off. Mortified that she was actually contemplating an encore, she wiggled against his erection and faked a coy grin. "You do know that we're just role-playing here."

A muscle jumped in his cheek, and she instantly regretted her taunt. She was out of her league. He was going to chew her up and spit her out. Fire her for insubordination or for endangering his covert surveillance.

Jaw clenched, he rose, set her gently aside and then took a cautious step back as though she were a ticking bomb. Her skin prickled with dread as he wiped his palms down the legs of his jeans and then picked up the shopping bags. "Let's get

74

back to the office and discuss your duties," he said, while nudging her toward the parking garage. "Seems there's more to you than meets the eye, Jinx."

Chapter Seven

A basic background check told Jake plenty and zip about Anthony Rivelli. Thirty-seven and never been married. No record of being a sexual predator or a deadbeat dad. No civil suits filed. No criminal record. Never been charged for DWI, although he'd been issued a couple of speeding tickets. Not surprising since he drove a BMW Z4. *Nice.*

Rivelli owned a condominium in Ventnor, the shore town bordering Atlantic City, and a house in Cherry Hill, a ritzy community midway between Atlantic City and Philadelphia, Pennsylvania. He was a college graduate who'd worked his way up from slot host to the vice president of a major casino in less than fifteen years. Anthony Rivelli was driven, rich, and squeaky clean.

At least on the surface.

Jake shut down his computer and wondered what he'd find

when he dug deeper. Generally he found dirt. People, in general, were a major disappointment. Six years with the Atlantic City Police Department had exposed him to the dregs of humanity. Near the top of his list were men who physically or emotionally abused women and children, and that included fathers who failed to pay child support. Intimidating deadbeat dads didn't pay well but it was damned satisfying. As far as he was concerned abandoning a child—emotionally or financially— was a top-ten sin. Children were innocents, and there weren't a helluva lot of innocents in this world. Almost everyone had a skeleton in their closet.

Afia St. John had three. Not in her closet, but six feet under.

That woman was a direct connection to the great beyond, and all he could think about was tapping into her. He'd caught a glimpse of heaven when she'd blindsided him with that mind-warping kiss. A divine warning? A smart man would have issued her walking papers. His intelligence wasn't in question, but neither was his integrity. He was a man of his word, and he'd promised to look after Afia for two weeks.

Day one and he'd already breached Harmon's trust.

What had he been thinking when he'd stolen that initial kiss? Hell, it wasn't even a kiss, just a brush of the lips, and he'd been thinking about how sexy she'd looked eating that frozen custard. He'd been thinking about her sweet, velvety tongue, imagining all sorts of wicked scenarios. He'd been thinking about how cute she looked in that cheap baseball cap and silently admiring her observational skills.

He'd been struck stupid.

He'd scrambled to cover his bone-headed blunder, but then

she'd engaged in her own role-playing, giving him a throbbing hard-on and a headache to match. One moment he had her pegged as an inept submissive, the next she was salvaging a surveillance op by taking creative initiative. She was a damned enigma, and every fiber of his body ached to investigate each enticing angle.

Thankfully, he had the Rivelli case as a distraction.

The phone rang and he promptly answered it.

So did Afia.

"Leeds Investigations," they answered as one.

"Isn't that cute," Joni quipped.

"I'm sorry," Afia said.

"Don't apologize, girl," Joni said. "You were doing your job. I think she's a keeper, Jake. What do you think?"

"I think you're a pain in my ass."

"Is that any way to speak to your sister?" Joni asked.

"Did you call for a particular reason or just to bust my balls?"

"I'm hanging up," Afia said.

"Bye," Joni said. *Click.* "Okay, big brother. Spill."

"You first." Certain Afia was no longer on the line, Jake leaned back in his chair and massaged his pulsing temples. "What did the doctor say?"

"The same thing he said at my last appointment, that those few weeks of bed rest cured what ailed me and pee-wee. I'm in peak condition, which is more than I can say for you. Have you lost your mind?"

"Not that I know of," he said, thanking God for his sister's good health.

"Men who get romantically involved with Afia St. John, die."

"We're not romantically involved."

"Yet."

"Ever." Upsetting his pregnant sister by coming clean and admitting that he'd already succumbed to temptation wasn't an option. He hunched over and rooted in his top drawer for a bottle of aspirin. "She's not my type."

Joni snorted into the phone. "She's a woman. She's beautiful and she's in trouble. She is *so* your type."

"What makes you think she's in trouble?"

"Intuition."

Joni's intuition was killer. They both knew it, so he didn't argue the point.

"What are you looking for?" She also had the hearing of a superhero.

"Aspirin."

"Bottom right drawer next to the multi-vitamins you never take."

"I get my vitamins the natural way. By eating right." Today's boardwalk binge not withstanding. At the time all he could think about was putting some meat on Afia's bones. "Speaking of food, I'll have to take a rain check on dinner."

"Got a hot date?"

Jake grinned at her suspicious tone, and the fact the aspirin bottle was exactly where she'd said. "New case."

"The mystery client from this morning?"

"She thinks her fiancé is cheating."

"What do you think?"

"I think you miss the job." Jake washed down three aspirin with a swallow of cold coffee.

Joni sighed. "To think I've been replaced by a slumming socialite."

"Slumming?" Per his promise to Harmon, he'd been careful not to mention Afia's financial fiasco.

"She's loaded, Jake. Why in the hell would she want to work for a small time P.I. other than to get a few cheap thrills?"

"I resent that remark." Jake's lips curled upward. "I'm not cheap."

"Maybe not. But you're sure as hell easy." His sister groaned. "You can't save the world, Jake."

"I'm not trying to save the world."

"Yes, you are. One underdog at a time."

"Very dramatic," Jake teased. "Feeling hormonal?"

"Asshole."

He laughed. "What happened to cleaning up your language now that the baby's almost here?"

"That *was* clean compared to what almost flew out of my mouth," she said with a smile in her voice. "Dinner tomorrow night?"

"Sure. Joni?"

"Yeah?"

"No one could ever replace you."

"Love you, too, Jake." She smooched into the mouthpiece and then hung up.

He dropped the receiver into the cradle and then sat there staring at the phone, contemplating Joni's approaching delivery date and forthcoming bills. He thought about diapers, formula, baby furniture, pediatric visits, and other kid essentials. He worried about upcoming school field trips, boy (or girl) scout expenses, and the price of a tuxedo or prom dress. As it was, Joni and Carson just made rent. If only Carson would augment his spotty musician gigs with a steady nine to five. But Joni didn't want her husband to compromise his art. Compromising, Jake had pointed out, wasn't the same as abandoning.

It was like talking to a brick wall. If Jake even hinted to Carson that he should get a "real" job, Joni would never forgive him. He'd decided to give his brother-in-law a year to come around or to make it big. If he failed, then, by Christ, Jake would risk his sister's wrath for the sake of his niece or nephew and provide the jazz pianist with some inspiration by knocking some common sense into his artistic brain.

He was obsessing over college tuition when Afia cracked open his door.

"I finished deep-cleaning the reception area," she said in a timid voice.

He glanced up to find her standing on his threshold, ponytail disheveled, her cheeks flushed from exertion, the souvenir T-shirt stained with blue scouring powder. She swiped a hunk of hair out of her eyes drawing attention to a pair of bright yellow rubber gloves and a smudge of dirt on her left jaw. She looked rumpled and sexy as hell.

Man, he was in deep shit.

He'd agreed to let her scrub and polish the outer room because he couldn't find anything else to keep her occupied after they'd returned to the office, and he hadn't been in the mood to train her on the computer. He didn't want to be in the same room with her let alone standing over her, breathing in her scent, risking physical contact. He couldn't remember the last time he'd been so affected by a kiss.

"You do know that we're just role-playing here."

He had definitely underestimated her skills. In addition to being observant, she was one hell of an actress. Both useful talents in the field, not that he intended to utilize them. He'd learned his lesson on that score. He needed to concoct projects, something to keep her busy while he investigated Rivelli. He needed to keep an eye on her while keeping his distance.

This was going to be the longest two weeks of his life.

He watched as Afia tugged at the fingertips of her gloves and glanced around his office. For someone who'd been so flip about that supposedly meaningless kiss, she looked suspiciously embarrassed now. She hadn't made eye contact with him since returning to the Bizby, not that he'd pressed the point, because quite honestly he wasn't up to the discussion. He needed to examine his own shocking reaction to that kiss and to get a handle on whatever was brewing between them before addressing the issue. You didn't need to be a P.I. to detect the sexual tension.

She cleared her throat and pointed to a dust ball peeking out from between the file cabinets. "Are you sure you won't change your mind about me cleaning up in here?"

And watch you scrubbing nooks and crannies on hands and knees? Subject myself to the sight of your wiggling butt? "It can wait."

"It looks like it's been waiting for some time."

All right, so the place was a little dusty. If he bothered to raise the crusty venetian blinds, he'd probably find windows smeared with two months of film. Probably why he hadn't raised the blinds of late. Disgust would prompt him to hire a cleaning agency, an added expense he didn't need just now, or to snatch up a rag and a bottle of all-purpose cleaner himself. Except he'd run out of cleaning supplies two weeks after Joni's last day, and had yet to replenish them. As far as his four ineffectual temps were concerned, every one had given him the clichéd, "I don't do windows."

Between checking up on Joni, keeping up with cases, and playing Mr. Fix-it around his money pit house, he'd easily overlooked a little dust. Hell, a *lot* of dust. Apparently Afia was less tolerant. So much so she'd toted in her own cleaning products. "Why do I get this feeling I could eat off of your kitchen floors?" he asked.

She shifted her weight, worried her bottom lip, and he instantly realized his blunder. She didn't have a home. *"She's living with a friend,"* Harmon had said.

Jake fought the urge to push out of his chair, to close the distance between them, and to worry that enticing lip for her. *Don't think about that mouth, that kiss.* He cleared his throat and glanced at his watch. "Speaking of home. It's quitting time."

At last she risked his gaze. "But I haven't put in a full day."

"Again, we don't keep regular hours." He stood, strapped on his gun, and snagged a thermos and a set of high-powered binoculars. "You've done enough today, and I need to head back toward the Carnevale. Rivelli told his fiancée he'd be getting off work between five and six o'clock."

"Are you going to follow him?"

"That's the plan." He crossed the room, trying to ignore the eager look on her face.

"Do you need any help?"

"No." He shooed her over the threshold, closed the door behind him, and breathed in a lethal dose of lemons and bleach. He surveyed the reception area, adding another skill to Afia's list of talents. In less than three hours, she'd scrubbed and polished the sparsely furnished reception area until the walls gleamed and the hardwood floor shined. Even the couch looked resurrected.

Wait a minute. Hardwood floor? "Where's my carpet?"

"I can't imagine why you'd want that ugly shag when you have such beautiful hardwood floors." She peeled off her gloves, giving him her back as she tossed them into a pail and needlessly rearranged her cleaning products. "Besides it clashed with the walls and the sofa."

Evasive. Twitchy. *Uh-oh.* "Where's my carpet?"

She groaned and pointed toward the hall. "It was an accident."

Without another word, he walked past her to investigate. His first thought was how did she manage to roll up the good-sized area rug and maneuver it out into the hall all by her skinny little self? His second thought, when he unfurled the first quarter, was what in the hell were those white splotches all over his midnight blue shag?

He leaned down and sniffed. *Damn.* "How in the—"

"I used bleach to disinfect the toilet bowl. I thought I had screwed the cap on tight, but when I came back in I tripped.

There was a buckle in the carpet, and the bottle tipped, and—"

"The cap fell off and bleach splattered."

"I'll replace the carpet."

The hell she would. He'd bill Harmon. Sticking it to the old man for sticking him with the "bad-luck-beauty" had warped appeal. He looked over his shoulder and caught her stroking her charm bracelet, a habit he'd noted throughout the day. Given the influence of a superstitious mother, she no doubt considered those charms good luck. He hated to break it to her, but maybe it was time to swap those fourteen-carat gold charms for a cheap pink rabbit's foot. It sure as hell couldn't hurt. "Don't worry about it. Like you said, it was an accident." Ignoring her look of distress, he straightened and dragged the rolled carpet down the hall. "I'm going to store this in the cargo elevator for now. Grab your purse. I'll give you a ride."

"But-"

"Lock the door behind you." He tossed her the keys and then rounded the corner, carpet in tow. Maybe he could salvage a portion, utilize it somewhere else, or maybe he'd just chuck the damned thing. Joni had been nagging him to replace the seventies shag for months.

By the time he got back to his office, Afia had changed back into her tailored red shirt, knotted a silk scarf around her neck, and twisted her hair into a sophisticated bun. He caught a whiff of expensive perfume and noted the high-quality of her red leather handbag. If he wanted to harden his heart all he had to do was envision her closet, no doubt the size of his living room, stocked with a hundred pairs of shoes and racks of designer clothing.

And then there were people like Joni. People who clipped coupons and shopped at Price Clubs. People who could barely afford decent medical care.

Jake cringed at his unkind thoughts. Afia couldn't control being born into money anymore than she could choose the day she was born. Rich did not equal selfish and thoughtless. All the same, this moment, he couldn't wait to pass her off to her *friend*, the same person who'd probably provided her with this morning's limo and the chauffeur who looked as though he could double as bodyguard. He needed a breather. Time away from her to collect his normally superb senses.

"I really am sorry about the carpet," she said, handing him back his keys and gazing up at him with those lost puppy dog eyes.

"Forget it," he said, resisting the urge to give her hand a reassuring squeeze. Touching was bad. Touching led to stroking, holding, and kissing. "The reception area never looked better. Thanks."

She smiled. "You're welcome."

Don't focus on her mouth. Don't think about that kiss. He nudged her toward the stairs. "What's your address?"

"That's very kind," she said, descending the first of four flights. "But I called a friend. I'll just wait out front."

"I'll wait with you." He wasn't about to leave her alone. Though not the worst of areas, Afia St. John was an easy target. Pretty, gullible, and jinxed. The urge to play guardian angel, to deliver her to his own doorstep, to cook her supper, and to tuck her away in his bed was overwhelming. She was *not*, he reminded himself, a stray. She'd lost her fortune, not her friends, most who lived, he assumed, quite comfortably. Tonight she'd be sipping cocktails in a million dollar home with her socialite girlfriend, while he chugged bitter coffee in the front seat of his '99 Mustang and endured the tedium of tailing a suspected skirt chaser.

He wouldn't have to worry about Afia, wouldn't have to *think* about her until tomorrow when she showed up for another day at the office. By then he'd have a plan. A way to keep her busy for the next two weeks while keeping her at arm's length.

In spite of the disturbing sexual attraction simmering between them, in spite of her vulnerable aura, he'd be damned if he'd give in to the temptation to "save her." She had Harmon, and Harmon had Oscar Kilmore. Between the two of them, they'd track down her money, and she'd go back to doing whatever rich widows do. Then Jake could get back to his real life and to the people who truly needed him.

By the time they hit the street, he'd worked up a decent head of steam. He couldn't pinpoint his frustration, which made him all the more pissed.

Afia hiked her leather bag higher on her shoulder. "You really don't need to wait—"

"Yes, I do."

"I don't want you to miss Mr. Rivelli—"

"I won't." He leaned back against the Bizby's brick front and lit up a cigarette, hoping to take off the edge. Afia started to say something and then apparently decided better. Smart girl. He was in no mood for a lecture. Besides, he'd already made a pact with Joni. Not wanting to be a bad influence on the baby, she'd agreed to temper her foul language if he gave up smoking. They both had up until the day the kid was born. He'd already cut down from a full pack to five cigs a day. The way he saw it, he was ahead of the game.

Afia copied his stance, settling in and leaning back against the wall, which was fine except that she was standing a little too close for his immediate comfort. "About that kiss," she said, tweaking his unease. "We haven't really discussed—"

"It was good. You were good. Rivelli didn't suspect a thing. Nice cover." He blew out a stream of smoke and glanced down in time to see her frown. What? Was she disappointed because he'd only rated her good? Had he wounded her pride? Sorry, but no freaking way was he going to own up to what he really thought of that kiss.

"Thank you. But, I have to confess you inspired the action."

"How so?" *For the love of God,* he thought, *don't admit you have the hots for me.*

"You insulted me."

His mouth fell open, the cigarette dangling from his lower lip. "When?" When the hell had he insulted her?

"When you said I don't have what it takes to be a private investigator." She straightened her shoulders, and although she didn't meet his gaze or raise her voice, he could tell she was upset. "I wasn't going to say anything," she continued, her voice shaking with each earnest word. "But I thought about it all afternoon, and . . . I changed my mind. You don't know me. How could you possibly know what I am or am not capable of? I want to learn the tricks of your trade, and I'd appreciate it if you'd take me seriously."

Why did he have the feeling that she wasn't used to speaking up for herself? Again he was shocked by her vulnerability and obvious insecurities. He snuffed his cigarette and nabbed her chin. "Look at me and say that again." It was a move meant to intimidate.

She met his gaze, and it was then that he saw gold flecks of determination sparking in her big brown eyes. "I want to learn your business." She steadied her voice, grasped his hand and squeezed. "I want you to take me seriously."

"Fair enough," he said, tempering a smile and the wild beating of his heart. Christ, Joni was right. Afia *was* his type. Although instead of rescuing her from an abusive lover, he needed to rescue her from herself. Afia St. John was the victim of low self-esteem.

Jake was a breath away from kissing some confidence into her when a Harley-Davidson roared up curbside and broke the mood. Afia hurried forward. He slowly followed.

A six-foot-something mass of cut muscles, wearing tight black jeans and an even tighter black T-shirt took off his helmet revealing a head of short, equally black hair. The neatly trimmed goatee perpetuated biker boy's devilish look. The man smiled at Afia then nodded at Jake and offered his big hand in greeting. "Rudy Gallow."

"Jake Leeds." He shook the hand of the man he recognized from this morning. The man he'd mistaken for Afia's chauffeur. The man she called *friend*. Gallow's grip was strong and confident, his gaze direct and assessing. Jake tried to size him up in return, but couldn't get a bead on him outside of the notion: *He's not what he seems.*

Afia took up a spare helmet and slipped it on without direction, leading Jake to believe she was no stranger to this man's bike. She glanced at Jake while tightening the strap beneath her chin. "What time would you like me to be here tomorrow?"

So much for chitchat, he thought as he watched her climb up behind Gallow and straddle the motorcycle seat. Now that her friend was here, she seemed in a hurry to get away. He imagined the striking couple going for a spin and ending up back at the man's posh home. When she wrapped her arms around Gallow's ripped abdomen, Jake speculated about the sleeping arrangements and a muscle jumped under his left eye. He couldn't fathom why he was ticked. He'd known Afia for all of six hours. So she had a boyfriend. So what? "Nine o'clock."

She smiled. "I look forward to it."

Jake eyed biker dude, subtly scoping for clenched fists, narrowed eyes, any body movement to imply propriety or jealously. The man merely smiled, an enigmatic twinkle in his eyes that confirmed he was going to be a pain in Jake's ass. With a cheeky salute, he eased his bike into the steady flow of traffic.

What the hell? Jake climbed into his Mustang and watched as they drove away, more frustrated and intrigued by the minute. Afia was right. He didn't know her. Every freaking time he thought he had a handle on her, she up and threw him a curve ball. Seeing her transform from demure socialite to biker chick had definitely shaken his assumptions. On impulse, he snatched up his cell phone and hit speed dial as he pulled away from the curb and headed toward the Carnevale Casino. "Joni? Fire up your laptop."

Without realizing it, Afia had just issued him a challenge.

Chapter Eight

"What do you want this morning, Afia? A bowl of oatmeal or a cup of fruit?"

"Do you have the makings for a ham and cheese omelet?" Rudy cast a concerned glance at his friend, decked out in her cheetah pajamas and furry black slippers, and pondered her sanity as she rooted through one of the six clothing racks stationed on either side of his oak dining table. He'd known Afia for five years. Her breakfasts had always consisted of oatmeal, fruit, or dry wheat toast with a glass of orange juice. Last night she'd blown him away by asking Jean-Pierre to pick up a pepperoni pizza with double cheese on his way back from the video store. Then, right in the middle of *Casablanca*, she'd asked if they had any microwave popcorn—buttered. Now this. Something was definitely up.

Pulling his "ABBA" T-shirt over his head, he padded across the kitchen floor in his boxers and bare feet and then opened the refrigerator door to check out the food situation. "I can whip you up an omelet with spinach and low-fat provolone."

"What about pancakes with maple syrup? Oh, and maybe some bacon."

He nabbed a bag of hazelnut coffee beans, shut the fridge door, and then moved to his sleek soapstone countertop. "Okay," he said, filling the coffee maker with bottled water and scooping the beans into a grinder. "What happened yesterday at the office?"

"You mean aside from me filing, cleaning, and ruining Jake's carpet?"

"Yes, aside from that."

"Nothing."

"You're stressed," he shouted over the grinding ruckus.

"No, I'm not."

"Depressed."

"No."

Rudy rolled back his shoulders as the grinding ceased and rich black coffee dripped into the glass pot. "Lonely?"

She crinkled her nose. "How could I be lonely? I'm living in a cozy two-bedroom townhouse with two warm, intelligent men."

Rudy surveyed his sheet and pillow strewn sofa (Afia's temporary bed since she refused to accept his offer to swap places), his quaint kitchen, dining, and living area made even smaller by her suitcases and boxes, and Jean-Pierre's clothing racks and bolts of glitzy fabric. What she called cozy, he considered cramped, though he'd die before speaking his mind. His home was Afia's for as long as she wanted-ed. Their employer/employee relationship had blossomed into a full-fledged friendship over the past few years. She'd even helped him to launch his freelance chauffeur business. Afia was tolerant, generous, and pure of heart, and Rudy adored her even with all of her quirky hang-ups and superstitions.

As for Jean-Pierre, well, as much as he liked the costume designer, the man had a few irksome habits. Such as referring to people by pet names, and hand-stitching trim on dancers' costumes while watching the Classic Movie channel. The next time Rudy stepped on a straight pin in his bare feet, he was going to punch Jean-Pierre in his chiseled jaw.

"Then you must be horny," Rudy said, heading back toward the fridge. He heard Afia gasp, and he smiled. For an open-minded person, at times she was pathetically easy to shock.

"Why do you say that?"

"Because you're eating to fill some void. You used to shop. Now you don't have any money, so you're eating comfort food. Not that I'm complaining. I always thought you were too skinny."

"You did?"

"Absolutely, honey." He pulled out a carton of eggs, a bag of fresh spinach, and a loaf of wheat bread.

"Why didn't you say something," she asked quietly.

He turned and noted her crestfallen expression. "Because of that," he said, gesturing to her pout. "I didn't want to hurt your feelings." *And because you had too many other people telling you what you should and shouldn't look like.*

She tugged at the hem of her pajama top and straightened her shoulders. "I'm not that sensitive."

"*Oui, ma petite,* you are." Jean-Pierre Legrand, Rudy's latest roommate and newest pain in the ass, sashayed into the living room wearing Pink Panther draw-string pajama bottoms and a sexy smile. He crossed to Afia and kissed her on each cheek. *"Bonjour, Chou à la crème."*

She blushed and giggled. "Good morning, Jean-Pierre."

Rudy couldn't imagine why she was so charmed since Jean-Pierre had essentially called her a cream-puff. As she was working hard to assert herself these days, he didn't think she'd appreciate the nickname. But Rudy had to admit even an insult sounded sexy with a French accent.

As if reading Rudy's mind, the man cast a thousand-watt smile over his shoulder. *"Bonjour,* Gym Bunny."

"Jean-Pierre." Rudy snagged a skillet from the baker's rack, trying not to stare at his roommate's defined pecs. He had a lot of nerve ribbing Rudy about his love affair with free weights, when he himself had the wiry, hard body of an avid runner. The least Jean-Pierre could have done was throw on a shirt, not that Afia seemed bothered. No. The only one apparently affected by Jean-Pierre's bare chest was Rudy. *I am open and ready for a serious, long-term relationship,* he silently affirmed. Jean-Pierre was *not* relationship material. "Omelet?"

"Merci, Bunny.

Rudy wanted to pummel him. He also wanted to get him in a lip-lock. Neither action seemed prudent.

The chestnut-haired man held Rudy's gaze for an uncomfortable moment and then turned to Afia, utilizing his moderately-accented English. "So, what are we doing here?"

She flipped her hair over her shoulder and sighed. "Looking for something to wear."

Jean-Pierre noted the crammed clothing racks with a coy

smile. "I can see where that would be difficult."

"Something subdued," she said, thoughtfully tapping her finger to her chin. "And not too tight."

"Something boring," Jean-Pierre said.

Afia beamed. "Exactly."

"So we should pass on the paisley turquoise and lime silk suit."

She blew her bangs off of her forehead. "Afraid so."

"Pity." Jean-Pierre raked his wavy hair off of his clean-shaven face and tied the shoulder-length mass into a low pony-tail, his compact shoulders rolling with the effort.

Rudy suppressed a groan, and cracked six eggs into a ceramic bowl. "Go and pour us a cup of *café, Chou à la crème*," he heard Jean-Pierre say, "and leave this to a profes-sional."

Two seconds later, Afia was standing beside Rudy, straining to reach the mugs on the top shelf of his corner cabinet. "I real-ly like Jean-Pierre," she whispered.

"Of course, you do," Rudy mumbled. "He filched those racks from the wardrobe department so you could hang up your clothes, and to top things off he's hot, he's French, and he's *gay*."

"You noticed," she said with a grin.

He grunted then snared three mugs for her and set them on the counter. "So what happened with Jake?" he asked, firmly changing the subject. "You two were looking pretty chummy last night when I rolled up on my bike."

"For heaven's sake, *nothing* happened!"

Jean-Pierre started singing the theme to *Casablanca*. "You must remember this, a kiss is still a kiss . . ."

Afia's cheeks bloomed with two brilliant blotches.

"Jake kissed you?" Rudy exclaimed.

She averted her eyes and concentrated on pouring the coffee. "It was business."

". . . a sigh is just a sigh . . ."

"Do you mind?" Rudy called over his shoulder.

"*Moi?*" Jean-Pierre chuckled then opted to whistle the melody.

Rudy rolled his eyes and turned back to Afia. "I can't believe you confided in Jean-Pierre and not me. You've known him for less than three weeks."

"I didn't confide in Jean-Pierre," she said, shoveling four spoons of sugar into her coffee.

"Then how—"

"I don't know," she grumbled.

"You talk in your sleep, *Chou à la crème,*" Jean-Pierre said, coming up behind them. "Must have been the sangria. I was on my way to the bathroom when I heard you mumbling about a . . . um . . . *surveillance* op and Jake's tongue." Grinning, he presented her with a pair of taupe slim-fitting capris and a short-sleeved emerald shirt trimmed with brown and taupe ribbons. "Unassuming," he said. "Better than boring." Then he draped the outfit over a chair, picked up two mugs, and handed one to Rudy.

Rudy ignored the jolt when their fingers brushed and focused on Afia. "Care to explain how you ended up frenching your boss on a surveillance gig?"

She sipped her coffee and stared down at her slippers. "Can't."

"Can't?"

"It's related to a case, and Leeds Investigations prides itself on maintaining confidentiality."

Rudy stroked his goatee. "Hmm." He glanced at Jean-Pierre, cocked an eyebrow, and then looked back to Afia. "So how's the coffee?"

She puckered her lips and blew on the steaming java. "Hot."

Jean-Pierre winked at Rudy. "That is what she said about the kiss."

✱ ✱ ✱

Mrs. Kelly was trying to calm a cranky parent when Afia blew into the daycare center. According to Rudy, who patiently waited in the limo with the engine running, she had five minutes to coordinate her schedule with the woman who, with the exception of two assistants and an occasional volunteer mother, ran the center single-handedly. Since Jake hadn't mentioned a specific lunch hour and had implied she could be working sometimes as late as six-thirty, she figured her best course of action was to volunteer between six and eight-thirty in the morning. Mrs. Kelly had intimated that she could use an extra hand to do some cleaning and someone to help serve cookies and milk during morning story time. Afia looked forward to spending time with the children even if it meant mopping up spilled milk and crumbled cookies.

Children were wondrous creatures and a source of curiosity for Afia. Just like working for a living and asserting herself in uncomfortable situations. Standing up to Jake yesterday, looking him in the eye, and demanding that he respect her wishes had been an incredible rush. It had taken her the utmost control not to crow to Rudy and Jean-Pierre. Rudy, especially, would be so proud. But she feared, as excited as she was, if she started talking she might unwittingly divulge the details of the Brannigan/Rivelli case. So instead she'd indulged in pepperoni pizza, popcorn, and a classic movie with her best friend and her new friend, Jean-Pierre. They'd stayed up until two a.m. giving each other facials and getting tipsy on sangria. She hadn't realized what a small and sheltered life she'd led until Henry Glick had robbed her of her security. Yesterday had been the best day of her new life.

Today would be even better, because today Jake was going to teach her some investigative techniques. Today she'd start hunting down Glick and her money.

She looked around, frowning at the crayon-marked walls and the threadbare carpet. The daycare center could benefit from a dose of her money. Unfortunately, for now, Mrs. Kelly would have to make due with Afia's time, and time was ticking away. The last thing she wanted was to be late to the office two days in a row.

"Are you the hat lady?" A little red-haired girl, maybe three or four years old, tugged at Afia's blouse. "Mrs. Kelly says the lady who gave us the hats was pretty. You're pretty."

"Why, thank you." Afia stooped down to put herself eye to eye with the cute little munchkin. "And yes, I'm the lady who *gave* you the hats. What's your name?"

"Mya."

Afia smiled. "Did you like the hats, Mya?"

The little girl's mouth puckered into a frown. "Billy taked mine."

She raised an eyebrow. "Billy *took* your hat?"

The girl nodded. "He's bad."

"Maybe if you ask nicely, he'll give it back."

Just then a slight, skinny-legged boy galloped into the room wearing one of Afia's straw hats. The buttercup yellow number, with an up-turned brim and a big, red rose pinned due center. He looked ridiculously cute.

Mya disagreed. She wagged her pudgy finger chanting, "Sissy, sissy, sissy! Billy is a sissy!"

Afia gasped. "That's not nice, Mya."

She pointed to the man arguing with Mrs. Kelly. "Daddy said so!" she announced.

Afia was disgusted and absolutely speechless.

The little girl taunted the boy in a singsong voice. "Billy is a sissy! Na-na-na-na-na-na!"

Red-faced, Billy rushed forward and clipped Afia in the eye while tackling Mya. All hell broke loose and finally, Afia had Mrs. Kelly's attention.

❋ ❋ ❋

He wouldn't yell. He wouldn't lecture. He'd simply wait and see what kind of excuse Afia offered for being twenty minutes late. No wonder she couldn't hold down a job. She was clumsy, moody, and habitually late. Okay, maybe not moody so much as unpredictable. Her ability to transform from kitten to wildcat in the blink of an eye had kept him tossing and turning most of the night. Or perhaps it was the vivid dream showcasing Afia in stiletto heels and biker leather. If she was as adventurous in real life as she was in Jake's fantasy, no wonder her first husband had suffered a heart attack in the middle of sex.

Just one of the interesting tid-bits Joni had confirmed last night via cell phone as Jake had tailed Anthony Rivelli from the Carnevale Casino to his Cherry Hill home. Unfortunately, their conversation had been cut short when Carson had returned home early from a gig, surprising Joni with flowers and Chinese food. Joni had promised to phone Jake with the rest of her report as soon as she did some fact-checking. One thing about Joni, she never did anything half-assed. Which probably meant, if she dug deep enough, she'd discover the fact that Afia was currently broke. He'd cross that bridge when he got to it.

Anxious and without a laptop, he'd ended up calling a buddy on the force who'd gotten back to him in spurts during the six non-eventful hours he'd sat surveillance outside Rivelli's home. He'd quickly learned that Rudy Gallow, though he looked big, bad, and rich, had a clean record, a chauffeur's license, and a bank account comparable to Jake's, which wasn't saying much. He rented a townhouse in a new development in the Inlet, not the nicest of areas, though the city was working hard to build up that section of town. Gallow wasn't Afia's social equal. He was her ex-driver and current friend, possible lover. Harmon hadn't seemed thrilled that she was shacking up with her "friend," but he hadn't seemed overly concerned. Jake didn't know what to make out of any of it, and he hated that he couldn't let it go. Of course, he could call Harmon and ask him straight out. *What's up with Afia and biker boy?* But Harmon might wonder why Jake cared.

Good question.

Just because he was attracted to Afia didn't mean he had to act on it. Just because she seemed as though she needed to be saved, didn't make it so. She'd already proven herself quite the actress. What if the wide-eyed, vulnerable waif persona was an act? What if she'd seduced both of her husbands with that angel aura only to sprout horns? Two rich, older husbands. Two freak accidents. A missing fortune. A hot, young lover.

Black Widow.

Jake rolled his eyes and reached for a bottle of aspirin. He really had to stop watching late night film noir.

His door slammed open, and Afia skidded into the office wearing a preppy summer outfit, big black sunglasses, and a panicked expression. Her hair was unbound and tousled, her cheeks flushed. She'd either sprinted to work or just tumbled out of bed. Again, he wondered about her sleeping arrangements. Again, his left eye twitched.

She stood poised on his threshold, one hand pressed to her heart as she caught her breath. "I'm so . . . so sorry . . . to be late," she said in between pants. "There was an . . . incident."

Jake raised one eyebrow, waiting for her to elaborate.

"So," she said, ten seconds later as she moved forward and gingerly sat on the edge of an opposing chair. "Where do we begin? What would you like me to do?"

Jake chased three aspirin with a swallow of cold coffee, winced and then tossed the empty cup in the trash.

Afia clasped her hands in her lap, fingered her charm bracelet. Her leg started to bounce. "Would you like me to make a fresh pot of coffee? Check the messages? File some . . . files?"

He leaned back in his chair and crossed his arms over his chest. "Are you going to wear those sunglasses all day?"

She pushed them higher up her pert nose. "It's a little bright in here."

"Late night?"

"Rough morning." Her leg bounced faster.

He didn't know what that meant, but he didn't like the possibility that it involved sex. Jake stood, reached up under his retro bowler's shirt, and repositioned his gun. "Let's roll." He walked past a wide-eyed Afia, trying not to notice how sexy she looked with all that rumpled hair.

"Where are we going?" she called, chasing after him.

"To start your training."

She let out a musical squeal.

Jake suppressed a wicked grin. She'd be singing a different tune once she got a load of her first assignment. He stopped short, turning to explain the concept of "low profile" at the same time she tripped, stepped out of her strapless green slip-ons, and tumbled forward.

He caught her in his arms, all one-hundred pounds of her, feminine and flustered and smelling of cinnamon. His mouth watered. His pulse raced. "Afia."

She tilted her face up, moistened her lips, and he thanked God those sunglasses shielded her puppy dog eyes. "Yes?" she whispered.

"Do something with that hair."

Chapter Nine

"You can't be serious."

"Dead serious."

Afia squinted through her sunglasses to where Jake pointed, her nostrils flaring at the odor of rotting vegetables. "But it's disgusting, not to mention rude."

"It's an old and proven means of gathering valuable information." Jake tugged down the brim of his baseball cap and glanced over his shoulder. "We've got about an hour before the disposal truck comes by. Chop, chop, baby."

Afia knotted her hair into a low bun and cursed her chosen footwear. The backless slip-ons were pretty but impractical. Not that there was anything practical about "dumpster diving," as Jake had so eloquently tagged her appointed task. Mental note: Buy a pair of cheap sneakers. "Invading someone's privacy is a serious offense, you know."

"It's part and parcel of being an investigator." He slid his hand into the front pocket of his jeans and pulled out a pair of disposable, latex gloves. "So do you have what it takes or don't you?"

Afia bristled at the challenge and the implication that she

considered herself above a little dirty work. She wasn't a snob, and she certainly wasn't a wimp. She did, however, have scruples. Fighting her honest nature, she nabbed the gloves and snapped them on, ignoring Jake's toe-tingling smirk. It was really most annoying being attracted to a jerk. When she'd tripped and fallen into his arms this morning, her knees had gone mushy along with her brain cells. She'd stared up at his scrumptious mouth, hoping for a sizzling kiss, and all she'd gotten was yet another rude remark about her hair. Both of her husbands and almost every other man she'd ever met preferred women with long hair. Sleek, meek "Barbie dolls." As near as she could tell, Jake liked his women bald, fleshy, and aggressive. Even *she* wouldn't go so far as to shave her head to please a man. He'd just have to get over it.

Shooting the infuriating P.I. a sidelong glance, she scrunched her nose while nearing the six-foot, brown-metal dumpster of the ritzy high rise. "What are *you* going to be doing while *I'm* breaking the law?"

"Standing guard. If anyone starts down the alley, I'll distract them." He grinned as he offered her a leg up. "And for the record, you're not breaking the law."

"Then why don't you want anyone to see us?"

"Because I don't want to have to explain why we're scavenging through the trash. We're on a case, remember?"

"How could I forget?" He'd recited his views on confidentiality and covert surveillance on the short ride over to Anthony Rivelli's shore getaway. She'd appreciated the industry insight, if not the sarcasm. Inexperience might cause her to bobble, but she'd never purposely bungle a job.

Annoyance gave way to sinful delight when he encircled her bare ankle with one hand and cupped her bottom with the other. Her entire body tingled as her mind raced with a wicked fantasy. She had his pants around his ankles when he called her back to reality saying, "Nothing personal." *Kaching!* Another ding in her ego. Next he issued a "One, two, three . . ." and before she knew it, she was flat on her back amidst an ocean of rippling green garbage bags. How romantic.

"You okay?" he asked with a smile in his voice.

"Fine," she grumbled, squirming to find her footing. She swatted away a fly and crinkled her nose, trying not to gag on a noxious odor as she unknotted one of the garbage bags. At least it was a cool, cloudy morning. She didn't even want to know what this dumpster smelled like in the heat of a sunny afternoon. "What am I looking for precisely?"

"Anything with Rivelli's name on it. A bill, a magazine, an envelope. Even an empty prescription bottle. Anything that tells us that that trash is *his* trash. Then toss the whole bag down to me. We'll go through it back at the office."

"I just don't see the point," she grumbled. Picking through strangers' refuse. It was downright creepy. She quickly abandoned one bag for another.

"A credit card statement would list recent purchases. If he has a girlfriend on the side he might be buying her gifts." He paused, and she heard the flick of a lighter, smelled smoke, and knew he'd just lit up a cigarette. Mental note: Buy him a nicotine patch. "A phone bill would list phone numbers and frequency of calls," he continued. "If we're very lucky he might be hooked up with a woman who's fond of writing love letters."

"That's *if* he's hooked up," Afia said, leafing through Mrs. Robert Sheffield's copy of *Homes and Gardens*. Her heart stuttered when she came across the feature on holiday dinners and renovated Victorian houses. Banking on the power of affirmations, she mentally chanted, *"I am open and ready for a family and a home full of warmth, laughter and love."*

"Find anything?"

Startled, she flipped the magazine over her shoulder and promptly lost her footing. She fell backwards, bursting through a bulging bag of discarded food products from a recent barbecue. "Gross," she mumbled, flinging a leaf of wilted lettuce off of her elbow.

"Someone's coming," Jake said. "I'll take care of it. Just stay low and keep quiet."

She supposed now wasn't the time to whine about the barbecue sauce smeared all over her pants. Biting her tongue, she shifted her position and rummaged through a bag to her left.

Bingo.

Two minutes later Jake was back, and Afia had located two bags of trash belonging to one Anthony Rivelli. She tossed them over the side and heaved herself over the edge, ignoring Jake's command to wait. She'd be darned if she'd spend another minute in this disgusting dumpster. What if something lived in here? Like a rat? She scrambled over the side, nearly kicking him in the head. In her haste she lost her left shoe.

He caught her in his arms, his expression and voice laced with sarcasm. "I suppose you want me to go in after it."

She glanced down at her right shoe. The pointy-toe of her beautiful tapestry slip-on was stained with catsup and relish and something gooey that she didn't recognize. The heel had mysteriously disappeared. "Not really." She kicked its mate off and up into the dumpster. Darn, but she'd loved those shoes.

Frowning, she squirmed out of his arms, peeled off the soiled latex gloves and then tossed them into the dumpster as well. Pushing her Gucci sunglasses (the only thing of class left on her body) firmly up her nose, she gave him her back and then marched barefoot toward his car.

Jake came up behind her and swept her off of her feet. "Are you crazy? With your luck, you'll step on a piece of glass." He deposited her in the front seat of his sporty Mustang and then went back to retrieve the bags.

What did he mean, *with her luck?* He sounded just like her mother. Questioning her judgment. Anticipating the worse.

By the time he'd tossed Rivelli's trash in the trunk and slid behind the wheel, Afia was fuming. He'd just ruined what was supposed to be the second best day of her life by reminding her that she was jinxed. A normal person would have gotten in and out of that dumpster without incident. She looked like something the cat dragged in and smelled even worse. Randy and Frank would have been appalled by her appearance. Her confidence plummeted further, and it was all Jake's fault.

Why did she feel this expedition had been his way of teaching her a lesson? Arms crossed over her chest, she angled her head, and glared at him from behind her sunglasses. "So. Am I forgiven for being late?"

He eyed her bare feet, her stained pants, plucked a watermelon seed from her hair and then leaned forward and crushed his mouth to hers.

Tinder to dying fire. She burst to life under his heated touch, groaning as he coaxed her mouth open, his soft, velvety tongue stroking hers. His large, strong hands cradled the back of her head, holding her captive as he ravaged her mouth, seeking, taking. Her insides melted as desire pooled low in her belly. She turned toward him, channeling all of her frustration and longing into this wildly erotic moment.

Sizzle. Burn.

She grasped his shoulders, clinging for dear life as he nearly drove her to climax with a kiss that would melt steel.

She couldn't think. Couldn't breathe. Somehow she ended up straddling him, his rock-hard erection rubbing against her tingling crotch, her back pressed against the steering wheel.

Making out in a car in broad daylight.

She couldn't remember the last time, if ever, she'd been this turned on.

She knocked off his cap, raked her fingers through his hair, unfastened the top buttons of his shirt, and smoothed her hands over his muscled chest, frantic to feel skin on skin.

He swept off her sunglasses, nipped her jaw, her cheek . . . and froze. "What happened to your eye?"

"What?" Her hand stilled on his bare shoulder. She felt a muscle in his neck jump against her thumb, and her heart raced even faster. He was angry. Why was he angry? Still dazed from his kiss she tried to focus on his words.

He tenderly brushed his thumb under her left eye.

She winced.

"Rough morning, huh?" Frowning, he lifted her off of his lap and deposited her on her own side of the seat. "Bastard," he mumbled, keying the ignition, and shifting into reverse.

"It's not what you think."

"Don't you dare stick up for him."

Him? Him, who? "Oh, my God. Are you talking about Rudy? Do you think he . . . he . . . "

"Well, didn't he?"

"No!" Her stomach dropped as Jake backed out of the alley and peeled onto Atlantic Avenue. "God, no. It was Billy."

"Who the hell's Billy?" He sped through a yellow light, heading back toward Atlantic City. To where? His office? The Inlet? Did he know where she lived?

"He didn't mean it, Jake. It was an accident."

He worked his jaw. "Do you know how many times I've heard that one, Afia?"

His anger rattled her, and yet she wasn't scared. Just heart-sick. Why did she feel as if she'd just pushed some very old and sensitive buttons? He thought someone had intentionally harmed her. He was outraged on her behalf. She felt sudden-ly and horribly guilty for not being upfront with him this morn-ing. Why hadn't she been upfront?

She laid a calming hand on his forearm and squeezed. "Listen to me, Jake. It was an accident. Honest. Billy is a lit-tle boy. I stopped by The Sea Serpent-"

"The what?"

"It's a daycare center. I wanted to talk to the woman in charge about volunteering, but she was busy and well . . . There was this little girl, Mya, and she was teasing Billy, and . . . well,

111

he pounced on her, and I can't say that I blame him, although it's that girl's father that deserved a good smack, but anyway, Billy tackled Mya and clipped me in the process."

Jake glanced sideways at her, slowed the car to a lawful speed limit. "Are you serious?"

"Dead serious." She felt the tension easing in his arm muscles and tried to pacify him further with a teasing jab. "It's sweet that you care, but you're not going to punch out a four-year-old boy in my defense, are you?"

He let out a ragged sigh, ran a hand over his face then made a left onto the Blackhorse Pike.

"Where are we going?" she asked.

He glanced at her, an intense, soul-searing gaze that caused her breath to catch in her throat. "My place."

So you can toss me on your bed and pick up where you left off with that kiss? She rubbed her wishbone charm and gulped. "Why?"

"We need to talk."

* * *

Angela wanted a martini. Instead she ordered a diet soda. Daddy didn't approve of drinking before noon. God forbid she disrespect Vincent Falcone.

Head of the Falcone "family," Vinnie, a leathery-skinned, silver-haired man of sixty-nine flashed his capped teeth at their buxom waitress who looked all of twenty. "I'll have an iced tea, sweetheart." He dismissed her with a wink and a swat on the butt.

The young woman giggled. "Your father's such a flirt," she said to Angela and then skipped away.

Okay, Angela thought, she didn't skip. But she may as well have. "I swear the waitresses in this restaurant get younger by the day. Next week a sixteen-year-old will probably serve us."

Vinnie reached for the Italian bread and tore off the end. "I wouldn't mind being serviced by a sixteen-year-old." He chuckled at his own joke as he dipped the bread in balsamic vinegar and olive oil.

Angela frowned, worrying that he was only half-kidding. The older her father got, the younger his taste in women. It was disgusting. And yet he wasn't any different from any number of men leaving their wives, or longtime lovers, for younger, supposedly hotter women. Youth, according to Wall Street and Hollywood, equaled desirability.

Angela's mind floated to Anthony. He was only thirty-seven. But *she* was thirty-nine and three-quarters. She didn't care how well she ate, how much she exercised, or how much "work" she had done, she couldn't compare to a perky, supple, twenty-something. She just knew Tony was seeing a younger woman. While racking her brain for a list of candidates, she'd considered the various entertainers employed by the Carnevale. Given her fiancé's obsession with the performing arts, she could well imagine him becoming enamored with a costumed bimbo. Angela knew for a fact that the nine female dancers in the variety show that had opened three weeks ago in the casino's main room were all under twenty-five. What red-blooded male wouldn't be hot for a young, flexible dancer? What young, ambitious woman wouldn't be hot for a vice president of a major casino?

Then again he could be hiking any number of skirts at the Carevale, a glitzy, Euro-hip casino that appealed to the under-forty crowd.

Her cheeks prickled with heat as she curled her fingers into her lap so as not to slap the waitress when she skipped forward and placed their appetizers on the table. It didn't matter that the girl hadn't done anything wrong. She was wrinkle-free. That was enough.

"I'm having a small party Friday night," Vincent said to Angela, although his eyes were on the waitress's retreating backside. "I would like for you and Anthony to attend."

Angela smiled and nodded, knowing it wasn't a request so much as a summons. "Tony promised he'd be home no later than seven for the next few nights." He'd been especially attentive since the lipstick incident. Not that she was fooled. "If you don't mind us being a little late—"

"Just as long as you show. I want to introduce my future-son-in-law to a few old friends." He swallowed a raw oyster, chucked the shell and picked up another.

"We'll be there." Angela stabbed a cucumber with her fork, craving an entire plate of fried calamari, a big bowl of pasta, and two or three cannolis. She'd been eating like a bird for three years. She was starving. But it was worth it. She'd snagged Anthony Rivelli with this body, and by God she intended to keep him.

"Everything okay between you and Anthony?"

Angela's head jerked up at her daddy's wary tone. The last man who'd broken her heart had ended up at the bottom of the

Delaware River. "Everything's perfect."

At least it would be as soon as that P.I. discovered the identity of her competition.

✳ ✳ ✳

Jake nudged Afia to get her moving toward his front door. Any minute now the dark clouds looming above were going to split open and pour rain. He knew the 1890 Victorian wasn't much to look at just now, but she was standing on his front lawn staring up at the blue and pink house with its broken gables and warped balustrades as though it was the house in *Amityville Horror.*

"You live here?" she whispered.

"Amazingly." If she thought this was scary, wait until she got inside. Stripped hardwood floors, peeling wallpaper . . . oh, and the pet hair. "You're not allergic to cats, are you?"

"You have cats?" She blinked up at him as they traversed the creaky floorboards of his porch. "How many?"

"A few." Jake shifted Rivelli's trash bags to one hand and unlocked the front door. He needed a drink. A stiff shot of whiskey to burn off the last of his adrenaline. One look at Afia's injury and he'd been primed to kick some ass. It was the volatile side of him that had prompted him to resign from the force. He'd probably scared the hell out of Afia, but she'd handled the tense situation with a cool head and a sense of humor. The woman was full of surprises.

Jake pushed open his door, his dark mood lifting a shade at the sight of a friendly face. The senior feline of the house sat

115

just inside the foyer, a stuffed mouse clenched between his teeth. "That's Mouser."

Afia reached down and gingerly petted his head. "Hi, Mouser."

Didn't look to Jake as if she had much experience with cats. "He won't bite."

She nodded. "Despite his name, he doesn't look like much of a killer."

He chuckled. "He's not. He's a big fat baby." But lovable as hell. The old black and white greeted Jake at the door every-day. Mouser dropped his stuffed toy at Jake's feet. He bent down and scratched the cat's whiskered chin, thanking him for the gift. Content, Mouser waddled off to take up his place on the jade-velvet footstool. Same routine everyday. Jake straightened, placed his keys on the Queen Anne table and switched on the Tiffany table lamp flooding the small, dark foyer with muted amber.

Afia stepped in behind him, peered around his shoulder, and giggled.

"Rosco and Barney," he said, nodding at the twin silver tab-bies wrestling on the floor in front of the carpeted staircase. Unsettled by the sheer joy in Afia's laughter, he set the trash bags next to the coat rack and motioned her ahead into the liv-ing area. "Scamp and Velma are around here somewhere."

"You have *five* cats?"

"Not by choice. They're all strays." He reached down to break up Rosco and Barney's antics, smiling when Barney licked his hand. "I'm only keeping them until I can find them a home."

"How long have you had them?"

"One to four years, depending on the cat." He ignored the twinkle in her eyes, crossed to the bay windows and pulled back the heavy curtains to let in some light. No dice. The sky had darkened to a smoky shade of purple. One hell of a storm was brewing and he'd yet to patch the leaks in the kitchen's ceiling. Time to dig out the pots and pans.

He turned to excuse himself and found her circling the room, scrutinizing his sparse décor. "It's a work in progress," he said, feeling defensive. He only had so much time and even less money.

"It's charming," she said, eyeing the sculpted mahogany fireplace, shield back gentleman's chair, and lyre base coffee table. "And tasteful. The exact opposite of your office."

"I don't live at my office."

"I never would have guessed you liked antiques. Where do you shop?"

"Estate sales. Flea markets. Most of these pieces are repro-ductions, but every once in a while I get lucky." He motioned to the mahogany-finished Medallion sofa he'd picked up for a song. "Have a seat." The sooner they had their talk, the better.

She eyed the jewel-toned upholstery and winced.

"I'll get a lint brush." What had he been thinking bringing her here? This place was a hellhole compared to the mansions she'd probably lived in.

"It's not that. It's . . . me." She gestured to her stained clothes then held up her hands. "I'm afraid to touch anything. I'm a mess."

Jake thought she looked adorable but kept his opinion to

himself. He'd brought her here to clear the air. To address this infernal attraction. He'd expected her to refuse when he'd asked her to climb into that dumpster. The more she surprised him by going against type, the more he wanted to jump her bones. Which is basically what he'd done in the car. He'd learned every curve of her body in sixty-seconds flat. He still couldn't believe what a total ass he'd made of himself by losing control. To make matters worse, he'd overreacted when he'd gotten a glimpse of that puffy eye. The possibility that his feelings ran deeper than lust proved downright chilling. Christ, he needed that drink.

"There's a full bathroom upstairs," he said. "Second door on the right. Help yourself. I'll see if I can find you something to wear." *Then we're going to have that talk.*

She caught her lower lip between her teeth, scrunched her nose.

"What?"

"Are we pressed for time?"

"No. We can go through Rivelli's trash here just as well as back at the office. Why?"

She shoved her hair out of her eyes with the back of her hand. "I feel disgusting. Would you mind terribly if I took a shower?"

Great. He wanted to cool the attraction, and she wanted to get naked. He jammed his hands through his hair, trying to shake loose the image of her standing in his shower, water sluicing down her hot, little body. "The main bathroom has a claw-footed tub. It's antiquated but the plumbing works. I installed a shower in the small bathroom adjacent to my bedroom. It's my personal bathroom so it's kind of a mess. But, whatever, take your pick." Bath or shower, she'd still be naked, and he'd be burning in hell for his fantasies.

She moved forward and tugged at the hem of Jake's shirt, pointing out a food stain just north of his belt buckle. "Maybe I should take a bath and let you use the shower."

Maybe I should shoot myself, he thought. Now she was suggesting they *both* get naked. "Afia."

She tilted up her face, her eyes glazed with desire. "Yes?"

"About what happened in the car."

"I'm sorry about the barbecue sauce."

"I'm not talking about that." Thunder rumbled in the distance. Mouser streaked by, a blur of black and white fur, and dived under the sofa.

"I guess he doesn't like storms." She moistened her lips, her eyes now huge with dread. "I'm not fond of them either."

"Meaning?"

"I have the distinct feeling you're about to rain on my parade," she said. "I, for one, enjoyed what happened in the car."

He swallowed hard. "Mixing business and pleasure isn't smart."

She quirked a timid smile. "I'm not famous for making wise decisions."

"I'm not famous for playing second fiddle."

Her smile faded. "What's that supposed to mean?"

He didn't know exactly. He'd slept with women who were

seeing other men. Casual dating, casual sex, he'd never had a problem with the concept. Until now. Envisioning Afia doing the nasty with biker boy set his teeth on edge. Something about that guy bothered him.

And then there was Harmon. If Jake nailed his goddaughter, the man would have his balls.

"I don't understand, Jake. Is it because of my hair?"

"What?"

"Because I'm not opposed to getting a little kinky, but I draw the line at shaving my head."

"Who asked you to shave your head?" And what exactly did she consider kinky? Damn. He shifted to disguise an infuriating boner.

"Are you or are you not attracted to me?"

He tried to ignore the hitch in her voice, the confusion in her eyes. He tried to rise above his carnal lust, and failed. He grabbed her up and kissed her hard, deep, and long. One hand cradled the back of her head, while the other cupped her tight, little ass, and he pulled her flush against his body. Instead of pushing him away, she moaned into his mouth and squirmed against his erection, sending shock waves throughout his lower half. Thunder rattled the windowpanes, and Jake swore he'd been zapped by a bolt of lightening. Every molecule in his body pulsated. He was on fire.

When he set Afia to her feet she was glazed-eyed and short of breath. He was no better off. "And that's the last I want to hear on the subject," he rasped, backing toward the stairs. "You and me . . . it's not gonna happen."

She blinked at him, her lips swollen from his arduous kiss. "Where are you going?"

"To take a cold shower."

Chapter Ten

"Rudy, I want to have a fling."

"That's flattering, honey. But you're missing a piece of equipment that I'm rather fond of."

"Not with you, silly." Afia sank lower in the old-fashioned bathtub, careful to keep her cell phone above the bath water. "With Jake. I want to have a fling with my boss." Five minutes after that mind boggling kiss-off, and she was still trembling. If that . . . *interlude* was any indication of his lovemaking skills, she'd probably climax before he even got her pants off. And wouldn't that be bliss? She'd never had multiple orgasms, but sensed a testosterone-charged dynamo like Jake wouldn't settle for less. She adjusted the faucet, cranking up the cold water as she assessed the wainscoted room's eclectic bric-a-brac. Her pulse fluttered at the thought of the big, bad P.I. scanning a flea market for porcelain perfume bottles and ceramic soap dishes. "Nothing serious," she said as much to herself as to her friend. "Just . . .

fun. Just . . . sex. Does that make me awful?"

"It makes you human. You forget, honey. I've seen Jake. I'd be worried if you didn't want to get horizontal."

She wondered what Rudy would think if he knew how close she'd come to "getting horizontal" in the front seat of Jake's Mustang. She'd straddled the man, for God's sake, unbuttoned his shirt, and groped his chest. Could she be any more sluttish? Then thirty minutes later she'd been ready and hoping for a toss on his sofa. His kisses were like some sort of cosmic aphrodisiac, rocketing her libido to the next galaxy. Wiping perspiration from her brow, she used her toes to turn off the brass faucet. The scented water rose two-inches shy of the deliciously deep tub's rolled rim. "So you approve?"

"You're a grown woman, Afia. You don't need my approval. Or anyone else's for that matter."

She recognized that disgusted tone. "*Anyone else* being my mother."

"You do tend to let her influence your relationships."

"I don't want a relationship with Jake. I want to have a fling." Short, hot, and memorable. She couldn't imagine long-term with him. He was too intense. Too unpredictable. But mostly he was bossy. Henry Glick had cured her of blindly following a man's directive. "Besides," she said "Mother's in Tahiti. By the time she hits U.S soil, the fling will be flung."

"You're not the love 'em and leave 'em type, honey."

Although he'd probably meant that as a compliment, it felt like a slap in the face. *Afia's a goody two-shoes. Na-na-na-na-na-na.* "That was the old me. The PG me. I would like one X-rated night before I die." Lightning flashed outside the small window, a shock of white light bouncing off of her beloved bracelet curled on the porcelain vanity. Rudy had claimed that losing her fortune and her moneybag charm on the same day had been pure coincidence. Giselle St. John would cite the consequences of being born on Friday the thirteenth. Thunder boomed. "With my luck, come tomorrow, I'll be knocking on Heaven's door."

"That's your mother talking," Rudy said. "Please don't make me reach through this phone and slap you."

"Sorry."

"Forgiven. So your husbands were duds in bed, huh?"

She could almost envision the teasing grin on his face. "No." She smoothed a cool washcloth over her burning cheeks, mindful of the swelling beneath her left eye. She'd never discussed the specifics of her sex life before with Rudy, and there were limits to how much she'd say now. It was too personal, and okay, maybe a little embarrassing. "They were both very . . . attentive."

"Boring."

"Conventional."

Rudy grunted. "Like I said, boring."

She heard the pipes groan, registered the silence of pulsating water, and immediately envisioned Jake stepping out of the shower in all his naked glory. Water rippling over the hills and valleys of all that sinew. His biceps flexing as he finger-combed his hair off of his chiseled face. Her eyes rolled back in her head.

Sizzle.

All she had to do was climb out of the tub, hurry two doors

down, and climb all over Jake. Surely, he wouldn't be able to resist a naked, willing woman. Surely, that would kick start a fling or at least a one-night stand. It was brazen and risky, and darn it, she just couldn't do it. "So, how do I seduce a man who doesn't want to be seduced?"

"How do you know he doesn't want to be seduced? What about that kiss on the boardwalk?"

She glided a bar of heather-scented soap over her legs and smiled. "That was nothing compared to what happened today," she said, marveling that the macho P.I. had actually purchased fragrant soap.

"If I have to hear about this through Jean-Pierre, so help me, Afia—"

"Jake kissed me this morning in his car," she said, lowering her voice to an excited buzz. "Actually he ravished me, and it was . . . incredible, but unfortunately it went no further than a ten alarm kiss."

"Was there tongue involved?"

She blushed to the roots of her damp hair. "Um . . . yes. Then later," she hurried on, "when I questioned the attraction, he floored me with a second scorcher. Rudy, he makes the backs of my knees sweat."

"Wow. I'm jealous." Her friend cleared his throat, as if dismissing a dicey image. "Wait a minute. Why are you worrying about seducing this guy? He's all over you."

"*Was* all over me. He doesn't believe in mixing business with pleasure. Or something to that effect," she mumbled. *"You and me . . . it's not gonna happen."* He'd sounded so adamant. And what had he meant about playing second fiddle?

"Maybe he's intimidated by your wealth," Rudy said. "Blue-collar, alpha-men are funny that way."

"You think?"

"Why are you whispering, honey? I can hardly hear you. Where are you?"

She heard Jake walking along the hall, padding down the creaky stairs, and immediately pulled the rubber plug from drain. "In Jake's bathtub. Where are you?"

"A.C. International. A high-roller's flying in from Florida. I'm supposed to drive him . . . Did you say Jake's bathtub?"

"Don't ask me to explain. It's case-related which makes it confidential. Let's just say I ended up wearing someone else's lunch."

"That's disgusting."

"That's what I said." She climbed out and snatched up a fluffy towel while maintaining her grip on the cell phone. "So what should I do?"

"Soak and scrub, and hope that he owns some talcum powder. It's not like you know him well enough to borrow his deodorant."

Afia rolled her eyes, trading the towel for the T-shirt and sweatpants Jake had given her just before he'd escaped into his own bathroom. "Hold on." She laid down the phone to pull his faded gray T-shirt over her head, breathing in the distinct scent of fabric softener. There was something undeniably intimate about wearing her host's clothes. Smiling, she tugged on the dark blue sweatpants, pulled the drawstring tight and then put the cell back to her ear. "You have approximately sixty seconds to give me a crash course in flinging."

Rudy sighed. "You're absolutely positive you don't have feelings for this guy?"

"I've known him for less than two days."

"Takes less than two minutes. Cupid's a quick shot."

She blocked out the image of Jake fired up and ready to pummel her "assailant," his affectionate behavior toward his five "stray" cats, and the knowledge that he spent his free time shopping for antiques to furnish his charming Victorian home. She focused on his sexual charisma—his hands, his tongue, the hard evidence of his desire—while shaking her hair loose from its bun. A plethora of feelings had rocked her body, but she was certain it had nothing to do with affection and everything to do with lust. "If you don't want to help me, Rudy, just say so." She leaned over to roll the too-long hem of the overly baggy sweat pants to above her ankles. "I just thought, well, you have more experience than I do."

"Ah."

Afia cringed at her friend's flat tone. "I didn't mean to imply that you're . . ."

"The king of quickies?"

"I'm sorry, Rudy." This morning he'd received three new self-help books from Amazon.com. He'd probably been sitting in the airport waiting area engrossed in an enlightening read when she'd called. Afia crumpled onto the toilet seat, feeling like an insensitive heel. "I know you're trying to alter your lifestyle. I wasn't thinking. I shouldn't have said . . ."

"Afia."

"Yes?"

"Always do what you want and say what you feel, because those who mind don't matter, and those who matter don't mind."

She relaxed and smiled. "Shakti Gawain?

"Dr. Seuss."

"I love you, Rudy."

"I love you, too, honey. Now here's what you need to do."

* * *

Showered, dressed in comfortable black cargo shorts and a faded blue T-shirt, Jake sat at the oak butcher-block table petting Velma with one hand while sorting through Rivelli's discarded magazines and receipts.

The afternoon storm raged. Rainwater dripped into the three stainless steel pans, an annoying audible plop that registered every five seconds. Rosco and Barney wrestled in the laundry room. Mouser cowered under the sofa waiting for the storm to subside. Wary of women, Scamp had taken refuge under Jake's bed and wouldn't be showing his whiskers until Afia left the house. Jake almost wished he could join the skittish puss.

He stretched his muscles, but the tension remained. The woman had him tied up in knots. His "talk" hadn't gone precisely as planned. No, he'd had to complicate matters by sticking his tongue down her throat for the second time today. *Smooooth*. He'd spent ten minutes under an icy shower spray trying to numb the craving to join her in that claw-footed tub. He couldn't remember the last time he'd been this stupidly hot for a woman.

Probably because this was a first.

His head snapped up as Afia padded into the kitchen wearing his sports socks, sweatpants, and police academy shirt. He'd purposely provided her with worn workout gear guaranteed to fit her like a potato sack. The T-shirt fell to mid-thigh. His sweats, rolled to above her ankle, bagged in all the right places. She had absolutely no shape. Her face was scrubbed clean of make-up, and her damp hair was divided into two long braids. She looked all of seventeen.

Perfect. He'd never been attracted to jailbait.

Just think of her as off-limits, which she is, and you'll be fine.

Right.

So long as she follows my dictate and doesn't raise the subject of our mutual attraction, everything will be cool.

Sure.

He focused on Rivelli's crumpled receipts and continued to stroke Velma, who'd sprawled out on the left half of the butcher's block. He'd tried to break the tiger cat from jumping up on the tables, but she was stubborn and needy, and hell, it's not like he ever used the butcher block anyway. "Feel better?" he asked Afia without turning. *Be cool, man. Don't bring up the kiss.*

"Much better," she said. "Thank you."

"There's a T.V. in the parlor. Make yourself comfortable. We're not going anywhere for a while. It's raining like a bitch out there."

"I can see that."

He heard the scrape of metal against tile and glanced over

129

his shoulder to find her adjusting the placement of one of the three pans. *Plop. Plop.* He waited for a snide comment regarding his leaky ceiling but, naturally, she disappointed him. She motioned toward the receipts. "How's it going?"

"Not good."

"Oh." She worried her full, naturally pink bottom lip while sitting down on the stool next to him. Just his luck she didn't have a favorite afternoon soap opera. "So I guess you found some incriminating evidence," she said, her disappointment as evident as the welt beneath her eye.

"Just the opposite. I found zip." A surge of protectiveness washed over him. Accident or not, *Billy* had clocked her good. "How's your eye?"

She glanced sideways at him. "You're not going to get riled again, are you?"

He cocked an eyebrow. "Four years old, huh?"

She quirked a lopsided grin. "He was defending himself. Someone called him a sissy."

"Ah, well in that case . . ." He resisted the urge to touch her, to kiss away the pain. Touching was bad. Kissing was worse. "I'll get you some ice." He escaped toward the freezer and some frosty air.

"I like the way you decorated your kitchen. It's . . ."

"Rustic?"

"Homey."

He found it hard to believe that she actually liked the scarred walnut table and mismatched wicker chairs. The appliances were ancient. The collection of old-fashioned kitchen utensils a flea-market whim. Then again little-rich-girl was full of surprises. He returned with a folded dishcloth full of ice cubes. "Here. Try this."

"Thank you." She pressed the makeshift icepack to her cheek.

He focused back on the receipts, silently cursing the flowery scent wafting from her glistening clean skin. That's what he got for setting out the soap Joni had given him, one of her perpetual housewarming gifts. *"What if you have a female guest,"* she'd said, *"like me. If you think I'm using your manly deodorant bar on my sensitive skin, you're nuts."* He wished to Christ he'd tossed his sister's advice along with that flowery-smelling "guest" soap.

"So Rivelli's trash was," she shrugged, "clean?"

"No empty drug or liquor bottles," he said, biting back a smile, "or hefty receipts to suggest he's a drug or alcohol abuser. Not even a wine bottle to suggest casual drinking."

"Or an intimate dinner for two," Afia added. "No love letters?"

"Nope. No condom wrappers or empty tubes of spermicide, which implies no sex, unless he's having unsafe sex."

"Or unless she's on the pill. That's assuming there is a *she* other than his fiancée. Did you question Ms. Brannigan about her choice of birth control?"

"No, I did not. Good call, Jinx." He glanced sideways, impressed by her reasoning, intrigued by the tinge of pink in her cheeks. Either she was pissed off by the nickname (Good. Insurance that she'd keep her distance) or she was embarrassed by the topic of discussion. The woman had been married twice, and she was possibly, *probably* screwing around with her ex-chauffeur. Surely birth control had been addressed. She was childless after all. So what method did she prefer? He wondered. The pill? The ring? A diaphragm? Not that it mattered, because they were *not* going to have sex. And even if they did he'd still wear a condom. He didn't bed hop, but he did have a healthy sex life and a string of casual girlfriends. Protection was second nature and a matter of respect for one's self and one's partner.

He wondered if biker boy wore a pocket rocket.

He wondered a lot of things about that guy. He knew through Joni that Afia had bought him that limousine. What kind of a man accepted a gift like that from a woman? A gigolo? A gold digger? A lazy bum? She'd claimed that a four year old had given her that shiner, but how did he know for sure? Was her relationship with Gallow on the rocks now that she'd lost her fortune? He'd only met the man once, but he'd bet his P.I. license Rudy Gallow's interest in Afia wasn't rooted in her feminine charms.

Jake clenched his jaw, cursing his obsession with Afia's mysterious "friend." He'd known this woman all of two days, and he was acting like an overprotective, over-possessive ass. He couldn't help wondering if she'd affected her father and husbands this way. First they lost their minds, next their lives.

Jinxed.

"Didn't find a phone bill," he said, smoothing his palm over Velma's exposed belly in a bid to calm his nerves. "And there's nothing suspect about the receipts I did find."

Velma stretched out, bumping her paws against Afia's elbow.

Using her free hand, she reached across the table and scratched the cat's head with her fingertips. "Maybe Rivelli's not having an affair." Velma purred, and Afia grew bold, using her entire hand to massage the tiger's furry neck. "Maybe Ms. Brannigan's unduly insecure."

"It's possible," he said, flinching when her hand connected with his.

"But not probable?" she asked, pulling away and fisting her hand in her lap.

"I still have another bag of trash to go through." He rose to check on the rain-catcher pans. "We'll see." Dammit, if she didn't abandon the ice pack to follow him, sliding a spare pan into position while he emptied a full one into the sink.

"I guess your line of work has made you cynical," she said, from behind him. "That's understandable, but people aren't always what they seem."

"I'll agree with you there."

"I mean sometimes they have secrets, but it's because they're embarrassed about something, not because they've done anything immoral or illegal."

Thunder rattled the kitchen windowpanes as a different kind of tension charged the air. This was no longer about sexual awareness. This was about deceit. Intrigued, Jake abandoned the pan, turned and caught Afia stroking that damned bracelet. A practice she indulged in whenever she was nervous, which bothered the hell out of him because it suggested she was relying on a superstitious talisman rather than self-confidence. He leaned back against the counter and crossed his arms over his chest. "Are we still talking about Rivelli?"

"I wasn't bored," she blurted.

"Excuse me?"

She stepped in next to him, avoiding eye contact, and turned on the faucet. "I told you that I wanted this job because I was bored. That's a lie." She soaped up a sponge and attacked the stainless steel saucepan. The way she scrubbed you'd think it had been filled with burnt pudding instead of rainwater. "My business manager embezzled all of my money. I'm . . .I'm . . ." she scrubbed harder. "Well, I don't have any money. I need to work to pay off my bills and I wanted to work for you because I thought maybe . . ."

"Yes?"

"I was hoping to acquire the skills to . . ."

"What?"

"To track down the man who stole my money."

"I see."

She scrunched her brow. "You're being very calm about this."

"Very little surprises me, sweetheart." Actually, she had surprised him. He'd expected a confession regarding her ex-chauffeur, not her traitorous accountant. He would have preferred to know where she stood with Gallow, as he already knew the specifics of her financial status. Of course, *she* didn't know that he knew. He had two choices: play dumb or fess up about Harmon. Since Harmon had hired him, and the man therefore was a client making Jake's "assignment" confidential, the latter was not an option. "So you're embarrassed because you're broke?"

"No!" She jerked back, soaking the front of her shirt with

soapy water. "I'm embarrassed because I was stupid enough to give Henry Glick power of attorney."

Jake relieved her of the pan, trying not to stare at her chest, because, dammit, she wasn't wearing a bra. Her nipples pebbled against the thin, wet cotton, teasing him, taunting him. Hell. "Intelligent people get ripped off all the time, Afia." *You weren't the only one who was conned by Glick,* he wanted to say. *He was a trusted acquaintance of your mother's.* Instead he said, "Look at it as a life lesson." How lame was that?

But she wasn't paying attention to him. She was hyperventilating. "Oh . . . my . . . God . . . my . . ."

Jake's heart pounded as he watched her fingering her bracelet and gasping for air. He wrenched open the door beneath the sink and yanked out a paper bag. "Breathe into this." He placed the bag over her mouth. "Slow. Easy."

She knocked away his hand and the bag and felt around the sudsy bottom of the sink. "Charm . . . lost . . ."

"I'll find it." Heart in throat, he maneuvered Afia onto a kitchen chair and forced the bag over her mouth. "You breathe."

* * *

Some seductress. Not that she'd been in the actual process of seducing, but she'd been laying the groundwork, tearing down one possible barrier by coming clean about her finances or lack thereof.

She'd gotten flustered.

She'd lost a charm.

Now she sat in a cushioned wicker chair, red-faced with humiliation, a paper bag crumpled in her lap. Three weeks ago she'd come close to losing it, but she'd never suffered a full-blown panic attack. Not even when Randy had collapsed on top of her in the middle of sex. She'd been frantic on the inside, of course, but she'd reacted in a calm, clear-headed manner. She'd bottled her anxiety. She was very good at that. At least she used to be.

Afia massaged the tightness in her chest, watching as Jake wielded a wrench to loosen the kitchen drainpipe. He'd said he'd find her charm, and he seemed determined. Probably feared she'd freak out if he didn't produce. She wouldn't freak because, in the three lung-crushing minutes that she'd been gasping for air, she'd resigned herself to the notion that the charm was forever lost. She felt it in her bones. In her heart.

The hamsa hand. The magical charm that served as protection from the evil eye. The sentimental loss was nearly as crushing as the symbolic significance.

"It's not here," Jake said, thoroughly inspecting the pipe. He shot her a cautious glance, as if braced for a psychotic outburst. "Maybe you lost it upstairs," he said calmly. "Did you wear the bracelet in the bath?"

"No. I took it off. I . . ." she pressed her lips together, tears blurring her eyes as a thought occurred. "I probably lost it in the dumpster when I was rummaging through all that trash. And it's too late to go back and look because you said the disposal truck was on its way."

Jake secured the drainpipe then shimmied out from under

the sink. "That was over an hour ago. Wouldn't you have missed it before now?"

"I had other things on my mind." *Like trying to get you in bed.* What had seemed difficult before, now seemed impossible. As if he'd want to have a fling with a hyperventilating flake. Not that sex was even the issue. She hated that she'd lost control. "I'm sorry I overreacted," she said, brushing away a renegade tear. "It's just that it was a shock and a disappointment and . . . the hamsa hand."

"I take it the hamsa hand is a charm of major significance?"

Velma rubbed up against her ankle. Afia reached down and stroked her fur, feeling oddly calmed by the action. "It's a magical charm that serves as protection against the evil eye."

Jake dabbed a towel to his water-splattered T-shirt and then walked over and pulled up the wicker chair opposite Afia. He sat, jammed his hands through his spiky hair. "So now you think you're open season for this . . . evil eye? Is that why you got so upset?"

Velma trotted off toward another room, leaving Afia alone with the stern-faced P.I. She frowned, easing her knees away from his. "You're making fun of me."

"No," he said, leaning forward and bracing his forearms on his thighs. "Just trying to understand."

Though compassion shimmered in his emerald eyes, she knew he was a realist and not easily swayed by ancient superstitions. Her mother's rendition of the evil eye was too lengthy and dramatic, so she opted for a passage she'd read in an academic essay. "The evil eye is in essence a transmitted sickness. When an envious person gazes upon a coveted person, object, or animal too long, they're giving the evil eye, dooming said object to 'dry up.' "

He angled his head. "What do you mean 'dry up'?"

"Fruit withers on orchard trees. Children vomit. Nursing mothers or livestock lose their ability to produce milk. Men lose potency."

His brow furrowed in disbelief. "Damn."

She bristled. "I'm not making this up. It's an ancient belief."

"Superstition, you mean."

"In Sicily and Southern Italy they believe there are those who have the power to deliberately cast the evil eye," she plowed on, "while other cultures consider the act unintentional."

He raised a lone eyebrow. "At the risk of insulting you, you don't actually believe that you're in danger of drying up just because you lost that charm."

"The hamsa hand," she repeated with a shiver. The thought of "drying up" and never having children had been enough to incite that panic attack. "I don't know what to believe, Jake." She settled back in her chair with an exhausted sigh and studied her bracelet. "My dad gave me this bracelet on my thirteenth birthday. It had thirteen charms based on the concept that unlucky thirteen represents reversed bad luck. Each charm provided protection against one of my mother's pet curses or offered plain 'good fortune.' " She quirked a sad smile. "He figured I needed all the luck on earth."

"Because you were born on Friday the thirteenth?"

"Because I was born to Giselle St. John, a fanatically super-stitious woman. My name, Afia, means 'born on Friday.' I guess she didn't want me to forget, as if I could. Anyway, Lord knows I've had my share of misfortune. The last few years have been . . . difficult, but I managed." *Thanks to shopping and Rudy.* "Then three weeks ago I lost my moneybag charm, the same day I learned Henry Glick had absconded with my fortune."

"Coincidence." Jake took her hands in his and rubbed his thumbs over her knuckles.

Her pulse fluttered. If only he would pull her onto his lap, into his arms. This moment she longed to feel safe, coddled. A dangerous thing for a woman striving not to need a man. She cleared her throat, quirked a crooked smile. "You sound like Rudy. Actually his exact words were, *'Your life is out of control because you have no control in your life.'* Hence the Glick incident."

Jake tightened his grasp on her hands, glanced up, and rattled her with a piercing glare. "How can you be with that guy?"

"My mother recommended him and—"

"Not Glick." He practically growled the name. *"Gallow."*

Afia's mouth went dry. "You sound as if you don't like Rudy."

"I don't."

Her heart hammered against her chest, her breathing quickened. "But you don't even know him."

"I know his kind. That's enough."

So, what? He'd sized him up in one look? Caught a "vibe?" Mortified, she snatched back her hand. She knew Jake was alpha and macho and all that, but he had cats, and he liked antiques, and . . . her heart shriveled. He didn't even *know*

Rudy, and yet he was judging his lifestyle? "Well," she said, rising with as much dignity as she could muster while wearing sweatpants and a soaked tee, "I may be superstitious, but you're . . ." A homophobe? A bastard? ". . . a narrow-minded jerk!"

"Hold up." Jake stood and towered over her.

"I can't work for you."

He looked incredulous. "What? Wait a minute. I'm just trying to help-"

"By insulting Rudy and *his kind*?" She turned on her heel, too fast she realized too late. Lightheaded, she toppled back against his hard body. "Let me go," she snapped, trying to squirm out of his embrace.

"If I let you go, you'll fall. You're still dizzy from that attack." He tightened his hold, dropped his mouth close to her ear. "I'm sorry," he said, his warm breath fanning her neck. "I spoke out of turn. Your relationship with Gallow is none of my business."

Her knees weakened at the feel of his moist breath and scent of herbal shampoo. She closed her eyes and took a deep, resolving breath. She refused to be attracted to this man. "Rudy's a wonderful, warm-hearted human being." Her limbs trembled with conviction.

"I'll take your word for it." He turned her in his arms and eased her back down onto the wicker chair. "Let's back up and pretend that I didn't insult your . . . friend. And that you didn't quit."

She shook her head, a lump the size of the Hope diamond wedged in her throat. "I can't work for you."

"You can't leave me high and dry without an assistant." He cocked his head, his voice low and seductive, his eyes shining with a combination of stubbornness and desperation. "Give me two weeks notice at least."

"I can't—"

"I'll help you find Glick."

Her heart pounded against her ribs, thunder boomed, lightning cracked, and a cat howled low and long from the room beyond as Afia slowly nodded her agreement.

God help her, she'd just made a pact with a jerk.

Chapter Eleven

"Have you got the stuff?"

Jake ducked a giant moth as it zoomed toward the motion detecting security lamp and then held up a white paper sack. "Double cheeseburger with extra pickles, large order of onion rings." He held up a second bag. "A quart of Rocky Road."

Joni narrowed her eyes. "You didn't get that low-fat frozen yogurt crap, did you?"

"God forbid."

She threw open the front door, snatched the bags out of his hands and then bid him inside the McNichols' small, but tidy, two-bedroom apartment. The country-style décor, a pleasant mix of checks, stripes and flowered print, echoed the softer side of his sister's personality. "What took you so long?" she snapped, easing herself down onto her red and white checked sofa. "I'm starving."

Tonight, Jake noted with amusement, Joni clashed big time with the warm, inviting furnishings. "Considering I was on my way back from Cherry Hill when you called with your *emergency,* and that there aren't a helluva lot of fast food restaurants open at this hour, I think I made pretty good time." He opted to sit in the quilt-printed rocker glider, a safe distance away from his hormonal sister. "You could have sent Carson."

"Carson got a last minute call to sub for the pianist in the pit band for that new show at the Carnevale. The regular guy broke his wrist. Bad for him, good for Carson. This could turn into a steady gig," she said with a big smile. "He has a rehearsal after the show. I don't expect him until around three a.m."

Jake frowned. "What if you need him before then?" Sure, he was happy about Carson's potentially steady job. But if it meant leaving Joni alone late at night, every night . . .

"He's got his cell phone," Joni said, nibbling on an onion ring. "Stop being such a mother hen."

Since their own mother had passed on from cancer six years ago, and as Carson's parents lived in Ohio, Jake figured he had the right to hover and nag. It didn't matter that Joni had always been a tough little rug rat, or that she'd married an adoring husband, he still considered himself his little sister's protector. Just now he was cursing himself for indulging her late night craving. His stomach rolled at the sight of all that grease. "How can you eat junk like that after midnight?"

She licked her fingers. "I'm pregnant. I can eat junk like this anytime."

He thumbed up the brim of his baseball cap and watched her devour a quarter of the double cheeseburger in two bites.

"That's not your supper is it?"

She smirked. "No. I had spaghetti and meatballs with Carson around five. We missed you."

"Sorry I had to cancel again. It's this case." This time he'd tailed Rivelli to Angela Brannigan's home, an upscale townhouse on the outskirts of Cherry Hill. He could have bailed at that point on the assumption that Rivelli would spend the night in his fiancée's bed, but something prodded him to extend the surveillance. Sure enough, around ten o'clock, the casino V.P. exited Angela's townhouse, hopped into his BMW, and sped off. He'd driven straight home and after an hour his lights were off, and all was deadsville in Rivelli's primary residence. Maybe he was humping his secretary in the office supply room, because there sure wasn't any action late at night. Not the past two nights anyway.

"Tell me about it," Joni said. "Maybe I can help."

Jake pointed at the quart of ice cream sitting on the honey-oak coffee table. "You want me to put that in the fridge?"

"No. I'm going to eat it in a minute."

The health nut in him cringed. "The whole thing?"

"Stop busting my ass. I get enough grief from Carson." She reached for another greasy onion ring. "According to the doctor, I'm fine. Now tell me what's up with the cheater. And don't look at me with that 'it's confidential' face. I'm still part of the team. I'm just on extended leave."

He grunted. "Like you're ever coming back." Once she had the baby, she'd forget all about nailing cheaters, abusers, and deadbeat dads. She'd be immersed in the daily grind of rearing her kid and making sure he or she got the right moral guidance so that they didn't end up a cheater, abuser, or lazy bum. She'd never be able to dump her kid at daycare. Speaking of which . . . "You know anything about a daycare center called The Sea Serpent?"

"Funny you should ask. It came up when I was researching Afia. Sorry I haven't filled you in before now, but there was a lot of interesting info on that girl, and I wanted to try to sift through fiction and fact. I'll go and get my notes," she said, rising with fried food in hand. "Be back in a sec."

Interesting, he thought as his sister padded out of the room in her striped pajamas, didn't begin to describe Afia St. John. He swept off his cap, tossed it on the end table, and massaged the back of his neck. Every time he thought about that woman he got a spasm. She'd twisted him into a knot of emotions this afternoon, and he'd yet to unwind. After their blowout, they'd retreated to their own corners to wait out the thunderstorm. She'd curled up in the parlor with Velma, the traitor, to watch a classic movie while he'd searched through the second bag of Rivelli's trash. The day hadn't been a complete bust. Bag number two had produced three press-on fingernail tips and a pair of black fishnet stockings with a major run. Of course they could belong to Angela Brannigan, surely she'd spent a night or two at her fiancé's shore getaway. But per her specific instructions, he wouldn't be able to ask her until *she* called *him*. Clearly, the woman was paranoid. He wondered why, but he didn't obsess on the point because he was too busy obsessing over Afia and her weird behavior.

First she'd hyperventilated over losing a charm. Then she'd freaked out when he'd insulted Gallow, which he hadn't meant to do, but, hell, it had just come out. She'd been so offended, she'd tried to quit her "job." Yeah, that would've gone down real well with Harmon.

So he'd salvaged his "assignment" by offering to help her locate Glick. Harmon wouldn't like that either, but he didn't intend to follow through, so no harm done. He'd stall her for a while, and if pressed they'd do some surface prodding. As much as he'd like to show up Kilmore, he could very well botch whatever progress the Philadelphia P.I. had already made by diving in cold.

He didn't want to jeopardize Afia's chances of getting back her money. If that's what made her happy . . . money and Gallow. The knot tightened when he thought about Afia's staunch defense of her friend. He applauded her loyalty even though he didn't understand it. Did she think so little of herself that she'd settle for a gold digger? Was she that insecure? It bothered him that her mother had crammed all of that superstitious nonsense down her throat. Instead of instilling her child with confidence, she'd convinced her that she was jinxed. It made his blood boil. According to Harmon, Judge St. John had been enormously fond of his only child. Had Giselle been jealous? He'd dealt with women like that, jealous of their own children. Had she beat Afia down to build herself up? The judge was no longer around but Giselle had a new husband. Did she worry he might take an interest in Afia? Would she go so far as to sabotage Afia's life by setting her up with a crooked accountant? *Or* was she plain and simple a nutcase?

"What's got your underwear in a twist?" Joni reentered the room carrying a notebook and a bottle of beer. She handed

Jake the beer. "You look like you're ready to punch something . . . or someone."

He took a swig, knowing he'd need at least three beers to cool his jets tonight, but what the hell, one was a start. He nodded toward the notebook as Joni took her seat. "Whatdaya got?"

She drummed her fingers on the open pages. "Why do you want to know?"

"She's my employee. I have a right to check into her background."

Joni snorted. "Shouldn't you have done that *before* you hired her?"

Jake took another swig, leveled her with a pointed stare. "Don't make me confiscate your Rocky Road."

She narrowed her eyes. "You have a death wish?"

Maybe. He had a thing for Afia. Wasn't that the same? "What about that daycare center?"

"The Sea Serpent," she said, still drumming her fingers. "A daycare center designed for low-income families. It was founded twenty years ago by Judge St. John and a couple of other Atlantic City dignitaries. Relies heavily on contributions, funding from the Seashore Charity Committee and such. Afia served on the SCC for years."

"Past tense?"

"She resigned a couple of weeks ago."

About the same time she'd lost her fortune. "Reason?"

Joni shrugged.

Jake let it go. At least he knew that there was an actual connection between Afia and the daycare center. Maybe she really had been clipped by a four-year-old boy. "Okay. Let's move on." He glanced at his watch. "Hit the hot spots for me. It's one o'clock in the morning. You and the kid should be in bed."

"Yeah, yeah." She propped her fuzzy bunny slippers on the coffee table and thumbed through her notes. "Afia St. John's hot spots. Here we go. Born twenty-seven years ago to Bradley and Giselle St. John on, get this, Friday the thirteenth." She whistled. "No wonder she has such rotten luck."

Jake rolled his eyes. "Not you too."

"What?" She waved him off and continued. "Honor roll student. Went on an African safari with her father, Judge Bradley St. John, to celebrate her high school graduation. Freak accident #1: The judge was skewed by a rhino." She shuddered. "Can you imagine?"

He recalled the fondness in Afia's voice when she'd spoken of her father and grimaced. "She didn't witness the act, did she?"

Joni shook her head. "No. But it must've been traumatic all the same."

Jake agreed. He hadn't been that close to their dad, a remote man who'd cared more about being a cop than a father or husband, but he'd felt like hell for months after Sergeant Richard Leeds had died in a fouled robbery.

Joni tucked her bobbed hair behind her ears and then eyed Jake. "Did you know that both of her husbands were, like, twenty years her senior? In fact, they were both friends of her father's. Don't you think that's weird? I mean it's like she looked for someone to take her daddy's place."

Someone who could stand up to her mother. He took a pull off the long neck and waved his sister on.

148

"No college. No career," she said, glancing back at her notes. "Unless you consider being a trophy wife a career, which I guess it could be. Probably had to arrange a lot of dinner parties, frequent snooty galas, crap like that." She shuddered. "Anyhow, she married a hot shot defense attorney, Randy Harper, when she was, uh, twenty-two. Lots of old money. They were married two years, no children and then . . . Freak accident #2: Harper died in bed. With Afia." She raised her eyebrows. "Apparently they were . . ."

"Got it." Jake chugged a quarter of the beer, trying to dislodge the disturbing image. "Next."

"Hold up." Joni reached for the ice cream, peeled off the lid, and grabbed a spoon. She scooped out a glob of Rocky Road and then leaned back holding the spoon like a lollipop. "Moving on . . . A little under two years later she marries the CEO of a pharmaceutical company. We're talking stinking rich here. Married less than a year, no children, wham . . . Freak accident #3: Frank Davis gets whacked in the temple by a renegade golf ball during a charity golf tournament. And, yes, you guessed it, Afia was there, or on the grounds anyway. She's the one who registered him in the tournament."

"Tell me something I don't know," Jake said, growing more irritable by the minute. He'd read most of this in the newspaper. "You can skip the speculation. The gossip about her being responsible for her husbands' deaths."

"The black widow reference."

He scowled. "That's the one." Sure he'd toyed with the idea once or twice over the last couple of days, but his gut told him Afia wouldn't harm a fly. Gallow on the other hand . . .

"All righty." Joni licked her spoon and scanned her notes. "Here's one that hasn't hit the newspapers. She's broke." Her head snapped up. "Can you believe it? All that money . . . gone. The IRS confiscated her houses, one in Ventnor, one in Philly. The creditors took the rest. No wonder she needs a job." She smirked. "I told you she was in trouble. Man, oh, man. I wonder if she has a gambling problem?"

"Her business manager embezzled her funds." Jake figured he could let Joni in on that much since Afia had spilled the beans this afternoon. Besides, he didn't want her thinking that the woman had a gambling addiction. Her character had withstood enough speculation.

"All of it?" Joni asked wide-eyed.

"Apparently."

"That sucks."

"Yep."

Eyes sparking, Joni jabbed her spoon into the tub of partially eaten ice cream. "We should track the scum. Bilking a widow. What a creep!"

"*You* aren't going to do anything. You're supposed to be taking it easy."

"How many times do I have to tell you and Carson? I did my bed time. I'm fine. Do you really think I'd endanger this baby?"

"Of course not, but we're not taking any chances. I shouldn't have asked you to do this much. Now you're all worked up."

"Better worked up than bored to death doing word search puzzles." She jabbed a finger in the air. "Don't lock me out of this. I'm serious, Jake. I've relaxed enough for a lifetime. You try sitting around for days on end with your thumb up your ass!"

He howled. "It's not my fault you couldn't think of anything better to use than your thumb."

She tossed a throw pillow at his head. "Not funny."

"Very funny," he said, taking the hit. He polished off the beer and then regarded her with a calming smile. "As for locating the accountant, you can relax. The wheels are already in motion." He let her assume that he was the one conducting the search. If she knew it was Kilmore, she'd ask why, and he wasn't up to concocting an answer.

"Oh." Her color faded from bright red to healthy pink. "Well, good." She drummed her fingers on the notebook, cocked her head, and waited for Jake to give her direction. When he didn't, she heaved an exasperated sigh. "This is the part where you tell me how I can help."

"Sure thing. You can start by going to bed and getting some rest."

"In other words you're shutting me out." She scowled. "You're an ass."

"That seems to be the general consensus today." Afia's opinion of him had definitely dipped after that crack about Gallow. He shoved the gold digger out of his mind and considered the con artist. Henry Glick could be half way around the world by now operating under any number of aliases. He wondered if Kilmore had made any progress.

Jake's conscience smarted like hell. He'd told Afia he'd help her find Glick. Joni *assumed* he was on the case. He couldn't step on Kilmore's toes. Well, he could, but he wouldn't. Yet.

He dragged a hand over his face. When had this gotten so complicated?

The moment Afia St. John had walked into his office and zapped him with those lost puppy dog eyes.

Who was he kidding? He was going to save her whether she wanted his help or not.

"All right. I give up," Joni said with a yawn. "I can't talk to you when you're in protector mode. It's too damn wearing." She rose, snatched up her ice cream and headed out of the room. "I'm going to bed."

"Good."

She cast a wary look over her shoulder. "What are you going to do?"

He smiled at his tough-as-nails sister, unable to resist one last tease. "Help myself to a couple of your beers and sit out here with my thumb up my ass until Carson gets home."

Chapter Twelve

"Maybe she'll talk to you."

Jean-Pierre stirred sweetener into his coffee while peering up through his thick lashes at Rudy. "Why would she talk to me? You are her best friend. If she is going to confide in anyone it would be you, no?"

"No. I mean you'd think so." Rudy creased his brow as he gave the matter some thought. Afia had been suspiciously quiet for two days. When he'd asked her about the progress of the seduction, she'd said, "I changed my mind." Every time he asked her about Jake in general, she changed the subject. All he knew was that she was "learning the ropes," and very soon she'd be tracking down Glick. Which should have made her happy since that was her reason for wanting to work for the P.I. in the first place. Instead she'd been unnervingly reserved. As her friend he wanted to know why. Maybe he could help. But Afia had shut him out of that portion of her life. She'd even declined his offers to drive her back and forth to daycare or the Bizby, opting to rely on public transportation. Harmon wouldn't be happy about his goddaughter taking the jitney, but he was still out of town, and damned if Rudy was going to call and tattle.

She was taking control of her life. Acting without guidance. Asserting her independence. This was a good thing. So why did he feel so blue? So . . . lonely?

Shaking off a surge of self-pity, he took a sip of his coffee and then frowned across the dining table at Jean-Pierre who was freshly showered, shaved and shirtless, and merrily pouring skimmed milk over his granola cereal. "Did you spike the coffee with cinnamon?"

"*Oui.*" Jean-Pierre glanced up, his huge brown eyes glittering with mischief. "I am trying to spice up your life, Bunny." He paused, shoved his damp wavy hair off of his pretty boy face, and then flashed a coy smile. "Do you object?"

Rudy cursed the double meaning and the stirring south of his waistband. This was the closest Jean-Pierre had come to making an out-and-out pass, but the sparks had been flying since he'd moved in. The old Rudy would've been dancing in the sheets with Frenchie days ago. The man was young, hot and hung. He'd nearly swallowed his tongue the first time he'd gotten an eyeful of Jean-Pierre in his spandex running shorts. But Rudy wanted more than great sex. He wanted conversation, companionship, Christmas in Vermont. He wanted a life partner, and he wasn't going to get that with a good-time Charlie seven years his junior. He cocked a lone brow meant to intimidate. "I object to the nickname."

Jean-Pierre merely chuckled, calling attention to the tiny crinkles at the corners of his sparkling eyes, the brackets framing his full mouth. Laugh lines never looked so good.

Rudy slathered raspberry preserves on his wheat toast, cursing his roommate's ability to light up a room on four hours of sleep. Due to an upcoming "special performance" for the Atlantic City elite, he'd been forced to bring home a few of the dancers' costumes for some requested embellishments. Apparently the vice president of the Carnevale Casino was an enthusiastic fan of all things that glittered. Jean-Pierre's instructions had been succinct. More rhinestones. More sequins. More cleavage.

Knowing that Jean-Pierre was overwhelmed, Rudy and Afia had pitched in, and the trio had stayed up until two in the morning adding enough "glitz and glam" to make a drag queen drool. Throughout, Afia had gabbed along with a smile—asking questions about the show, the performers, the hands-on V.P.—until Rudy had casually asked about Jake.

"All I can think of," he said, returning the discussion to safer ground, "is that Jake nixed the nookie, and Afia's too embarrassed to discuss it."

"Or," Jean-Pierre said, toying with his cereal, "they are hot and heavy, and she is too embarrassed to discuss *that*."

"If they were hot and heavy there'd be a spring in her step. Have you seen any 'springing'?"

Jean-Pierre angled his head, pursed his lips. "No. *Chou à la crème's* spring does seem to be sprung." He took a sip of coffee. "Perhaps she is simply tired. The past two mornings she has risen before dawn in order to be at The Sea Serpent by six-thirty. Two hours with the children and then eight more with Jake. Then last night—"

"It's more than that," Rudy interrupted, growing more agitated with Leeds by the second. "If you could have heard her on the phone the other day. She was gushing. I've never heard Afia *gush* about any man. All she wanted was a fling. How could he not be into that? She's beautiful. Inside and out."

"Perhaps he wanted more than a meaningless fling. Have you thought of that, Rudy?"

It was the sound of his name that caused his head to snap up, and the sincere look in Jean-Pierre's eyes that made his stomach drop. In the month that he'd known the man, he'd never known him to be less than a smart-ass. Sincere was way more unsettling.

"Perhaps Jake senses that Afia is special. Special warrants more than a few passionate encounters, would you not agree?"

Pulse hammering, he gently set his empty cup in the saucer and stroked his bearded chin, unable to articulate an answer.

Jean-Pierre picked up the insulated carafe, rounded the table and then leaned into him and filled his cup with more "spiced" coffee. "I suggest the best course is to relax, to take one day at a time, and to keep an open mind, no?"

Rudy grunted, his mouth going dry at the feel of Jean-Pierre's hand on his shoulder and the mingling scents of cinnamon and Calvin Klein's Eternity. "We are talking about Jake and Afia, right?"

Jean-Pierre merely chuckled.

* * *

She was late. Again.

Afia stood in front of the Bizby, dreading having to explain to Jake why she was late for the fifth morning in a row. Not that he'd ask. He never asked. He just sat there looking at her with those unsettling green eyes—assessing, waiting—until she blurted out something stupid.

Yesterday she'd apologized without offering any explanation at all, because the truth was too embarrassing. Even though she'd left the daycare center on time, two jitneys had passed her by before a third had finally curbed at the shuttle stop and let her board. Unfortunately, she'd ended up in the Marina district instead of downtown. The shuttles were extremely affordable but had different routes and destinations, and she'd hopped the wrong one. Not wanting to risk another fiasco, she'd hired a taxi to drive her back into town. Still, she'd walked into the office twenty-five minutes late. If looks could burn, she'd be a pile of ash.

Today she was only fifteen minutes late, but she wagered she'd get far more than a withering glare. Jake would take one look at the shopping bag in her hand and assume the worse. He might not say it, but he'd think it. She'd blown off work to go shopping. Had she no sense of responsibility? No control?

She might actually have to offer up an explanation for this one. It was either that or be a doormat. Could she actually say it? *I'm inept with children.* Two days ago, Billy had given her a black eye. Yesterday, Sasha had bitten her. Today, David had slashed a black marker across the thigh of her pink denim pants with the intent of giving her a *tattoo*. Then Mya, the munchkin from hell, had soaked her striped silk blouse by heaving a cup of cranberry juice in the heat of a full-blown tantrum.

Not having time to return to Rudy's apartment, on a whim she'd slipped into the discounted clothing store two doors down from the Bizby. She'd purchased and changed into an inexpensive pair of drawstring pants and a Mighty Mouse T-shirt. While she was at it she'd picked up those cheap white sneakers she'd been wanting. Though not the most chic of out-fits, she was certainly dressed well enough for dumpster diving (should that be on today's agenda).

With her soiled Chanel ensemble rolled into the shopping bag, she groaned and fell back against the Bizby's brick front. She was exhausted. Too many days of too little sleep and too much drama. It was a beautiful day. Clear and sunny. She breathed deeply, wanting to go for a stroll on the beach, know-ing she really had to get inside. Several people walked by. Not one gave her a second look. Dress to blend. She couldn't help but smile. There was something to be said for being invisible.

Even her shopping spree had been low-key. In and out in less than ten minutes. She'd spent under twenty dollars, and she'd still felt a little rush. It occurred to her that she didn't have to spend a fortune to achieve instant gratification. According to Rudy, compulsive shoppers shopped to fill a void, to cope with feelings of loneliness or anxiety. She didn't like to think of herself as a shopaholic. But over the past few years she had spent a lot of money. She'd amassed an enormous wardrobe, including coordinating shoes, handbags, and hats. Then there was the art and furniture she'd purchased to renovate Frank's cold, contemporary homes. She *had* been lonely, even when she'd been married.

Her brow crinkled. As much as she hated to admit it, Rudy was right. She'd hooked up with men she had no chance of connecting with emotionally. Wealthy, career-driven men who'd treated her like a fragile ornament. Men who made her feel safe and treasured, but not exactly challenged or sexy. Friends of her father's. It was a sobering thought.

Especially since these days she felt extremely challenged. Dealing with the children at the daycare center was almost a snap compared to dealing with Jake. He'd taken her interest in learning the investigative trade more seriously than she'd expected. Over the last two days, he'd lectured and quizzed her on body language, street sense, and the nuances of gathering information via standard and not-so-standard interviews. In addition, they'd worked on her computer skills by intensifying the investigation on Anthony Rivelli, an investigation that was thus far dead in the water. Jake was a demanding teacher, and though there were times she wanted to scream in frustration because she was technically challenged, he'd remained calm and supportive telling her that in time she'd "get it."

As for the investigative end, although she was uncomfortable poking into people's private lives, she understood the need in certain instances and found the process fascinating.

Almost as fascinating as Jake. In the midst of returning a folder to one of the locking file cabinets, she'd noticed several cases involving spousal abuse and missing children. No wonder he'd reacted so strongly to her swollen eye. He operated in an ugly world where people did unspeakable things. She wondered how he slept at night, but then she realized that it was probably *because* of his work that he found some peace. Instead of standing on the sidelines, he actively aided and protected the persecuted. Obviously, he was a man of great compassion. So, how was it possible that he was intolerant of the gay population? And how was it possible that she was still attracted to him knowing of this offensive glitch in his make-up? The questions had plagued her for two days and made her squirm with guilt every time she looked into Rudy's eyes. She felt like a traitor, and yet she'd aborted the seduction. What's more, she'd gone out of her way to shield her friend from Jake's contempt by making sure they didn't come into contact.

I haven't done anything wrong.

Heart pounding, she glanced down at her watch. Great. Now she was *twenty* minutes late. She pushed off of the wall at the same time Jake pushed through the front door, nearly plowing her over.

He caught her before she teetered backwards. "You own a cell phone, Afia. Use it. If you're going to be late at least have the courtesy to call so I don't have to worry."

She blinked up at him, flustered by his penetrating glare. "I'm sorry. I . . . I . . ." He'd been worried? "You have my number. You could have called *me*."

"I tried. It helps if your phone is actually turned *on*." He released her, pressed the office key in her hand and then headed for his car. "I'll be back in a while."

She trotted after him. "Where are you going? What's wrong?" Something was definitely wrong. This wasn't just about her. It couldn't be. "Is it your sister? Is she okay?"

"Joni's fine. Just go up and . . . do some research on the next dancer on the list." He wrenched open the car door and climbed inside.

So this was about Rivelli? Yesterday Angela had denied ownership of the black fishnets they'd found in her fiancé's trash, suggesting they investigate the cast of the *Venetian Vogue,* the Carnevale's featured show. After talking to Jean-Pierre, Afia had to admit there might be cause for worry. She opened the passenger door and slid in next to Jake. "As it happens I have quite a bit of information on each of the girls. I spoke to someone last night and—"

"Get out of the car, Afia."

"No." Okay, so this wasn't about Rivelli. Jake wouldn't be this tense over a suspected playboy. She tossed the shopping bag in the back seat then buckled her safety belt, determined to ride this out.

"We'll talk about it when I get back."

"Okay." She locked her door. "So where are we going?"

He narrowed his eyes and lowered his voice to a menacing growl. "We're not going anywhere. *I'm* going to help a client. Now please get out of the car. I don't have time for this."

"Then you better get going." She crossed her arms over her chest in defiance.

He keyed the ignition. "You're a pain in my ass."

She feigned a relaxed smile, nearly choking on the charged air. "So who's this client?"

"Nancy Ashe." He pulled away from the curb, made a U-turn, and then a left on Atlantic Avenue and headed south.

"Who's Nancy Ashe? And be warned," she teased, frantically trying to ease the strain, "if you say a client, I'll punch you." He didn't smile, not even a smirk, and that worried her. She leaned to the left, peeked at the dash. It also didn't bode well that he was going 45 mph in a 25 mph zone. "Is she hurt?"

"Not yet."

Afia swallowed hard, not liking the answer, not liking his tone. She especially didn't like the way he reached up under his shirt and adjusted the gun she knew was there. "Maybe we should call the police."

"She doesn't want the police. That's why she called me."

Afia bit her tongue as he slowed at a red light, looked both ways then drove on. Oh, boy.

"There's a restraining order against Marty. If she calls the police, they'll put him in jail."

"But if there's a chance he might hurt her, if there's a restraining order, well, obviously this Marty's dangerous and he *should* go to jail."

"I agree." The tires squealed as he swerved right onto Route 40. "When he's drunk, Marty Ashe is one mean bastard. But Nancy isn't going to budge. She barely had the courage to kick the son of a bitch out, she's not about to piss him off further by putting him behind bars. He'd only retaliate when he got out. They always do."

She cringed at his jaded tone. "Marty's her husband?"

"Unfortunately."

She thought about one of the cases she'd skimmed. The pictures she'd unfortunately peeked at. The bloodied lip. The broken arm. Her voice jumped an entire octave. "And he's with her now?"

"He's pounding on the back door. Making threats. Apparently he wants to move back in. She hasn't buckled yet and, thankfully, neither has the door."

Afia shook off a shiver. "What does she want you to do?"

He gunned the accelerator and flashed a smile that held no mirth. "Scare the hell out of him."

Stunned into silence, she rubbed her goose-pimply arms and focused on the road. She had no doubt that Jake Leeds was capable of scaring the hell out of Satan. And any man who beat up on a woman was surely in league with the devil. "If you end up having to shoot him, don't worry. I know a good lawyer."

He laughed then, breaking the eerie tension, and just like that Afia knew somehow, some way, everything was going to be all right. But just in case . . . She unclasped her charm bracelet, leaned over and dropped it in Jake's shirt pocket. "For good luck."

She expected him to roll his eyes, or to make her take back the bracelet. She didn't expect him to snag her hand and to press a kiss to the inside of her wrist. "Thanks, baby."

Chapter Thirteen

Jake attributed his rounding the corner of the house just as Marty had pried open the back door to exquisite timing. That Marty had turned when he'd beckoned him, rather than continuing over the threshold toward a white-faced Nancy, he chalked up to human reflex. His ability to coax the inebriated bastard into the backyard was due to his police training and superb bullshitting skills.

It was the black cat that had lunged out of nowhere, streaking across Marty's path and tripping the bastard just as he'd aimed a revolver at Jake that had him presently cruising the Internet. The bullet that had whizzed by his ear might have gone through his chest if not for that cat. A cat that had duly disappeared. A cat that no one in the neighborhood claimed.

Coincidence or luck?

Jake sat at his desk, eyeing the polished cat charm on Afia's bracelet while typing SUPERSTITIONS into the search engine and contemplating his brush with disaster. Marty Ashe was a bully. A man who attacked with obscenities and fists. The fact that he'd obtained a gun was a surprise and, in a warped way, a blessing. Unlike Nancy, Jake wasn't afraid to press charges.

Marty was looking at some deserved jail time.

A multitude of listings came up on the computer screen. Jake clicked on one after another, noting in particular the superstitions pertaining to black cats. Depending on the culture, beliefs differed. In the Orient, black cats symbolized poverty and ill-health, while Scottish superstition claimed a strange black cat on your porch brought prosperity. Though considered unlucky in the European and European-American traditions, in the African-American sporting world, the black cat granted invisibility and the return of lost love as well as money luck.

The clichéd and most common belief was that black cats conjured bad luck, while others touted exactly the opposite. Apparently there was an "evil" black cat and a "good" black cat.

To see a black cat cross your path brings bad luck.

To see a black cat walk toward you brings good luck.

And assorted variations.

Any way you looked at it, if one was given to superstition, Marty Ashe had been foiled by a black puss. The bastard's bad luck had been Jake and Nancy's good fortune.

Jake's skeptical brain spun in circles as he fingered Afia's bracelet. A gift from her father. A father she adored. A father who'd told her that she needed all the luck on earth, not because he believed her to be jinxed, but because her mother had an absurd fear of Friday the thirteenth, amongst other things. He wondered what an intelligent man like Judge Bradley St. John could've seen in such an irrational woman. He typed PARASKEVIDEKATRIAPHOBIA into the search engine only to learn that over twenty-one million Americans suffered from the phobia. Amazingly, fear of Friday the thirteenth appeared to be the most widespread superstition in America. So it wasn't as if Giselle was a freak of nature. As for the judge, well, whether the man was superstitious or not he'd given Afia a gift that perpetuated the belief in lucky talismans.

Since Jake subscribed to the notion that children are products of their parents, Afia's easy acceptance of ancient superstitions made perfect sense. Had he been reared in a whimsical household, perhaps he'd be walking around with a lucky token in his pocket. When it came down to it, how was rubbing a rabbit's foot any different than stroking rosary beads? How did believing in the power of the supernatural differ from believing in the power of a Supreme Being? Who was he to judge?

When Afia had slipped the bracelet into his pocket he'd been touched and, okay, a little amused. As if a charm bracelet was going to offer more protection than his Glock and honed boxing skills. But then there'd been that cat, and although logic supported coincidence, curiosity, and Afia, had him contemplating luck.

"I just got off of the phone with Nancy."

Jake glanced up from the computer screen as the woman of his obsession walked into his office and sank down in the chair across from his desk. She slumped rather than sitting rigidly in her usually prim way. She looked exhausted, but gratified, and his heart tripped at the jazzed twinkle in her eyes.

"She thought it over and decided to take my advice. She's going to visit the Atlantic County Women's Center on Monday. I'm so relieved."

"So am I," Jake said, amazed and grateful that Afia had been able to convince Nancy to seek professional help. While he'd been filling in the patrolmen on the details of the attempted shooting, she'd been in the house "having a talk" with Nancy. Considering the volatile situation, Afia's calm demeanor had impressed him. "I've been trying to talk Nancy into visiting the center for months." He minimized the "superstition" document and leaned back in his chair. "How is it that you know so much about a place that councils battered women?"

Cheeks tinged with pink, she shrugged and looked away. "I served on the Seashore Charity Committee for years. I'm familiar with most of the non-profit social service agencies in Southern Jersey. But I'm ashamed to say that I don't have much hands-on experience. I've never actually been to the ACWC. I told Nancy I would meet her there. For support. With me there, maybe she won't back out." She glanced at Jake with a shaky smile. "I need to take an active part in society rather than standing on the sidelines."

He shifted in his seat, uncomfortable with the adoration shining in those chocolate-brown eyes. "You served on a charity committee and organized functions to benefit those in need. That's more than a lot of people do."

"It's not the same as getting personally involved."

He noted her cartoon T-shirt with a faint smile. A super-hero mouse, cape flying, fist thrust in the air . . . *"Here I come to save the day!"* He remembered how Afia had stormed around the corner of the Ashe house, wide-eyed, pigtails swinging, thirty seconds after the gunshot, ten seconds after he'd pinned Marty. He'd wanted to blast her for leaving the safety of the car. Instead, he'd said, "Call the cops," and she'd disappeared inside the house chanting something under her breath. His heart tripped knowing how easily she could have been hurt had Marty been the one in control. "Helping people one-on-one can be rewarding," he admitted. "But it can also be disappointing, draining, and, at times, dangerous."

"That doesn't stop you," she said, clasping her naked wrist. "The danger part. If Marty hadn't tripped over that cat . . ." Her voice cracked, and she looked away.

"I still would have been fine," he told her, although he was-n't sure if he bought that line any more than she did at this moment. He'd gone into the situation with a cocky attitude, swearing Marty didn't have the stomach for firearms. He would have paid for his arrogance if not for that cat.

Afia's leg started to bounce, and he guessed now that the adrenaline was no longer pumping, her composure was at last slipping. Though a far cry from the fragile socialite who'd teetered into his office five days ago on three-inch heels, she still radiated a vulnerability that brought him to his knees. An appealing yet frightening trait as it pegged her a gentle soul. Gentle souls invariably get trampled. He'd tried to toughen her up over the past two days, to teach her a few practical skills. Skills she could utilize in her personal life as well as just about any field.

What if it turned out that Glick and her money were history? What if she had to make her own way?

The thought of her out there, operating alone in the big ugly world, set his teeth on edge. Trouble followed this woman like a faithful dog. Although he attributed her mishaps to coincidence or lack of confidence, it didn't matter what he thought. If Afia continued to believe that she was jinxed, she'd continue to act as a bulls-eye for misfortune.

"You can't save the world, Jake," Joni had said. Maybe not. But he could damn well make a difference in Afia's life by instilling her with more confidence. He had another week to work his magic. She needed to trust her instincts, to believe in herself.

She needed to break free of her influential mother. As soon as that woman returned from Tahiti she'd start pushing old buttons, and if Afia didn't have the gumption to stand up to her, she'd be right back where she started.

Maybe the judge was right. Maybe Afia needed all the luck she could get.

He palmed the charm bracelet and rose. "You were incredible today. Grace under pressure."

She stood and held out her arm, offering up her delicate wrist as he rounded the desk. "Let's just say that I'm good at containing my emotions." She cleared her throat. "Usually."

"That's funny," he said, securing the bracelet, his fingers tingling at the feel of her silky skin. "I'm pretty good at maintaining control myself." He gazed down into her big brown eyes, now glassy with tears, and his own throat constricted. "Usually."

It was a mistake, of course, to draw her into his arms. He did it anyway, his heart pounding like a son of a bitch as she leaned into him and rested her face against his chest. Compassion and lust warred as he smoothed his palm down her rigid spine trying to ease her trembling, his own body pulsating with caged desire. A vivid fantasy exploded in his head involving bath bubbles and champagne. *Jesus.* She was upset, and all he could think about was getting her naked.

Clinging to his shoulders, she stood on her tiptoes and tilted back her head, seeking, offering. Her lush pink lips and glittering doe eyes shattered the last of his so-called control.

With the primitive groan of a man who'd lost his grip on his good intentions, Jake framed her face within his hands and lowered his mouth to hers, intending to sate the hunger that had gnawed at him for two days. But when their lips connected, tenderness coursed through his being instead of raw passion. Affection instead of lust. He swept his tongue inside her welcoming mouth, offering comfort. An unfamiliar need burned strong in his gut. The need to cherish.

A siren wailed in his ears. *Step away from the subject.*

Wetness trickled along his fingertips. He eased back, thumbed away the tears escaping through her lowered lashes. "Afia." She met his gaze and the siren blared louder. She had the distinct look of a woman in love. She opened her mouth, and he braced himself for the three words that would serve as well as a curse.

"You and me," she croaked. "It's not gonna happen."

* * *

Roses. Two-dozen long stemmed yellow roses meticulously arranged in a blue crystal vase. Angela tipped the delivery boy, shut the door, read the accompanying gift card, and promptly hurled the vase against the wall.

He'd *promised!* Tony had promised that he'd be home in time to attend her father's party. He'd assured her that he could clear his calendar. He knew how important it was that they showed. Or maybe he didn't. Maybe she should have articulated the unspoken. *Don't screw up our life by screwing with my daddy. He's a mob boss.*

Tony had to know. He was an intelligent man. He read the newspapers. Though he consistently eluded prosecution, Vincent Falcone had been at the root of more than one criminal investigation. What, did he think that was *another* Vinnie Falcone? Did he truly think her daddy's catering business was legit?

Angela sank down on the sofa and stared at the carnage of her rage. Was the shattered vase an omen of shattered dreams? She balled her trembling hands in her lap, contemplating the disturbing notion that she was engaged to an imbecile. Either Tony was too stupid to put two and two together or too stupid to be afraid of Vinnie Falcone. Either way she felt her anger ebbing as she focused on those long-stem roses. Tony was a hard worker. A straight arrow. A gentle soul and a gentle lover. He treated her like a lady. The fact that he was messing around with another woman hurt deeply, but she could bear the pain, just as she'd deal with that woman because, in her heart, she believed that Tony truly cherished her. No man had ever cherished Angela Falcone. They'd used her to get ahead. To get close to her father. If Tony were interested in taking advantage of a mob connection to further his career and finances, he would have found a way to sidestep his boss's directive.

Swallowing an uncharacteristic bout of tears, she reread Tony's card.

Sorry, honey. Dunkirk unable to attend SCC Gala. Insists I represent the Carnevale in his absence. My regrets to your father. Will call you later tonight. I love you, Tony.

So casual. So calm. No, clearly, he didn't understand the importance of attending her daddy's party. He was being responsible. Following his boss's orders. That's if indeed George Dunkirk, president of the Carnevale Casino, had issued that order. What if Tony wasn't going to that gala at all, but rendezvousing with his tart?

Angela crumpled the note and tossed it aside, angry tears coursing down her cheeks as her stomach twisted painfully with jealously and mistrust. It's not as if she could waltz into that gala decked out in her finest under the guise of attending as the V.P.'s dutiful fiancée. No, she had to make an appearance at her daddy's stupid dinner party and somehow cover Tony's ass. Surprisingly, the prospect of dealing with her father wasn't nearly as upsetting as the vision of Tony burning up the sheets with a twenty-something bimbo.

She rose on shaky legs and crossed to the bar. Sniffing back tears, she mixed a double martini, downed the drink in one long swallow and then snatched up her cell phone. There was one sure fire way to know where Tony spent his evening.

* * *

"What makes you so sure we're not going to have an affair?"

An affair? Afia tried to back away from Jake, but he tightened his grasp on her forearms. She supposed she should be grateful for his vice-like grip, as her knees were five seconds from buckling. She cursed herself for losing her composure, for allowing him to offer comfort. His idea of comfort was a slow, tender kiss that wrapped around her heart and ignited images of cuddling in bed, talking about their day and their kids. Longing had swirled in her stomach like a cyclone, overwhelming in its power. It was like having a glimpse of what you'd always wanted, and feared you'd never have. It was torture. "You said so yourself two days ago. *You and me. It's not gonna happen*," she mimicked, swiping away her tears and steeling herself against his seductive gaze. "I distinctly remember you saying that."

He focused on her mouth and then looked deep into her eyes, searing her soul with a white-hot declaration. "As much as I hate to admit it, I'm not always one hundred percent right."

Nerves jangling with anticipation, she suppressed a sigh of relief when he released her and headed for the door. At least one of them had regained their good sense. But then he turned the deadbolt, locking out the rest of the world, and her heart threatened to burst through her ribcage. Her own world spun as he took a deep breath and slowly closed the distance between them. She took a step back. Then another.

He followed until he'd backed her against the desk.

"Maybe we should stop fighting this thing," he said. "See where it takes us."

"By having an affair?" she croaked. An affair sounded even more risky than a fling. So passionate. So *emotional*. No, no, no. She couldn't risk getting emotionally involved with Jake. Men she cared about, men who cared about her, died. Somehow Rudy had escaped the curse. Or had he? For the first time she pondered the wisdom of moving in with her dear friend. Today, the powers that be had given her a not so subtle reminder of her ability to attract fatal danger in the form of Marty Ashe. That black cat could've been Jake's doom as easily as his savior. Thank goodness she'd had the wits to arm him with her protective charms.

"What are you afraid of, Afia?"

"What?" Her thoughts muddled as his hands slid to her backside. The next thing she knew she was sitting on the edge of the desk, Jake's big body wedged between her thighs.

"Is it the difference in our social status?" He worked his right hand up under the hem of her T-shirt, smoothed his palm up and over her bare back, his fingers brushing the clasp of her bra.

Her breath hitched as a wave of shock and excitement rippled through her body. He wasn't going to feel her up right here on his desk, was he? "You forget. I'm not rich anymore."

"Your friends are rich," he said, leaning closer.

"No, they're not." Not her real friends. Oh, God. Was her bra undone? She shifted. No. Still clasped. Darn. No, good. No . . . She leaned back, trying to gain breathing room, but bumped up against his left arm. She glanced over her shoulder and caught him shoving aside notepads and receipts. Why was he clearing the desktop? Her mind danced with X-rated possibilities.

"Your mother's rich."

"Filthy rich," she squeaked, her vision clouding as she breathed in the scent of herbal shampoo and raw masculinity. "Now that she's married to Bartholomew."

"Bart's Bonbons," he said, close to her ear, his breath hot on her neck. "The man's practically an icon. I'm not an icon."

"No." Her eyes lazed shut as he nipped her earlobe and suckled. That felt good! No, great! No . . . "You're an every-day guy." Though far, she thought hazily, from ordinary.

"Your mother would hate me," he said, easing her back until she was pressed flat against the top of the desk.

She nodded, her breath coming in shallow pants as he inched up her shirt, pressing kisses over her taut stomach. "She would strongly advise me against," she swallowed hard, "see-ing you."

"Do you always do what your mother tells you to?" he asked, rolling up her shirt to reveal her bra.

Always. "Mostly," she whispered as he skimmed his fin-gers over the swells of her breasts. Her skin tingled, her body pulsed. He pressed his erection against the juncture of her thighs, and she instinctively wrapped her legs around him. *Do it!* She gripped his shoulders, trembling with anticipation. *Take off my pants, rip off my panties. Do it! Do it!* She felt naughty, feverish. She'd never had sex on a piece of furniture other than a bed. "Too conservative," she mumbled.

"Your mother?"

Actually she'd been thinking about her husbands. Her

cheeks burned. Now wasn't the time to bring up her boring sex life. "Her choices . . . safe," she managed as she risked meeting Jake's heated gaze. Passion and excitement danced in his emerald-green eyes, promising a wicked adventure. He'd looked sexy and dangerous, and out-of-this-world gorgeous.

He smiled down at her, squeezed her nipples through the thin, lacy fabric. "Ready to take a walk on the wild side?"

Walk? She was ready to leap, run. Hell, she was eight steps ahead of him. She blinked, unable to articulate a dignified answer, warning bells clanging in her head. No, wait. Not clanging. Ringing. The phone was ringing six inches from her ear.

"Let the machine get it," he said, smile fading.

"What if it's Nancy?" she whispered. What if Marty made bail? The thought was as effective as being doused with cold water. She snatched the receiver before Jake could stop her. "Leeds Investigations," she said, her voice sounding unnaturally husky. She cleared her throat. "Hello? Oh . . . hello." Sincere worry faded to wariness. Client or not, Afia didn't like this woman. "Yes. One moment, please." She glanced up at Jake, who'd yet to remove his hand from her breast. He didn't look very happy, and she suspected this call wouldn't help her case. Quirking an apologetic smile, she offered up the receiver to Jake, and mouthed, "Angela Brannigan."

He mouthed a word that started with an "F" and this time she was positive it wasn't fudge. Frowning, he took his hands off of her to take the call. "I'm working on the dancer angle, Ms. Brannigan. Nothing yet. Mmm. Uh-huh." He straightened and raked his fingers through his hair.

Afia shimmied off of the desk and yanked down her shirt. Two seconds ago she'd been ready to have wild, dirty sex. Just now . . . she didn't know what she wanted just now, but she certainly wasn't in the mood to lie there half naked while Jake conversed with a client. She tried to escape, but he nabbed her hand, stroking his thumb back and forth across the sensitive skin of her wrist.

"The Summertime Gala, hosted by the SCC," he said into the phone while snaking his arm around her waist. "Yes, I've heard of it." He tugged her close and maneuvered the receiver so that they could both listen to Angela speak.

"This year the event is being sponsored by the Carnevale Casino. Tony just informed me that his attendance is mandatory," the woman said in a strained voice. "I want you to go to that gala. If he's there, watch who he interacts with. If he's not there . . . find him and, and . . ."

"Photograph who he interacts with," Jake finished for her.

"I don't know how you're going to get in," Angela went on. "I just called and the event is sold out, and obviously I can't ask Tony to put you on a guest list."

Afia poked Jake then patted her chest and gave him the thumbs up.

He raised an eyebrow, telling Angela, "I'll get in."

Afia smiled and nodded.

"Good," Angela said, relief evident in her tone. "I'll check in with you tomorrow morning." Then she disconnected.

"If it weren't for those fishnets and press-on nails," he said, replacing the receiver, "I'd be questioning that woman's suspicions. Five days into the investigation and Rivelli still smells as sweet as a rose. Either he's really good or I'm really slipping."

"Or he's innocent." Afia pulled clear of Jake and backed toward the door with a sigh. "Not that I'm convinced after talking to my friend."

"That's right. You have additional info on those dancers."

"And some scoop on Rivelli. Don't worry," she said, leaning back against the door and fiddling with the hem of her shirt. "My friend doesn't know why I asked. I used some of the interviewing techniques you taught me, and I'm pretty sure I did it right."

"No doubt." He cocked his head and studied her with a smile. "Why don't you come over here and we'll talk about it." Her gaze slipped to the bulge in his jeans. "Because if I come over there . . . just now . . . we won't end up talking."

He laughed and propped a hip on his desk. "Good point. Okay. What have you got?"

"Not that much, but it may lend credence to Angela's 'dancer' theory. Even though Rivelli oversees all of the departments—gaming, food and beverage, hotel—his main interest lies in entertainment. Thanks to Anthony Rivelli, the Carnevale has the most aggressive entertainment program in Atlantic City. Public areas, the lounges, the restaurants, and of course the showroom. He really pushed for the current variety show, *Venetian Vogue*. Glitzy, over-the-top costumes, dancing and singing, and plenty of T&A. Vegas meets Broadway, according to my friend."

Jake crossed his arms over his chest. "This friend of yours have a name?"

She didn't want to drag Jean-Pierre into this. What if it somehow got back to Rivelli? What if it compromised his job? "Surely you don't expect me to give up the name of my snitch?"

Jake snorted. "You've been watching too much television. All right. So Rivelli's hot on entertainment. That doesn't make him hot on an entertainer. Unless your friend, who I am assuming works at the Carnevale, heard some in-house gossip."

"No. Nothing like that. No one in particular, that is. It's just that he shows up at a lot of rehearsals and performances. Apparently he's very friendly with all of the cast members. More than one of the dancers has been seen sitting in his lap, but that doesn't mean anything. Show people tend to be touchy-feely."

"I've been known to get that way myself." He raked a slow, hot gaze over her body. "Anything else?"

So that's what it felt like to be undressed with someone's eyes! She ignored the tingling between her legs and crossed her arms over her chest. "Just that Rivelli engineered a special performance for tonight's gala. One of the flashy dance numbers from *Venetian Vogue*."

"So our nine lovely suspects will be in the same room with Rivelli tonight, and we'll be there to see if he gets touchy-feely with any one in particular." He smiled. "Excellent. So how are we getting in? Your friend?"

"Actually, I have two tickets. I bought them months ago. I attend the gala every year. I'll just go home and get them." She needed a breath of fresh air, time away to clear her mind. She still couldn't believe what she'd almost done on that desk.

"Just bring them with you tonight," Jake said with an amused grin as he watched her struggle with the deadbolt.

"I'm not going with you." In light of her financial fiasco, she'd decided to skip this year. The cost of her tickets had gone to a worthy cause. That's all that mattered.

He walked over, gently nudged her aside, and released the deadbolt with ease. "I'm not going to that fancy shindig alone."

"Then take a date."

"I'm planning on it. What time should I pick you up?"

She wasn't sure which was more frightening: Facing the SCC board members or going out on a "date" with Jake.

He tugged on her pigtail. "Come on, sweetheart. Think about it. You know these people. You know this event. With you by my side I'll mix right in. I need to be as inconspicuous as possible."

She gazed up at him, entranced by his chiseled jaw, full mouth and twinkling eyes. Why couldn't he be butt-ugly? If he were hard on the eyes maybe he'd be easier to resist. But she knew that wasn't true. Jake's beauty radiated from his confidence and his determination to protect the innocent. "So this date . . . it's just business?"

He grinned. "Mostly."

Her knees and will weakened. Devastated by a smile. She was pathetic. Then again, he was right. She did know these people. Her being there would make his job easier. Being skittish just because he'd suggested they have an affair was childish. "I'll meet you there."

He angled his head. "I'll pick you up."

Jinxed

She worried her bottom lip. He knew where she lived. He'd dropped her off the other day after that rainstorm. But she hadn't let him come inside. She hadn't wanted him anywhere near Rudy. Now she was wondering if perhaps she'd been taking the wrong course. Maybe if Jake got to know Rudy, he'd realize how absurd it is to be threatened by a person's sexual preference. He'd admitted that he wasn't always one hundred percent right. Maybe she and Rudy could help him to see the error of his homophobe ways. "All right. You can pick me up." She cracked open the door, her body tingling with the thought of making a positive difference in Jake's life. "Oh, and by the way," she said as she slipped out the door, "the Summertime Gala is a black-tie affair." She smiled. "Dress to blend."

"Afia."

"Yes?"

"If you're interested in picking up where we left off . . ." He winked. "Dress to impress."

181

Chapter Fourteen

"What do you think?"

Rudy set aside his book, sipped his power-smoothie and took in Afia's radiance with an appreciative smile. He adored the way she'd twisted her hair into an up-do reminiscent of Audrey Hepburn in *Breakfast at Tiffany's*. Her make-up was exquisite, dramatic without being over the top. But he'd told her that before, and he knew that her worries now centered on the dress. She pivoted, allowing him a full view. The strapless, satin orchid gown with the A-line skirt suited her figure and color and reeked of sophistication. "You look beautiful, honey. Very classy."

Her face crumpled. "You mean boring."

Rudy leaned back in his recliner and dragged a hand over his face. They'd been at this for over an hour. Where was Jean-Pierre when he needed him? He'd pluck an evening gown off Afia's packed clothing racks, spout something in French, and, *ta-dah*, she'd be transformed into whatever she was striving to emulate. "Sweetie, you've had on four evening gowns. Each one looked fabulous."

"Classy," she snapped. "Your exact words have been: classy, sophisticated, regal, and sweet. None of which are acceptable."

Rudy slapped a palm to his brow. "I lost track of time, didn't I. It's that time of month isn't it?"

"No, it's not that time of month." Afia blew her bangs off of her forehead. "Honestly, Rudy, I just want to look, I want to be . . ."

"What?"

She slapped her hands to her sides in frustration. "Irresistible. Sexy. Hot! Is that so hard to understand?"

"No. Yes. I mean, this is the Summertime Gala, right? The coming together of the upper crust of Atlantic County? Any one of the four gowns you've modeled thus far would have sufficed. No. More than sufficed," he said, holding up a hand in defense. "Perfect. They would have been perfect. Is there something wrong with perfect?"

"Yes. Perfect is boring."

Rudy cocked a suspicious brow. "I thought you said this was a business date."

"It is." Her cheeks flushed. "Mostly."

"Ah." He stroked his goatee, his suspicions confirmed. "So you're not looking to dazzle the *crème de le crème*, you're looking to 'wow' Jake. I thought you decided against a fling."

"I did. But I'm thinking I might have been hasty. Maybe I

should stop fighting the attraction and see where it takes us. He's a great guy." She broke eye contact. "Mostly."

"Mostly?"

She turned her back and rummaged through her clothing racks. "Everyone has flaws," she mumbled.

"Absolutely." Rudy sipped his smoothie and studied Afia. He had the distinct feeling that Jake's "flaw" was at the heart of her reserved behavior these past two days. He thought back on the way the P.I. had given him the once over the day he'd picked her up on his bike. He'd sensed curiosity and a tinge of hostility. He'd chalked up the hostility to the fact that he'd broken up what looked like a cozy moment. He'd been amused, but maybe he'd misread the situation. "He doesn't like me, does he?"

She sighed and, after a long minute, confessed. "He doesn't know you. If he knew you, he'd like you. I'm sure of it."

So there it was. The reason she'd nixed the seduction. The reason she'd avoided all talk of Jake. Until tonight anyway. Honestly, he didn't give a damn if the P.I. liked him or not, but obviously it was crucial to Afia. Rudy set his glass alongside his book and pushed out of the recliner. He moved in behind his friend and braced one hand on the end of the rack while she continued her search. She didn't look up. "Is he jealous?" he asked.

"What?"

"He's attracted to you, and you're living with two other men."

"He doesn't know about Jean-Pierre."

"Does he know we're . . . I'm gay?"

She nodded.

Now we're getting somewhere. "You told him?"

"No. But he's pretty good at reading people."

Rudy scrunched his brow. "So you think he took one look at me and assumed I'm queer. Most people don't, you know."

Her mouth curved into a soft smile. "Jake's not most people."

He noted the almost reverent tone in her voice. She really liked this guy, and she'd been putting him off because he disliked her best friend. His heart bumped up against his ribs as his affection for Afia swelled. "So, what? He out-and-out said he doesn't like homosexuals?"

She frowned. "Not out-and-out."

"So you're assuming, basically."

"I really don't think I could have misunderstood."

He placed a hand on her bare shoulder and squeezed. "But it's possible."

Her hands stilled, and at last she met his gaze. Confusion swam in those big brown eyes. "What if you're right? What if Jake is this wholly incredible person, and we fool around, and it turns serious? Consider my track record. We could be walking through a casino, and, *Bam!* a chandelier could fall on his head! Or a wrecking ball could demolish the Bizby with him inside! What was I thinking? Sleeping with Jake would be selfish and thoughtless. With my luck—"

"Afia." Rudy dipped his chin and spoke as calmly as possible. "When the odds are against you, trust your heart and seize the day."

She blinked up at him, sighed, and quirked a lopsided grin.

"Advice from one of your books?"

"Advice from me. Here," he said, spying a glittering, slinky number. "If you want sexy try this."

"Oh," she said. Just *oh*. She took the hanger and disappeared into the bathroom.

Rudy stared after her feeling like a victim of a runway model's meltdown. His thoughts flew to Jean-Pierre. How did the man cope? He dealt with emotional divas and wardrobe crises everyday. In truth, he was probably dealing with a few just now as he readied the dancers for tonight's special performance. Since the Carnevale had booked a headliner for the weekend, the cast had expected to have the night off. Most of them, Jean-Pierre had pointed out, were happy to donate their time for a good cause. Rudy imagined Jean-Pierre trying to soothe the disgruntled few and took solace knowing he merely needed to appease one insecure female. No matter what Afia looked like when she came out of that bathroom, he was going to say she looked *hot!*

"Rudy!"

He rolled his eyes, tramped down the hall, planted his hands on either side of the jambs and spoke through the closed door. "Yes?"

"I have to adjust my makeup to suit the color of this gown. I'm trying to hurry, but if Jake gets here before I'm ready . . ."

"Stop worrying, honey." He smiled, warmed to his bare feet by the sincere concern in his friend's voice. "Jake and I are going to get along just fine." He'd make sure of it.

✴ ✴ ✴

Jake stared up at the star-filled sky and took a long drag off of his cigarette, seeking a dose of tranquility before he actually knocked on that townhouse door. He could do this. If Afia didn't have a problem with him picking her up at her lover's house, why should he? Not that he was all that convinced anymore that Gallow *was* her lover. He found it hard to believe that she'd jump into bed with one man when she was sleeping with another. It didn't fit her character. And she definitely wanted to burn up the mattress with Jake. Hell, they'd practically done it on his desk. His heart pounded remembering the way she'd wrapped her legs around him, the way she'd succumbed to his touch. The only glitch was the affection he'd seen swimming in her eyes. If she fell in love he'd be screwed and not in a good way. What kind of future did they have? No future at all if she found out Harmon had hired him as her babysitter. He knew Afia well enough to know that she'd be hurt and furious.

He took another drag, sucking in the smoke, tamping down the guilt. If only he'd been able to resist her sexy innocence, to maintain professional distance, he might have survived this assignment with his dignity intact. Instead he'd dug a deeper hole by suggesting they have an affair. The moment she'd said, *"It's not gonna happen,"* he'd known for a fact it was. He couldn't think about next week, next month, or next year. He could barely wrap his mind around tomorrow.

He glanced at the door just as it opened, and Rudy Gallow stepped outside.

All of his energy was geared to navigating this moment.

"Got an extra?" Gallow motioned to Jake's cigarette as he

neared. "I haven't smoked in years, but I could sure use one now."

Jake reached into the inner pocket of his tuxedo jacket and pulled out a pack of Winstons. He offered Gallow the pack and a lighter, while noting his casual attire. Trendy, low-riding sweat pants and a tight fitting T-shirt that accentuated every muscle in his upper body. This guy was ripped. His biceps bulged with the simple effort of lighting a cigarette. If he wanted to kick Jake's ass, he just might pull it off.

Gallow inhaled and passed him back the goods. "Nice tux," he said, after blowing out a quick stream of smoke.

Jake could have said, "Thanks" or "Nice sweats." He nodded, took another long drag instead.

"Right. Okay." Gallow glanced up at the second story window. "Let's do this before Afia realizes I'm missing."

Jake snuffed his cig on the odds that Mr. Universe here was going to take a swing. He'd been caught off guard once today. Once was enough.

Gallow took another quick puff, and then chucked his cigarette as well. "I just happened to glance out the window and saw you. How long have you been out here?"

"A few minutes."

"Anxious about your date?"

He cocked an eyebrow. "Are you?"

Gallow furrowed his brow and then smiled. "Afia's mistaken. I don't think you know."

Jake waited.

"I'm gay."

He might as well have said, "I'm Elvis reincarnated." The news couldn't surprise him more.

Gallow braced his hands on his hips, dipped his chin. "Does that bother you?"

"No." Hell no! It made his day.

Mr. Universe rolled back his broad shoulders and smiled. "Good. Somehow Afia got the impression that you're a homophobe."

"You sound as if you don't like Rudy."

"I don't."

"But you don't even know him."

"I know his kind. That's enough."

"Christ," Jake mumbled, as several pieces of the puzzle snapped into place.

"I guess you know where she got that idea. Anyway, I'm glad she's wrong. You see Afia's protective of her friends. She doesn't have many. There's me and . . . Jean-Pierre." He paused, massaged the back of his neck, and then nodded. "Yes, Jean-Pierre is definitely her friend. He's our roommate. Also gay."

"Why are you telling me all this?" And how was it possible that someone as sweet as Afia only had two friends?

"Because Afia likes you, and she won't give whatever's between the two of you a chance if she thinks you're an asshole. You're not, are you?"

"An asshole?" Jake smiled. "Depends on who you ask."

Gallow laughed.

He's not what he seems. Jake should have listened to his gut on first meeting instead of letting his imagination run amok. Gallow wasn't a taker, he was a *care*taker. So Afia had bought him that limousine. That didn't mean that he'd accepted it without an argument. Or that he didn't intend to somehow pay her back. He glanced at the moonlit townhouse. Maybe this was the payback. Taking her in when she didn't have a place to stay. Nurturing their friendship when she'd lost her fortune. "You really care about her, don't you?"

Gallow sobered. "Yes, I do." He crossed his arms over his massive chest. "You?"

Jake didn't flinch. "Yes."

Gallow nodded then stroked his devilish goatee. "I have some other concerns, but they'll have to wait." He urged Jake toward the door. "Afia's probably ready by now. A word of advice," he said as they moved inside and climbed the stairs to the main floor. "I don't care if she looks like a regal princess, tell her she looks hot."

Jake didn't comment on the advice, as he was busy taking in the surroundings. Modern, eclectic furniture popped with color—bright teal, muted orange, soft taupe. An impressive entertainment center boasted a vast collection of CDs and DVDs. Framed Broadway posters decorated the butter cream walls. There was a spacious, organized quality about the living room and kitchen.

In contrast, the dining room was a disaster. Boxes piled high. Racks crammed with clothing. Was this the sum of Afia's material possessions? He thought about all she'd had, all she'd lost, and realized with a jolt that he'd never heard her whine about her situation. Not once. True, his house was old and in need of repair, his furnishings sparse, but each and every one was a treasured belonging. If he lost all he owned to creditors, he'd be heartsick. Was there nothing in her old life that she missed? Nothing that she treasured? And what was up with having only two friends, who were not even in her social circle? He had a sudden itch to interview Afia, to learn every aspect of her. Her hobbies. Her dreams. Really, what did he know?

He noted the industrial sewing machine and bolts of fabric. "Afia sews?"

Rudy shook his head. "No. Those belong to Jean-Pierre. He's the costume designer and wardrobe master over at the Carnevale."

"Ah," Jake said with a smile. Afia's snitch.

"Beer?" Rudy asked.

"Sure." He hitched back his jacket and stuffed his hands in his pockets while following Gallow into the track-lit kitchen. "So, you and Jean-Pierre are a couple?"

"No." Rudy glanced over his shoulder as he opened the refrigerator door and frowned. "What makes you say that?"

Jake shrugged. "This is a two bedroom place. I just assumed Afia had one room and—"

"Jean-Pierre and I are *not* sleeping together."

"Okay." Jake wondered at his terse tone, but let it slide. He wasn't all that interested in this man's love life, just ecstatic that Afia wasn't a part of it.

"Afia sleeps on the couch," he said, shutting the door and passing Jake a beer. "Glass?"

"No, thanks."

"I worry about her back sometimes. I mean how comfortable can it be sleeping night after night on a couch? I wanted to give her my room, but she wouldn't take it. She refused

Jean-Pierre's offer as well. Said she didn't want to put us out. There's no arguing with her. Trust me. We tried." He clinked his bottle to Jake's. "Cheers."

"Cheers." Jake tipped the long neck to his lips just as Afia stepped into view. "Wow."

"Hot," Gallow prodded out of the side of his mouth, but then Afia stepped closer and he got a better look. He set down his bottle on the counter and moved into the living room. "I thought there was a little bit more to that dress. Now that I see it on . . ." He jammed a big hand through his stylish hair. "I don't know, honey."

"I like it." Jake took a long swig of beer, needing to lubricate his desert-dry throat. Hot? She was on fire. The beaded gown flowed over her curves, leaving very little to the imagination. Scandalously low-cut, the sable brown fabric matched her hair and eyes perfectly while accentuating her creamy skin. Maybe it was her hair, twisted in a high chignon, or her lined, luminous eyes, or her slender bone structure, but damn if she didn't look like a sexed-up Audrey Hepburn. He'd always had a thing for Audrey.

She looked from Rudy to Jake and back again as if trying to gauge the tension.

"We're fine, Afia," her friend grumbled. "We're having a beer together for chrissake. It's that dress . . ."

She waved off his concern and glided toward Jake on glittering, three-inch heels. "Are you really . . . fine? With," she fluttered a hand, "everything?"

He set down the beer, buttoned his jacket and tried not to drool. "More than fine."

She smiled and smoothed her palms down the satin lapels of his single-breasted jacket. "You look very nice."

His heart raced in triple-time. "So do you." How in the hell was he going to make it through an entire dinner dance without feasting on those cherry-red lips?

She crinkled her nose. "Just nice?"

He glanced at Gallow who was standing behind her, wide-eyed. The man palmed his forehead and groaned. Jake thought it was because he'd failed to say "hot" until Afia stepped back and did a slow one-eighty. Holy shit. He'd thought the front was low-cut. The back . . . *there was no back*. The material dipped dangerously low, very near to the base of her spine. "Impressive," he choked out.

She spun and zapped him with a toothy smile. "I'll just get an evening bag, and we can be on our way."

Jake moved in next to Gallow, and they watched as she slinked to the far corner of the dining room and bent over to root through a box.

"I can't believe I picked out that dress," Gallow said.

"Thanks," Jake said, enjoying the rear view.

The other man grunted. "Keep your eye on her tonight."

"No problem."

"I don't mean . . ." He elbowed Jake. "Get your head out of your pants for a minute and listen to what I'm saying."

Jake glanced sideways.

"Afia's sensitive. A couple of the women on the SCC don't like her. Screw that, they despise her. Just—"

"Got it!" Afia straightened with a tiny brown clutch purse in hand.

"I got it, too," Jake said to Gallow as she shoved some essentials into her bag and snatched up a sheer wrap. "No problem."

She hurried forward and gave her friend a hug. "I don't know what time I'll be home tonight."

He glanced sideways at Jake and then kissed her on the cheek. "Have fun."

Jake put his hand at the base of her back and ushered her to the stairs. The feel of her satiny skin sent a bolt of desire directly to his loins. He ached to slide his hand beneath the thin fabric of that clingy dress, to smooth his palms over every satiny inch of her body, to finish what he'd started this afternoon. Knowing that he had to get through an entire dinner dance and a possible tail before earning the green light was a real bitch. Talk about control. But he knew without a doubt it would be worth the wait. She'd been willing to make love on a desk, she wasn't opposed to kinky, she was beautiful inside and out. In short, she was every man's dream.

He hung back as she started down the stairs, glanced over his shoulder at Gallow. "By the way," he said with a crooked smile, "you don't have to worry about Afia's comfort. She won't be sleeping on your couch tonight."

Chapter Fifteen

The five-minute ride to the Carnevale Casino was excruciating. Conversation was out of the question. She wasn't sure what had happened between Rudy and Jake, but she was certain she'd felt no tension, and relief had freed her of all of her doubts. Now Afia couldn't form a thought that didn't revolve around sex. Jake was as devastating in a tux as he was in a T-shirt and jeans. Every time he glanced sideways at her, her skin heated and her nipples hardened. The memory of how he'd palmed her breast, squeezing her buds through the sheer, lacey cups of her bra, burned strong. Tonight, she wasn't wearing a bra. He could bare her breast simply by pulling aside the slinky fabric of her bodice. Just the thought of it made her squirm.

Jake noticed her fidgeting and smiled. Had he read her mind?

He steered his car into Valet, handed over his keys, and rounded to Afia's side to help her out. His grasp on her elbow was strong and assuring as they breezed through the chaotic *porte cochère*. The valet attendants gawked. The bellhops gawked. She adjusted her wrap higher on her shoulders, draping it across her chest. Minutes ago, she'd felt scandalously sexy. Just now she felt supremely self-conscious in her barely-there dress. And she still had to face the women of the SCC along with the other three hundred or so dignitaries that ceremoniously attended the gala. Even the mayor would be there.

Jake wrapped his arm around her waist and hurried her inside as if sensing she was losing her nerve. "You look beautiful," he whispered in her ear as he ushered her through the bustling lobby.

Her heart fluttered at the compliment and provided her with a smidgeon of confidence. Her heels clicked against the Italian marble, mingling with the chatter and laughter of a Friday night crowd. As the Carnevale was the newest, and one of the most heavily themed casinos in the city, it was also currently the most popular. She tried very hard to focus on the stunning Venetian design rather than the patrons' leers and grumblings. Maybe they weren't staring at her and gossiping about her husbands' untimely accidents. Maybe they were griping about their gambling losses, or the exorbitant amount of money they'd shelled out for a gourmet dinner.

Once she and Jake got upstairs and into the ballroom, she had no doubt *she'd* be the focus of speculative conversation. In attendance would be acquaintances and so-called friends of her past. She realized suddenly that instead of helping Jake to blend in, she'd only draw undue attention. *Look, here comes the Black Widow with her next victim. How much do you think he's worth? Poor guy's a goner. Maybe he'll get lucky and go like her first husband.*

Panic surged through her veins, her past and present colliding as they neared a massive, blown-glass chandelier.

When Jake veered her toward the elevator, she broke off and slipped into a cocktail lounge called the Rialto. Gilded paintings of Venice's Grand Canal graced the cobalt walls. An arched bridge rose behind the bar, doubling as a stage for a mandolin player and an electric violinist. Romantic music strained to be heard above the cacophony of buzzing voices and clinking glasses. The room was crowded and dimly lit. The perfect place to get lost.

Jake walked up beside her, scratched his head. "What are you doing?"

She took one ticket out of her clutch and pressed it into his hand. "You go on up, have dinner, circulate, and watch Rivelli. I'll wait down here."

Jake scanned the mostly-male clientele seated along the bar, and frowned. "You're kidding, right?"

"I'll sabotage the surveillance."

"What?"

"Instead of helping you blend, I'll only create a stir. I'm the 'Black Widow,' remember?"

Impatience flickered across his handsome face. "That's old news, Afia. Let it go. I guarantee you most gossip mongers have moved onto fresh blood. It's human nature. I hate to tell you this, sweetheart, but no matter how you slice it you're going to draw attention. You're goddamned gorgeous."

Afia blinked, stunned by the husky declaration. Men had

been singing praise to her beauty her entire life, but never had a compliment sounded so sincere. Maybe because she knew that Jake found her attractive even when her clothes were smeared with barbecue sauce or when her hair was shoved up under a two-dollar baseball cap. She'd gained at least three pounds this week, and he still wanted to see her naked. She breathed deeply, while massaging a strange ache in her chest.

He took her hand and pressed a kiss to her palm. "You can sit down here and hide, or you can take an active part."

He was reminding her of her conviction earlier today. She appreciated the not-so-subtle nudge. She'd agreed to help him tonight, and if he didn't consider her a liability, it certainly wasn't fair to pull out. If anyone made a nasty remark, she'd handle it as she always did . . . with dignity. She certainly wouldn't make a scene. They were on a case. This was work. Feeling foolish, she handed over her ticket. "All right."

He pocketed both gala tickets, noted her crinkled brow, and ran his hand over his face. "What?"

She shifted, glanced over her shoulder to make sure no one was listening. "It's just that . . ." She cleared her throat and whispered, "I'm not wearing any underwear."

"None at all?"

Wide-eyed, she motioned him to lower his voice. "Well, a wisp of a thong, but that's it. Anything more would have ruined the lines of the gown."

He massaged his temples. "You had to tell me this now, baby?"

The sexy endearment quickened her pulse and caused her cheeks to flush. "I'm sorry," she said, trying to hold her voice to a whisper. "But I had to let you know how inappropriately I'm dressed. Now that I'm out in public, I'm feeling a bit self-conscious."

"You look sexy, not indecent. Relax. No one knows that you're naked under there. Except for me." He studied the ceiling and shook his head. "I need a drink if I'm going to get through this night."

"Me, too."

He grabbed her hand and practically dragged her to an empty space near the end of the bar. "What would you like?"

"What are you having?" she asked.

"Scotch, neat," he told the bartender.

"Make that two," Afia said.

Jake raised his brows. "You sure about that?"

"I need as much bolstering as you do. What's good for the goose . . ."

"You're the goose." Jake slapped a twenty down on the bar. "I'm the gander."

"Whatever." Afia thanked the bartender for her drink, thanked Jake for treating, and then raised the glass to her lips. The fumes went right up her nostrils, and she instinctively grimaced.

He laughed. "Let me order you a glass of wine."

"No, no. This is fine." *I will hold my own with this man.*

"Whatever you say." He raised his glass in a mock toast.

Wanting to get it over with, she downed the drink in one fiery swallow and then gave a full body shudder. Mental note: Scotch is disgusting.

"Jesus, Afia. You're supposed to sip it."

Since she didn't think she could speak yet without breathing fire, she simply smiled.

Jake swore and then matched her, downing his scotch in one shot. "Come on," he said, nabbing her hand.

"Maybe we should have one more," she rasped.

"No way."

She clattered behind him, feeling the burn of that hard liquor all the way up to the third floor ballroom. Music floated out through the open doors. *We Are Family*. No, *Boogie Oogie Oogie*. One of those overplayed seventies songs. Hard to tell since the orchestra was in the middle of a solo, no lyrics. Most of the attendees were already inside. Thank goodness. She wouldn't be forced to make chitchat while waiting in line. They could simply slip inside and find a seat, hopefully in the back at a table where no one knew her. Reserved seating was always up front, and since Afia was no longer a member of the committee at least she didn't have to worry about sitting next to Dora Simmons or Frances Beck.

Unfortunately, the wicked witches of the Eastern seaboard were manning the silent auction table.

It was impossible to move inside without passing them. The table was purposely situated in a high traffic area to elicit the most bids. As Dora and Frances were the most vocal of her critics, she decided to confront instead of avoid. They'd only track her down later. Better to get it over with. She stroked her charm bracelet, silently chanting, *I am willing to forgive their pettiness. I am encased in a protective bubble, shielded from their catty jabs. I'm rubber, you're glue* . . . No, no. Not that one.

"Well, isn't this a surprise." Dora was the first to speak. She was always the first, and the last, to speak. Sometimes Afia thought the woman was in love with the sound of her own voice. Other times she thought she was a controlling shrew. Probably she was both.

"Good evening, Dora," she said with an easy smile. "Frances."

"We didn't expect you, dear," Frances purred in a condescending voice. Baring her sculptured claws, she patted the first of several six-foot tables strung together in a very long "L." Each table featured donated goods and certificates from local businesses and artisans. "Please don't feel pressured to bid on anything. Pennies must be precious these days."

"Pennies are precious every day," Jake said, regarding the stylish, forty-something women with a disarming smile. "That's why we need to spend them on what matters." He winked at Afia. "We'll definitely bid."

Frances's surgically tightened face burned red, but her voice remained calm. "I'm sorry, and you are?"

"Afia's boyfriend," he said, offering his hand in greeting. A polite, no, dashing gesture, she thought. "Jake Blaine. Pleased to meet you."

She was glad that Dora and Frances were sizing up her escort instead of scrutinizing her heated blush. Boyfriend? Well, she supposed it made sense as they were undercover, but she wished he had warned her, although he had said this was a "date." *Boyfriend. Date.* Jake, she realized with a start, made her feel like a woman reborn, instead of the doomsday widow.

"Very kind of you, Mr. Blaine, as Afia has yet to introduce us," Frances said, with a haughty sniff.

"I'm so sorry." Afia pressed a hand to her racing heart. "It's just . . ." She smiled at Jake. "I'm sorry. Jake, I'd like to introduce Dora Simmons, president of the Seashore Charity Committee, and our, their, *the* vice president, Frances Tate."

"So how long have you and Afia been seeing each other," Dora asked, moving in for the kill.

"Not long," Jake said.

Frances raised her thinly tweezed brows at Afia. "I'm glad you had the good taste to break things off with your chauffeur, dear."

Maybe it was the scotch. Maybe it was her reluctance to be a doormat with Jake looking on. Or maybe she was just plain sick of these two hypocritical do-gooders. She smiled, a slow smile laced with innuendo. "Oh, I'm still living with Rudy."

Frances blinked and looked at Jake.

He nodded. "Great guy. A real man's man."

Afia stifled a giggle.

Dora crossed her arms over the black beaded bodice of her classic silk gown. "And what business are *you* in, Mr. Blaine?"

"The business of gathering information."

"Oh?"

"Data processing," he clarified.

"Oh. Sounds tedious. Although it must pay terribly well," she said, glancing at Afia.

"Not terribly," Jake said. "Just your everyday, blue-collar job."

Frances smoothed her fingers over her diamond choker and

chuckled. "Young. Middle income. You're certainly not Afia's type now, are you, Mr. Blaine?"

Zing! Afia felt an invisible arrow pierce her protective bubble, and she almost, almost lost her composure. *I am willing to forgive their pettiness.*

Jake's smile was intact, that same gorgeous, dimpled smile, but his eyes had turned dark and cold. "Here's a tip, ladies." He thumped two fingers against his heart. "Charity begins at home." He nodded toward the silent auction merchandise. "Amazing that you're able to do so much good when your hearts are so small."

"Well!" Dora said with a nervous titter. "I never!"

"I'm not surprised." Jake grasped Afia's hand and tugged her further down the table. "Come on, baby. Let's shop."

Afia had to press her lips together to keep from laughing. Jake, and not Dora, had gotten in the last word. "I don't think you made a very good impression."

"I don't give a rat's ass what those two think of me and neither should you."

"I know. I don't. At least, I'm trying not to. They do wonderful work, but they really are obnoxious. To me, anyway."

"And why is that?"

"They're afraid I've got my sights set on their husbands."

"Do you?"

She blanched. "Of course not!" *I haven't done anything wrong.* Then she saw the teasing twinkle in his eye. "Oh."

He stroked his thumb along her jaw. "To hell with them, Jinx."

"To hell with them," she repeated, that strange ache pulsing in her chest again. Her blood roared in her ears as he focused on her mouth. She moistened her bottom lip willing him to steal a kiss. Just one . . . just something to appease the hunger until . . . later.

He swallowed hard then broke away to peruse the merchandise. "So what should we bid on?"

Disappointment seeped into her bones, even though she knew he was right to resist her silent plea. If they started kissing now they'd probably end up in the janitor's closet instead of the ballroom. "Actually," she said on a sigh, "Dora and Frances were right. I can't really afford—"

"Sure you can. End of the week. Pay day. It's for a good cause, right?"

"Oh, yes." Her enthusiasm returned at the thought of all the good that would come from the gala. "Tonight's proceeds will be divided up among several worthy organizations. The Homeless Shelter. The Aids Alliance." She grinned. "Even the daycare center will get a small, but much needed slice."

"Then let's do it."

His insistence melted away her inhibitions and left her light-headed. Or maybe it was the scotch. Probably a little of both. "All right, Mr. *Blaine*." She squelched the urge to hold his hand while scanning the merchandise. "Where'd you get that name anyway?"

"It's cheesy."

"Tell me." She passed over a spa certificate and basket of Godiva chocolates.

"Casablanca."

She slapped his shoulder and squealed. "Get out! I just

watched that movie the other night! Humphrey Bogart as Rick Blaine. Except tonight you look more . . . I don't know . . . like Cary Grant in *Charade*. Except you're younger and have blond hair."

"Perfect casting," his gaze floated from her lips to her eyes, "since you resemble Audrey Hepburn . . . except you're sexier."

Embarrassed, she made light of the compliment, fluttered a hand, snickered. "Oh, go on. No really. Feel free to expound on my charms."

He grinned and fingered a certificate for a moonlight cruise dinner. "You're cute when you're tipsy."

Aching to plunge her tongue inside of his sexy mouth, she shook her head and inspected a beaded bag. "It's not the scotch. It's you. You make me feel . . ." *Alive*. It sounded so pathetic. "You're right, it's the scotch." She smiled, and massaged her temple. "Next time, I'll sip."

Five minutes later they'd placed a bid on a landscape painting by a local artist. Afia had insisted that the painting would look perfect on the office's reception area wall, and amazingly, Jake had agreed. They hadn't bid as much as she normally would have, but she was pleased all the same. She'd actually *earned* this money. *No contribution is too small.* How many times had she told someone that when she'd hawked raffle tickets at one or another charity event?

She heard the orchestra switch over from Motown to standards, and knew from years of attending social dinner dances that the salad was about to be served. She suspected the special entertainment would take place in between courses. "We should probably go inside and find a seat."

"Preferably somewhere near Rivelli," Jake said.

Afia stroked her bracelet. "He'll be seated up front along with any other attending casino executives."

"Is that a problem?"

She glanced over and caught Dora glaring at her. *I will not be intimidated.* "No," she said, with a practiced smile. "Not a problem. Just tricky. The tables closest to the stage are reserved."

Jake nodded and ushered her toward the ballroom entrance. "Let's locate Rivelli and take it from there."

Afia slid off her sheer wrap, draping it over her arms as they walked past Dora and Frances. She heard a unified gasp and wasn't a bit surprised. Obviously, the witches of the East were appalled by her backless gown. The surprising part was that Afia didn't give a *rat's ass.* Even more surprising was that she felt completely at ease as she navigated the ballroom on Jake's arm. Most of the attendees were already seated and engrossed in conversation while awaiting their salads. The room was fairly dark, and it's not as if there were a spotlight on her, although there was a time she would have imagined just that. She noticed a few curious glances, a few behind-the-hand whispers, but nothing that she couldn't endure.

Truth be told, Jake was turning his own share of heads. Female heads. He looked handsome and dapper, and entirely comfortable in this reserved environment. He was rather like a chameleon, she thought, possessing the capacity to blend in perfectly with his surroundings. "You really didn't need me here tonight," she whispered out of the side of her mouth.

"But I'm glad I came."

He smiled down at her. "So am I." Then he angled his head toward a table just left of the dance floor. "There's Rivelli. The tall, dark-headed man sitting in between the lady with the red curls and the man with the slate-gray jacket. See him?"

Afia nodded. "I think I also see a table not too far away with two open seats. The best part is I don't know another soul sitting there. Shall we?"

✻ ✻ ✻

Now Jake knew why this was a two hundred dollar a plate dinner. The food was incredible, prepared, according to Afia, by the city's top chefs. The wine: top notch. The floral center-pieces: works of modern art. The ten-piece orchestra: talented and polished, playing jazz standards during the courses and dance music in between. The way Afia kept watching the par-quet floor and swaying in time, it was obvious she wanted to dance. Several other men, including the husbands of the two bitches he'd met earlier, had noticed as well, stopping by the table at various times to invite her onto the floor. Jake had smiled, but he'd wanted to cold-cock each one. Afia had politely turned them all down saying, "Thank you, but all of my dances are saved." Then she'd smile at Jake.

He'd been touched and tempted, especially during the slow songs. As to the classic R&B she seemed especially fond of, well, it's not that he didn't like to dance, it's just that he wasn't sure if he was capable of watching Afia "shake her groove thang" without losing his mind.

Dinner had been torture. Every time she moved just so, he got a glimpse of her breast. Just a glimpse. Just enough to make saliva pool in his mouth. During the main course he'd felt bare toes creeping up his pant leg, sliding up and down his calf. Relatively certain they didn't belong to the burly doctor on his right, he'd turned to Afia and raised a cautionary brow. She'd merely waggled her eyebrows and taken a dainty bite of her filet mignon. That's when he'd moved her wine glass out of her reach. She'd only had one glass, but she'd also had that scotch, and maybe she didn't have a head for liquor.

Rivelli on the other hand could clearly hold his drink. Jake had had a clear view of the man most of the night. The casino V.P. had consumed more than a few glasses of wine, and yet his behavior remained above reproach. He'd conversed and laughed with his table companions during courses. In between he'd visited with the dignitaries seated at the surrounding tables. Outgoing without being obnoxious. Good-looking, well-dressed, and well-spoken, and as his fiancée had pointed out, charismatic. But he hadn't made eyes at any woman in particular, nor had he touched any one of them inappropriately. When he'd stepped out into the hall to make a call on the house phone, Jake had stepped out for a smoke and eavesdropped. The call had been strictly business. When he'd excused himself from the table twenty minutes later, Jake had followed again only to land in the men's room. Perfect. He'd had to take a leak anyway.

Now they were both back at their tables, both having dessert and coffee, and both awaiting the special performance from *Venetian Vogue*.

"This is it," Afia whispered as the orchestra left the stage and a host announced the Carnevale showroom pit band. Five musicians, resembling Gondoliers in their black and white striped shirts and red kerchiefs, readied their instruments.

Jake recognized his brother-in-law at the keyboard. This morning Joni had called to tell him, *"Carson got the gig!"* A gig with an open-ended contract and surprisingly decent salary. In that moment, Jake had felt lighter, less pressured on the financial end. If he could get Carson aside tonight, he'd congratulate him personally. Otherwise he'd call him tomorrow. Right now he needed to watch Rivelli as Rivelli watched the dancers.

The music kicked off, very Euro-techno, and nine women and five men exploded into the room from all sides. Their costumes were outrageous. Revealing and glitzy, bold and imaginative. Eleventh-century Renaissance meets Cirque du Soleil. He'd never seen anything quite like it. The women wore matching hairpieces beneath their hats and plumes and gilded masks that covered the upper halves of their faces making it difficult to distinguish one from the other. They all had great bodies, stellar legs. Every one of them wore fishnet stockings. Rivelli, as far as he could tell, wasn't focusing on any one, particular girl. He was watching all of the dancers, the choreographed numbers as a whole, with a fat-ass grin on his face. The man was mesmerized.

Ten minutes later, the mini-show ended, and the audience rose to their feet for a standing ovation. The pit band disappeared-meaning Jake would be calling Carson tomorrow-and the orchestra returned and launched into *It's Raining Men*. The

Venetian dancers stormed the floor, encouraging the audience to join in. One of the first to bite was Anthony Rivelli. He snagged one of the girls, and they promptly "hustled" their way to the center of the floor.

It seemed as if three-quarters of the audience followed suit. Atlantic City's elite packed the dance floor, effectively shielding Rivelli and his partner from Jake's view.

He stood and held out his hand to Afia. "I believe you saved a dance for me."

"Lots of them." She clasped his hand and flashed a coy grin. "You just want to get close to Rivelli."

He pulled her onto the dance floor and into his arms. "I want to get close to you." He slid both of his hands over her bare shoulders, down the smooth expanse of her sexy back and maneuvered her toward the middle of the floor. "And to Rivelli," he admitted with a nod.

"What did you think of the costumes?" she asked, backing out of his arms to do a funky move.

"Imaginative."

She smiled. "My friend designed them."

He had a bead on Rivelli now. The man looked to be in his glory, but he seemed more focused on his dance moves than his actual partner. "What did you think of the pit band?"

"Awesome," she said, gaining his attention by giving him her back and using her arms and hips as enticingly as any belly dancer.

His throat went dry as the beaded dress shimmied and shifted over her curves, reminding him of what lay beneath. A willing body and a sexy thong. He forced his mind back to the topic at hand. "The keyboardist is my brother-in-law."

"He's good."

"So are you. Where'd you learn to dance like that? Come here." He grabbed her hand and spun her into him, clamped his hands on her ass and pulled her tight against his groin.

"You're being touchy-feely," she said, grinding against him to the rhythm of the music.

"Yes, I am." Christ, he was turned on.

She peeked over her shoulder. "Rivelli's not."

"No, he's not. He even switched to another dancer. Did you notice?"

"Yes. I also noticed . . ."

"What?"

She shrugged. "I don't know. Something about the way he moves. I'm certain we've never met before, and yet he's familiar to me." She shook her head. "That doesn't make any sense."

"Doesn't have to make sense. It's a hunch. Let it simmer, and see what comes to you. Anything would help at this point. This guy hasn't even thrown us a bone." He shifted his hands to Afia's hips as they continued to rock and grind. Trying to keep his mind and eye on Rivelli was a challenge.

"You're a sexy dancer, Jake."

It pleased him that she thought so, although she'd inspired the grind. "Not as sexy as you. You're killing me, babe."

She tunneled her fingers through his hair. "Really?"

Christ Almighty. "Mmm." He glanced down, the ornery twinkle in her eye causing his arousal to twitch. "You've been teasing me all night."

"I know."

"You'll pay."

"I hope so." She smiled, glanced sideways, and then gasped. "He's leaving." Afia poked him in the shoulder. "Rivelli's saying his goodbyes."

He clasped her hand and gently guided her through the crowd. "We're out of here."

Chapter Sixteen

This was hell on earth. Sheer torture. Cruel and inhumane punishment for being a shameless flirt. Why hadn't it occurred to her that they'd have to tail Rivelli after he left the gala? Of course they had to follow through, see where he ended up. What if he'd planned a late night rendezvous with one of the dancers? Or *two* of the dancers? He'd hustled with two different girls. Maybe he was seeing *both* of them on the side.

A ménage à trois.

Afia's mind swirled with scandalous images, only they were of her with Jake and . . . Jake. She was seeing double. Mixing wine and scotch probably hadn't been the brightest of ideas. Only she didn't feel drunk, just deliciously uninhibited. And the two naked Jakes were only in her mind. The real Jake sat, fully dressed, on the other side of the car, driving west on the A.C. Expressway.

"I'm telling you this dude is going to drive straight home or to Angela's townhouse." He steered one-handed as he stripped off his bowtie and popped some studs off of his shirt.

The gesture was wholly male and had Afia cracking her window for a blast of refreshing air. "He could still veer off between here and Cherry Hill," she pointed out.

"Five bucks says he won't. He's careful. Does all the right things. You saw him tonight. He played the perfect host. Once he hit the dance floor, the whole room followed. Maybe his sole purpose in joining that dancer was to get the party jumping. After that his duties as V.P. were complete, and he was free to play dutiful fiancé." He flexed his fingers on the wheel. "Oh, yeah. He's going straight home."

"So you don't think there's another woman?" She kicked off her shoes and adjusted the seat belt, trying to get comfortable.

"Didn't say that. There's the issue of the lipstick, the nail tips, and the fishnets. Between what I witnessed tonight and what Jean-Pierre told you, there is definitely an obsession or fascination of some sort at play."

She squinted across the darkened car at him. "How do you know about Jean-Pierre?"

"You told me."

"I didn't tell you his name."

"Rudy did."

He sounded so nonchalant. "So you don't mind that I'm living with two men?"

"I mind that you *have* to live with two men. I mind that

Glick stole your money and left you homeless, but that's another case. Let's stick with Rivelli for now." He dragged his hand over his head, causing choppy strands to stick out every which way. "For the record, it helps that they're gay."

She touched her fingertips to her temples, trying to focus on his words rather than his moonlit silhouette. Could he be anymore sexy? "Are you saying you'd mind if they were straight?"

He glanced sideways at her, worked his jaw. "Let's get back to Rivelli."

She suppressed a smug grin. He would mind. He'd be jealous. It made him even sexier in her eyes, and she wondered how she was going to make it to Cherry Hill and back without touching him. She rolled her window down another inch.

"I had the air on," Jake said.

"I know, but I'm hot."

"That doesn't make any sense."

She frowned at him. "I needed some *fresh* air."

He grinned. "The wine?"

"Yeah," she said, fluttering a hand in the air. "Sure. Blame it on the wine. So!" she said a little too brightly. "You're thinking there was, or maybe still is, another woman, but since the lipstick incident he's decided to play it cool."

"Very cool. Very safe. Hike up your skirt."

She stared at him for a moment, unsure if she'd heard correctly.

"You said you were hot. We're going to be in this car for another two to three hours. You might as well make yourself comfortable. While you're at it, let down your hair."

It sounded a little bit like an order, and absurdly that turned her on. Her hands shook as she reached up and started pulling the bobby pins from her chignon.

"We're going to play a game," he said, tweaking her excitement. "It'll help pass the time."

"Wh . . . What about Rivelli?"

"I've got him in my sights. I'm also ninety-nine percent sure of where he's going." He glanced over just as she shook out her hair. "You look like a goddess."

His voice was thick and hoarse and spiked her pulse mercilessly as she finger-combed the tousled mess. "I thought you didn't like my hair. You're always telling me to do something with it."

He flashed a one-dimpled smile. "That's because it's distracting."

"Oh." She smiled back. It was a beautiful night—mild temperature, star-filled sky, bright moon. She was a little tipsy, a lot aroused, and alone with a sexy man who'd promised to take her for a walk on the wild side. Swallowing hard, she slowly inched up her ankle-length gown to mid-thigh. "What's the game?"

"Interview," he said, reaching over and sliding her skirt higher. "I ask questions, and you answer them."

Her eyes rolled back as his fingertips grazed her inner thighs. "Do I get to ask you questions?" Her voice sounded raw and distant to her ears.

"Maybe."

"Fair enough," she said, because just now she'd agree to anything.

He smoothed his palm down her thigh, caressed the under-side of her knee and gave a soft tug.

She shifted, allowing him to reposition her left leg so that her foot rested in his lap. Her gown pooled between her legs, otherwise he would have had a prime view of her thong. Deliciously aroused, she groaned and let her head fall against the back of the seat as he stroked her bare calf.

"What's your favorite color?"

"Pink."

"What's your favorite kind of music?"

"It's a toss up between rhythm and blues and Latin."

"List your top three favorite movies."

"That's a tough one." She closed her eyes and thought about it a minute, shivering with sensual delight when he traced circles around her ankle. "*Wizard of Oz*. Any James Bond Movie." She smiled. "And *Casablanca*."

He laughed. "Quite the variety. Okay. List your five clos-est friends."

"Rudy, Jean-Pierre, and maybe you."

"That's only three, and I was only a maybe."

She lazed open her eyes, glanced out the windshield, and caught sight of a doe up ahead, standing just clear of the road-side trees. Alone and vulnerable. She tensed, fearing for the gentle animal's well-being. *Please let it have better judgment than me.*

"True friends believe the best in you, no matter what," she said, willing the deer not to dart across the road. "They don't care if you're young or old, rich or poor, if you live next door or across the country, or if your luck is worse than most people's."

She didn't feel that she needed to explain any further than that and wasn't sure that she could. She'd had her share of fair-weather friends early on in her life, and her adult friends had been her husbands' friends. All had drifted away following the funerals. True friendship was rare and her most treasured possession.

He was quiet for a moment, and she breathed more easily when he whizzed safely past the deer and moved onto the next question. "Why have you been late for work every day this week?"

Only slightly less awkward than his previous question. When was he going to get to the fun part of this game? "Because I've been going into the daycare center first, trying to help out, and each day there's been some catastrophe or another. I'm not very good with kids, which, if you must know, is very depressing."

"Why?"

"Because I'd like to have children someday." Without thinking she laid her hand to her flat belly. What she wouldn't give to be in Joni's shoes. "What about you?"

He nodded. "Two or three kids would be nice." He massaged the sole of her foot, applied pressure along the sides. "You're probably a pushover."

"What?" She practically moaned the word. He stimulated more zones than her reflexologist.

"Kids need boundaries. Try being more assertive."

Her eyes drifted shut. "Yes, sir." She gave a cocky salute, but her heart was hopping up and down like a jackrabbit. He wanted kids, and he was probably good with them too.

"Why did you marry Randy?"

Her eyes flew open. She tried to jerk her foot away, but Jake held tight and continued the massage. "This game isn't going exactly as I'd hoped," she said.

He waited.

"It's kind of embarrassing."

He massaged.

If they weren't alone in a dark car, if she hadn't had a couple of drinks, and if he hadn't relaxed her into a stupor, she probably would have hedged. Instead the words flowed. "My mother told me to." She cringed at the admission. "I know how that sounds, as if I don't have a mind of my own, but, I was very young, and I had known Randy a long time. I was comfortable with him, and I admit I'd had a bit of a crush on him for some time. The dashing older man. He treated me like a princess, and he made me feel very safe. For a girl who grew up thinking any day could be her last, that was pretty important."

He rolled back his shoulders and nodded. "And Frank?"

"Pretty much the same reason. I felt particularly lost after Randy died. Confused. Guilty . . . for reasons that I'd rather not go into. I was a mess, and Frank was there to pick up the pieces. My mother pushed the marriage thinking it was the best thing for me. I didn't care about the money, but she did. After Frank died, after the rumors, I went a little nuts and indulged in an eleven-month shopping spree. I guess I still didn't care about the money because I essentially threw it away. Rudy said I shopped to fill a void."

Jake glanced sideways. "What do you think?"

"I think he's right." She swallowed a lump of regret. "I wish I would have gone to a therapist instead. Think of all the good I could have done with that money."

He squeezed her toes and smiled. "You're still doing good. Think about what you're accomplishing with Nancy and the children at the daycare center."

She snorted. "The children hate me."

He laughed, reached over and brushed his thumb tenderly across her cheek. "I'm sure they don't hate you. Who could hate you?"

Her skin tingled under his gentle touch. "Dora and Frances."

He leveled her with a stern look.

"But I don't give a rat's ass what they think," she added.

"Good girl." He turned quiet then, focused on Rivelli's taillights as they turned onto Route 73. She was about to ask if it was her turn to conduct an interview when he said, "One last question."

"Yes?"

He pinned her with a quick look. "Did you love them?"

"Randy and Frank?" Well, that was a humdinger of a last question. Uneasy, she rubbed her forehead in thought. "I cared for them deeply, of course. They were very good to me."

"But did you love them?"

She opened her mouth, closed it. Well, she'd certainly told them so. Actually, no. She'd never said "I love you." It had always been, "I love you, too," in automatic reply to one of them saying it first. Or maybe "love ya!" as she'd signed off from a phone conversation. Why hadn't she ever said it first?

She shook her head. No, no. This was crazy. Of course, she'd loved her husbands. "We were very comfortable together."

"Comfortable?"

She nodded and stroked her bracelet. "Yes. Things were quite pleasant."

He turned and looked at her, brows furrowed. "Pleasant."

She huffed an exasperated breath. "Would you please stop repeating after me?" She yanked her foot out of his lap. "Is it my turn to ask questions yet?"

He chuckled and focused on the road. "Sure, baby. Fire away."

She had a million of them. Where had he gotten that scar on his cheek? Why did he leave the police force? Had he ever been in a serious relationship? She opened her mouth and his cell phone rang. "Darn!"

"Sorry, but it might be Joni." He plucked the cell from his inner jacket pocket, put it to his ear. "Yeah? Uh-huh."

Afia planted her feet back on the floor and fidgeted with the confining seat belt, while trying to make sense of the one-sided conversation.

"Yes, he was. Working. Uh-huh. No, nothing suspicious. Yes, I am. He did? Yeah? Tomorrow and Sunday? Sure. No, I understand. Thanks." He ended the call, tucked away the phone and slowed to make a U-turn.

Afia perked up in her seat. "What's going on?"

"That was Angela. Rivelli called her from his car. Told her he was thirty minutes from her house. He felt bad for abandoning whatever social function she'd had planned so he's spending tonight and the next two days exclusively with

221

her. He took the weekend off."

"You don't have to follow him tonight?"

"Nope."

"Or for the next two days?"

"Uh-uh. She said she'd overnight a package with some information. I can do some record checking, but the man himself is off-limits until Monday. Angela doesn't want me anywhere near them."

Afia snorted. "I think we should be investigating her. She gives me the creeps."

"Hold that thought. We have a game to finish, and I have another question."

She blinked at him. "I thought it was my turn!"

"Change of plan." He took the entrance ramp that put them onto the expressway heading back toward Atlantic City and gunned the accelerator. "What's your number one fantasy?"

✳ ✳ ✳

Oh, yeah. She was every man's dream all right. The sweet-faced socialite had just knocked his socks off, and he was not a man easily shocked. "An X-rated night of sex? That's your number one fantasy?"

"You asked."

Holy shit. He slid her a curious glance. "What do you consider X-rated?"

"Anything other than the ordinary."

His eyebrows shot to his hairline. S&M? Multiple partners? What? "Define ordinary."

"Kissing and fondling and making love in bed. Oh, and only one orgasm in a night."

He bit back a smile. Christ, she was cute. And deprived. "That's pretty ordinary. Is that, ummm, what you're used too?"

She turned to look out the side window. "I'd rather not talk about it."

"Okay." He focused on the highway and accelerated to seventy-five. Afia had married conservative, older husbands, and though she may have felt affection for them, she sure as hell hadn't been in love. This night just kept getting better.

"So can you do it?"

And better. "Make you come multiple times in multiple locations?" He smiled. It would be his pleasure and privilege. He glanced sideways and caught her staring.

She licked her lips and swallowed hard. "You look awfully sure of yourself."

She looked awfully tousled and sexy. His heart bumped up against his chest as a primitive yearning snaked through his body. This woman was beautiful, sweet, trusting, and adventurous, and he was going to possess her body and soul. The realization was staggering, but surprisingly, not all that scary.

He'd fallen in love.

Well, hell. He couldn't define the moment it had happened. Or maybe he could if he was brutally honest. He'd never put stock in the notion of love at first sight, but since meeting Afia his belief system had been knocked off kilter. All that was clear was that he wanted this woman in his life . . . forever.

"I wanted you the moment I saw you, Afia. I've been fantasizing about you for days, and after what you put me through tonight . . . trust me. I'm up to the challenge. No pun intended."

She brushed her bangs off of her forehead and blew out a shaky breath.

"Second thoughts?"

She shook her head. "No, I'm just wondering what all it will entail, and . . . where are we going to do it?"

"Here, there, my place." For as long as you'll have me.

"Here?"

He reached over with his right hand and slid her dress off of her shoulder. The silky fabric fell away, revealing her left breast. "I've been wanting to do that all night." He smoothed his palm over her feminine flesh, perfect, round, firm, and just big enough to fill his hand. Then he pinched her nipple, eliciting the first of many gasps.

"This doesn't seem . . . safe. I mean you're driving, and . . ." Her head fell back against the seat, and her eyes drifted shut. Her soft sighs were music to his ears as he stroked, tugged, and caressed. True he had to keep his eyes on the road, he couldn't drink her in just now, but he could sure as hell make her feel.

"Take off your thong."

Her lids flickered open.

"I want you naked, all the way naked under that dress."

She groaned. "You're going to tease me all the way to your house, aren't you?"

He raised one brow. "You know what they say about payback."

She reached up under her gown and wiggled out of her panties, tossing them on the seat between them. A wisp of nude lace.

His mouth went dry as he applied more pressure to the accelerator and reminded himself that he had a whole night ahead of him. An entire night of X-rated sex with the woman he loved. She really was going to be the death of him.

The next fifteen minutes classified as an erotic blur. Phone sex, but in person. He described in X-rated detail exactly what he was going to do to her once he got her behind closed doors. At first he'd tempered his language, but then he'd lost himself in the erotic images and her throaty moans, and his descriptions turned graphic. Wanting to heighten her arousal, he'd forced himself not to touch her, even when she'd begged, even though he was dying to know her intimately. Then she'd nailed him with a look that made him tighten his fingers around the steering wheel and shift in his seat. Passion and frustration sparked in those beautiful brown eyes as she informed him she couldn't take it any longer. She nabbed his right hand, slid it up under her gown, and told him to keep talking.

Sweet Jesus. He stepped on the brake and eased off the road. Before she could question his actions he had his seat belt off and was all over her. He devoured her mouth, wet sloppy kisses, while sliding his hand up her dress and stroking her hot, slick folds.

She locked her arms around his neck, clinging, whimpering, and causing his heart to race like a stallion. When she cried her release, he nearly came with her. Hands down, it was the hottest sex he'd ever had.

She collapsed against the back of the seat, and without a word, he slid back behind the wheel and gunned the car home. Before he lost his mind. Before he took her on the front seat of his Mustang on the side of a highly populated highway.

Ten minutes later, he pulled into his driveway. She threw open her door, scrambled outside and across the lawn. He was right behind her. Noticing she was barefoot, he scooped her up and threw her over his shoulder.

"What are you, a caveman?" she whispered loudly.

He smacked her backside. "Ugh."

"Oh, goodie," she said and giggled.

He couldn't get the door open fast enough. He nearly tripped over Mouser who sat patiently, stuffed toy clenched between his teeth. Cursing, he set Afia to her feet, leaned down, scratched Mouser's chin in thanks for the gift, and then tossed his keys on the foyer table and flicked on the table lamp. When he turned back Mouser was gone, and Afia was naked, the gown pooled at her ankles. His gaze slid over her creamy body, slight, but toned, and his blood drained south to his loins. "Even better than in my dreams."

"You can admire me later," she said in a raspy voice. "I'm ready for a walk on the wild side." She shoved her hands up under his lapels and pushed the jacket off of his shoulders. He shrugged out of the sleeves, letting the tux jacket fall to the floor. She was already working on the remaining studs of his shirt, her fingers frantic and fumbling. With a curse and one hard yank, she ripped open his shirt front. Studs flew and clattered to the hardwood floor.

"Sorry," she said, not sounding sorry at all, and then seared his chest with hot, wet kisses while working the buckle on his belt. "Pants," she complained, between kisses, "off."

Heart pounding, he clasped her trembling hands, placed

them on his shoulders and had his pants and briefs off in record time. He backed her against the door and kissed her hard and long, pouring his soul into what he hoped would be a lifetime of lovemaking. Blood roared in his ears as she trailed her fingers down his chest, lower . . . lower . . . She wrapped her hand around his erection, and his pulse rocketed to the next galaxy.

She eased away and looked down. "Wow," she whispered.

"I'm glad you approve," he teased, gritting his teeth in sweet agony as she began to stroke his shaft. He was hot, hard, and two seconds from exploding. "Oh, no, you don't." He nabbed her wrists with one hand and hauled them above her head, pressed them against the door.

She gasped. "What are you doing?"

He swept his free hand in between her legs. "Fulfilling your fantasy." He held her captive, feasting on her lush mouth while stroking her to climax yet again. Her body trembled, her moans intensified, and when he felt her nearing the precipice, he slipped a finger inside her tight warmth and drove her over the edge.

She collapsed against him, her breath coming in short, ragged pants. "I'm so sorry."

He smiled down at the top of her head, smoothed his hand down the length of her glorious hair. "For what?"

"For . . . you know . . . so soon." She gasped to catch her breath. "It usually doesn't happen this fast. And . . . and . . ." She smiled up at him. "That was twice in one night."

Heart full, he brushed his thumb across her puffy lips, swollen from his demanding kisses. "Third time's a charm." He scooped her up into his arms and headed for the stairs.

She wrapped her arms around his neck and laid her head against his shoulder. "Where are we going? Kitchen? Living room?"

"Bedroom."

She jerked her head up. "But—"

"I promise you it won't be ordinary." He'd make love to her in every room, on the floor, on a table, the couch, or up against a wall, but this time, the first time, would be in his bed.

She didn't argue. She grasped the back of his head and pulled him down for a blood-stirring kiss, making it difficult to manage the stairs. He kept going. Midway down the upstairs hall she wiggled and squirmed in his arms, repositioning herself so that her luscious legs were wrapped around his waist. One arm locked around his neck, she used her free hand to reach down and fondle him. "Here," she rasped. "Now."

Ignoring her order wasn't easy. Cupping her bottom, he hauled her down the hallway, shouldered open his door, flicked on the nightstand lamp, and flopped her in the center of the bed. "Now."

Chapter Seventeen

How could she have ever considered having sex on a bed ordinary? Because she'd never had sex with Jake. Afia squealed and panted with pleasure as he kissed, licked, nipped, and stroked every inch of her body. He worked mind-boggling magic with his hands and tongue. She was enraptured. Delirious with want, frantic with need. Hours of foreplay had transformed her into a wanton woman, uninhibited and demanding. But regardless of her dictate to "hurry" Jake took his time, coaxing her toward another orgasm with his talented tongue. *Sizzle.* She felt her body tightening, quivering. Her bones melted, and her mind blurred as he brought her closer . . . . closer . . . and suddenly he was on top of her, inside of her, filling her with long, deep thrusts.

"Come for me, baby."

She screamed his name as an incredible orgasm rocked her body. She saw fireworks, the moon and the sun, stars. Heaven. She'd died and gone to Heaven. "Oh, God," she rasped, locking her legs around his back and holding on for dear life as she shuddered with indescribable pleasure.

"Not quite," Jake said, his voice strained. "Just me." He brushed wayward strands of hair off of her face, holding his body very still, the bulk of his weight on his knees and forearms.

He was buried deep inside of her, his erection thick and hard, filling her to capacity, and yet she wanted more. She wanted something . . . more. Swallowing hard, she met his gaze, entranced by what she saw. Raw passion and . . . affection. Her heart pounded faster, harder. Dare she hope . . . no, she didn't dare. Those who loved her died. She could scarcely breathe. "I . . . I think I'm having a heart attack or a panic attack or something."

He smiled down at her. "It's called a hell of an orgasm." He eased out and in, out and in, a slow, wicked friction meant to torture and titillate. "Ready for another?"

His tone and expression were playful, but his gaze was dangerously intense. Something had shifted between them today. Things were different. *He* was different. Or was it her? Yes, she'd definitely changed. She'd stood up to the wicked witches. She'd flirted outrageously in public, revealed her secret fantasy, and, God help her, she'd allowed a man to pleasure her in a car. All for Jake. Only for Jake. *Oh, God.*

"Stop thinking," he whispered, his breath like licks of flames on her neck. "Feel." He hooked his arms under her knees, boosted her legs high, and thrust deep.

"Condom," she squeaked, gripping the last of her sane thoughts. "We forgot—"

"I didn't forget. I'm quick and you were delirious."

"Delirious," she whispered as he suckled on her earlobe and drove into her hard.

"Where do you want it?" he asked, in a throaty rasp.

Her lungs seized. Yes, she'd asked for X-rated, but maybe she wasn't as adventurous as he. "Where do I want what?"

"Your next orgasm. Where do you want it? Kitchen table? Dining room floor? Tell me now, baby, because I can't hold out much longer."

Neither could she. "Here," she blurted. With a hard shove, she pushed him off of her and onto his back. "Now." She needed to be in control of something, her emotions had been sucked into a chaotic cyclone. She straddled his impressive column and rode him for all she was worth. He groaned and gripped her hips, uttering graphic orders that had her eyes rolling back in her head. New and exquisite sensations rippled through her body as she experienced her fourth earthshaking climax. He was right behind her, his incredible body bucking beneath her as he found his release.

She collapsed on top of him, sated, pliant, and for the first time in a long time, without a worry in her head. Worrying took energy, and she was sapped. He wrapped his arms around her, stroking his hands lovingly over her back as she fought to catch her breath. "Mmm. Feels good," she mumbled, her limbs growing heavy as her mind shut down. "Jake?"

"What, baby?"

The endearment wrapped around her heart like a fuzzy blanket, warming her to her soul. "Thank you for fulfilling my fantasy."

He chuckled, an intoxicating low rumble from deep within,

while brushing his fingertips over her bottom. "The weekend isn't over yet."

She almost thought he'd said weekend, but that couldn't be right. She'd only asked for a night. She started to ask him, but then she forgot. Exhaustion claimed her and dreams overrode conscious thinking. In her dreams, she said it first. "I love you."

✻ ✻ ✻

The cell phone rang, jogging Jake out of a deep sleep and a wet dream. He lazed open his eyes and glanced at the red numbers on the nightstand's digital clock.

Five o'clock in the freaking morning.

Couldn't be Gallow checking in on Afia. He'd told the man he'd be keeping her overnight. Maybe Joni or Carson. The phone continued to ring, and Afia, star of his erotic dream, stirred and moaned something indecipherable as she twisted in his arms. He kissed her forehead, gently disentangled himself, and rolled over to snatch the cell. "Yeah?"

"Sorry to call you so early, Jake. But I'm back in town and I . . ."

Harmon.

He bolted upright, sheets tangled about his legs, his pole at half-mast.

Afia moaned and pushed herself up on her elbows. "Jake?"

"I'll call you right back." He powered off and tossed the cell on the nightstand. "It's all right, baby. Go back to sleep."

"What time is it?"

Her voice was rusty, and her eyes were barely open. She was only half awake, if that. She looked tousled and adorable, and he wanted to sink deep inside of her and stay there until noon. He did not want to start off his morning getting into it with Harmon Reece when he could be getting off with Afia.

"Get your head out of your pants," he could hear Gallow saying. Right.

Sleeping beauty pushed a hunk of that damsel hair out of her face and started to roll out of bed. "Have to get to the day-care center . . . the office. Where's the jitney stop?"

Why the hell would she take the jitney? He smiled at her gibberish. Grasping her shoulders, he tenderly pressed her back to the bed. She looked good snuggled amongst his pillows, tangled in his comforter, smelling of cinnamon and sex. Like she belonged. In this house. With him. A hundred fantasies exploded in his head. He jerked his gaze from her bare breasts to her sleepy face and forced his mind out of the gutter. "It's Saturday, honey. The center's closed. So is the office. You can sleep in."

She closed her eyes and smiled. "Tired."

"I know." He traced his finger along the delicate curve of her jaw. She'd had a long day yesterday and a hell of a night. Just thinking about the way she'd climaxed again and again sent his blood flowing south. Last night was emblazoned on his mind, especially the part where she'd said, "I love you."

He wasn't even sure if she was conscious at that point. He wanted it to be real. Christ, he wanted it to be real. "I'll be back. I'm going to get a drink of water. Are you thirsty?"

"Yes, please." She sighed and rolled her face into a pillow.

"Scotch, neat."

He smiled and kissed her shoulder. She moaned and burrowed deeper under the covers. She was wiped. Dead to the world. Good. Meant she wouldn't tramp down behind him and catch him on the phone with her godfather.

He rolled out of bed with a silent curse and tugged on a pair of boxers. What was he going to tell the man?

Uh, Harmon, you know how you asked me to keep your goddaughter busy? Well, last night we got busy in bed.

I betrayed your trust, Mr. Reece. I screwed you over by screwing your goddaughter over . . . and over . . .

Or best of all . . .

Harmon, while you were away I fell in love with Afia, and, whether you like it or not, I'm going to ask her to marry me.

He was fucked.

He glanced over at the bed at Sleeping Beauty and smiled. She was so worth it. Up until this point he'd been content to live alone. Better alone than risk failing a woman he'd pledged to honor and cherish forever. He was certain his father, an essentially good-hearted man, had never planned to allow his wife and kids to play second best to his career. But instead of recognizing and rectifying his frayed relationships, he'd pulled farther away, unable or unwilling to adjust his priorities. To say that his parents' marriage had been strained was an understatement. Jake had vowed long ago not to walk in his father's shoes, yet his desire to battle wrongdoers burned just as strong.

His desire to spend the rest of his life with Afia burned stronger. For her he'd accept the challenge and conquer the odds. Failure was not an option. Commit and stay the course.

Respect and honor, rain or shine.

Heart pounding, he palmed the cell and crept out of the bedroom. Roscoe and Barney sat just outside the door. Velma peeked out of the guest bedroom and trotted toward him. Mouser was probably downstairs curled up on the footstool. Scamp was in hiding, and with Afia here, he probably wouldn't see the skittish cat all day. "Hungry, guys?"

All three cats meowed, trotting after him as he navigated the dark hallway and loped down the stairs. He headed for the kitchen, picking up Mouser along the way. Still no sign of Scamp. He flicked on the kitchen overhead, opened the cupboard and snagged four cans of the gourmet food they loved so much. The stuff that cost a fortune. Thankfully, Joni kept him stocked with coupons, or the finicky cats would eat him into the poorhouse.

Once the gang was fed, he washed his hands, downed an entire glass of water, and then dialed Harmon. "Sorry to cut you off like that."

"I didn't realize you had company," the man said. "I'm the one who should be apologizing."

"Company?"

"I heard a woman's voice."

Jake cleared his throat. "Yeah, about that."

"I don't care what you do with your nights, boy. It's your days that I'm calling about. Afia. How is she?"

"Great." He scraped his hand back and forth over his unshaven jaw, trying to banish images of last night. *She's a she-devil in the sheets.* "She has a natural knack for investigative work."

"Really? Interesting. Well, maybe it will come in useful someday, who knows?"

The lawyer's flip tone struck a raw nerve. "It's coming in useful now, Harmon. I'm serious. She's doing a good job."

"I'm glad. Now I don't feel quite as guilty about forcing you to take her on."

Jake leaned back against the counter and crossed his left ankle over his right. "You didn't force me, you paid me." Even worse. "I'm off the case, Harmon."

"What?"

"Afia doesn't need a babysitter, but I do need an assistant. I'm paying her just as I would Joni, or anyone else." Although he couldn't afford to pay her the salary he'd quoted per Harmon. He'd have to figure that one out.

"We had a deal, Jake."

"Deal's off." He'd find another way to help his sister and Carson, assuming they still needed a financial boost. As for his house, it could be a work in progress 'til the day he died for all he cared. He could live with leaks and warped floorboards. He wasn't crazy about living without Afia.

Harmon was silent a long moment.

Jake waited. He was a smart man. He'd figure it out.

"That was Afia's voice," he said on a sigh.

"Yes, it was."

"Goddammit, I trusted you, Jake."

"You can still trust me." He kept an eye trained on the door, listened for footsteps. "I have her best interest at heart. I'll protect her from the press. I'll handle the creditors if they come knocking, and I'll make sure she stays out of trouble in general. That's what you wanted, isn't it?"

"What's going on?" His tone was as direct as the question.

"I could ask the same thing," Jake said, pushing off of the counter. "What's up with Kilmore? Has he made any progress?"

"He's working on it."

He wrenched open the fridge door and nabbed a carton of pulp-free orange juice. "He's been working on it for three damned weeks. He has a few more days, and then I'm stepping in." Adrenaline pumping, he poured a glass of juice.

Meanwhile Harmon cursed a blue streak. "You fell for her didn't you? Just like Randy. Exactly like Frank."

The juice turned sour in his mouth. He swallowed hard and tempered his voice. "Don't lump me in with those two. It's not the same."

"It's exactly the same. It's her sweet nature, that helpless aura. Makes a man want to save her. Even I'm not immune."

He couldn't argue with the damsel-in-distress factor. However . . . "She can take care of herself if she has to."

The lawyer snorted.

"You don't know her, Harmon."

"I sure as hell know her better than you do."

Jake set his empty glass in the sink. "I'll rephrase. You don't know what she's capable of."

"Well, let's see," he said, taking on a condescending tone. "So far she's managed to lose her father, two husbands, and a small fortune."

Good thing they were on the phone and not face-to-face. He'd never punched a business associate, but the legal eagle had it coming. "That's low, man."

"That's life. Afia's life anyhow. Have you thought about what you're getting yourself into?"

He wasn't thinking, he was feeling, and his gut said he and Afia belonged together. "You don't believe she's jinxed anymore than I do."

Harmon let out a testy grunt. "Listen, Jake, I love my god-daughter deeply. No, I don't think she's jinxed, but she does have a way of attracting trouble. Are you ready for that?"

"Bring it on."

"Christ Almighty, you've got it bad, don't you? All right." He paused. Swore again. "What are your intentions?"

To love, honor, and cherish until death do us part. "I'd rather discuss it first with Afia."

"Here's the thing. I like you, Jake. Always have. But if you break her heart . . ."

"You'll hire Murphy to break my legs?" He palmed his brow. "I'm not going to hurt her, Harmon. Just . . . give us some breathing room, will you?"

"Sure. Fine. At least I know she's in good hands for the time being. But listen up, son. Next week I'll be the least of your worries. Giselle will be back in town, and you are not her idea of a son-in-law. Not even close."

Just the mention of that woman's name kicked his protective tendencies into overdrive. "I'll handle Giselle."

"You'll be the first," Harmon said and signed off.

✳ ✳ ✳

Someone was staring at her. Intently. Afia forced open her heavy eyelids and found herself looking into a pair of yellow eyes. She didn't scream. She didn't even flinch. The topaz orbs were downright mesmerizing. Almond-shaped eyes set against a triangular black face. A hairy face with long whiskers. No, not hairy. Fuzzy. Cat. Black cat. Sitting an arm's length away.

Stunned into awareness, she swallowed a gasp and lay stock-still. She didn't want to frighten the thing. If he streaked across the bed or ran away she'd suffer ill luck. But if he moved toward her . . . "Are you a good omen? Or bad?" she whispered. Heart in throat, she carefully touched her bracelet and counted the charms. All there. All eleven including the cat.

It was fanciful to think that this was the same mysterious cat that had saved Jake's life yesterday. Though she was given to the absurd, there could be a simple explanation. "Are you Scamp?"

No reaction to the name. No mew or angled head. The cat remained aloof and continued to stare.

Afia stared back, paralyzed with apprehension. *Are you a good omen? Or bad?* If this was Scamp, then he was the skinniest of Jake's "strays." No, not skinny . . . slender, sleek. His coat gleamed like polished ebony, reminding her of an Egyptian statue. "Black cats were sacred in ancient Egypt, you know." *Please don't run away.* Last night she'd followed Rudy's advice. She'd trusted her heart and seized the day. She'd had wild, pulse-pounding sex with Jake, and this morning she didn't harbor a single regret. She didn't feel sluttish.

She felt alive. And happy. *Truly happy.* She wanted to seize another day, and another. She was sick of living in fear.

"You remind me a little of Bast," she softly told the cat. "Bast was an Egyptian Goddess. Head of a cat, body of a woman. The Goddess of the rising sun, and the moon, and so much more. Enlightenment, sexuality, fertility . . ."

The cat angled his head, causing her to blink and focus on just one of Bast's roles. "She was a fierce protector of children and was often invoked by those desiring offspring." Afia worried her lower lip, a savage longing clawing at her stomach. "Did I invoke you?"

The question was little more than a whisper, and yet the cat responded by taking a tentative step forward, and then another and another . . .

Afia lay flat on her back, her breath stalled in her lungs as the sleek black feline climbed on top of her and proceeded to knead her stomach with his furry paws. Then he purred, a low comforting drone that had tears of joy springing to her eyes.

"I'll be damned."

Afia rolled her head to the side and saw Jake standing in the doorway holding two crystal tumblers. He was quite the early morning delight. Disheveled, unshaven, and half-naked. She imagined personal trainers everywhere paying homage to his corded upper body. She certainly appreciated the result of his obvious hard work. Blushing, she turned back to the cat. "Please don't scare him away."

"Sweetheart, Scamp's not afraid of me." He moved inside and set the tumblers on the nightstand. "He's leery of women." He climbed back into bed and regarded her with a cocked eyebrow. "Most women anyhow. I guess he sensed what I know."

"What's that?" she asked, reveling in his masculine aura and the feel of Scamp's busy paws.

Jake stroked the cat, but his eyes were on her, warm and caring. "That you're special."

"I've been called a lot of things," she rasped, "but never special." Scamp padded off of her lap and curled up at the bottom of the bed near her feet. *Like a protective Goddess.* The Goddess of pleasure and joy. Fertility and birth.

"Two or three kids would be nice," Jake had said.

Afia's eyes burned, and her throat felt raw. She tried to get a grip on her chaotic feelings while pushing herself up on her elbows. "Could I have a drink, please?"

"Water or orange juice?" he asked, studying her with wary eyes.

"Water, please."

He handed her one of the tumblers. She drank deeply, sighed and, passed it back. "Thank you."

He set aside the glass and then turned back and brushed his knuckles across her cheek. "Regrets?"

Concern and sincere affection burned in his eyes, quickening her pulse. She settled back against the plethora of pillows and smiled, basking in his tender regard. "No regrets." If Scamp and her racing heart were any indication, she'd made the right choice. "You?"

"Oh, yeah." He skimmed his finger down the hollow of her throat and over her collarbone. "Last night was torture." He palmed her breast, leaned down and suckled.

Desire rippled through her body as he feasted on her nipples, making her wanton and bold. Then her mind tripped up her pleasure. She wondered where they were going with this. A fling? An affair? A relationship? Where did the babies fit in?

Don't think, feel.

"Speaking of torture . . ." A wicked smile curled her lips as she put her hands on Jake's shoulders and pressed him back on the bed. "I owe you."

He smiled up at her, a naughty twinkle in his eye. "Bring it on."

✻ ✻ ✻

"Stop second-guessing yourself, Bunny."

Rudy adjusted the sheet over his lower half and lolled his head to the left. Jean-Pierre lay on his side, head propped in his hand, looking better than any man had a right to on two hours of sleep, if that. "I'm not second-guessing myself." He'd taken his own advice, trusted his heart, and seized the day. Or rather the Frenchman. When Jean-Pierre had dragged through the door after one in the morning, exhausted and bitchy because one of the dancers had just informed him that she was pregnant, Rudy had taken pity on the man.

Comfort had started by way of a bottle of wine and a massage and had ended up in bed. The interlude had been hot, gratifying, and, when Jean-Pierre had fallen asleep in his arms, oddly fulfilling.

"All right." The source of his insomnia pushed his hair off of his face and raised a skeptical eyebrow. "Then what have you been thinking about? You have been staring at the ceiling for twenty minutes."

Rudy grunted, embarrassed and aroused. "I can't believe you've been lying there watching me."

"You are very easy on the eyes, *mon amour*." He flashed one of the devilish smiles that simultaneously irked and stimulated Rudy.

"I wish you wouldn't use that word."

"What word?"

He sighed, rolled over, and pushed himself onto an elbow to face Jean-Pierre and his greatest fear. "Love. I don't take it lightly."

"Neither do I."

"Then stop tossing it around."

Jean-Pierre screwed up his face. "Tossing?"

"I ignored it last night because you were hammered."

"What is hammered?"

"Drunk."

Jean-Pierre's lips twisted into an annoyed smirk. "Rudy, I am French. I have wine in my veins. I was not drunk. I meant what I said."

Rudy's heart pounded in slow, aching thuds as his fears started to ebb. Maybe all of those affirmations had helped. Maybe what he was looking for was right here in his bed. Was Jean-Pierre the one? Dare he believe? Dare he put his heart on the line? An Erica Jong quote floated through his head. *"If you don't risk anything, you risk even more."*

"So what were you thinking about?" Jean-Pierre asked.

"Vermont," he said, taking a leap of faith. "I'd like to spend

Christmas in Vermont with you."

Jean-Pierre nodded. "And I would like to show you Paris in the springtime."

His heart swelled at the genuine affection swimming in his bed partner's eyes. Then a lone thought lanced his euphoric bubble. He flopped back on the bed, jammed his hands through his hair. "Shit."

"Now you are thinking about Afia." Jean-Pierre fell back beside him. "You are wondering how you are going to break it to her that we are in love. No doubt, she will want to move out to allow us privacy."

"When did you get so damned perceptive?"

Jean-Pierre chuckled, reached over and squeezed his hand. "Do not worry, Bunny. Last night I got a glimpse of Afia and Jake on the dance floor. I think she will be moving out regardless."

Chapter Eighteen

"I like your bed," Afia said. "A lot."

Grinning, Jake watched her stretch like one of his cats and then roll side to side on his mussed sheets while he zipped up his jeans. "I'm glad." He wasn't sure if she was referring to the queen-sized pillow mattress, or to what they'd done on it. Either way the sight of her filled him with bone-deep pleasure. She filled this house with warmth, goodness, and an enigmatic energy. Wrapped in a thick burgundy towel and still damp from their shower, she looked pretty as hell and hot to trot.

He was down for the count. Her idea of torture had been smothering his body with kisses, stroking him to the brink, and then rolling on a condom and climbing aboard. He'd flipped her over, managing to hold out for another twenty minutes, intent to give as good as she gave. Exhausted, she'd drifted back to sleep, and he'd slipped off to take a shower. Damned, if she didn't join him midway through to soap him up into another lather. The woman was insatiable.

"I'm going to go downstairs and fix us some breakfast. You," he said, pointing a stern finger, "put on some clothes."

Did those words actually come out of his mouth?

She rolled over on her stomach. The towel scrunched up, and he got a peek at three-quarters of her firm bottom. He shook his head at the tempting sight as she propped her chin in her hand and grinned. Velma curled up on one side of her, Scamp on the other. He still couldn't get over how the wary cat had taken to her so quickly. Then again, he'd fallen in love with Afia in under a week.

"I'll have to borrow something of yours to wear," she said. "My evening gown is a little dressy for breakfast, and all of my other clothes are at Rudy's."

"Not for long," he mumbled, pulling a T-shirt over his head.

"What did you say?"

"Nothing. We'll talk about it over waffles." He streaked a comb through his wet hair. "Do you even like waffles?"

Her eyes twinkled. "With strawberries?"

"Don't have strawberries. What about bananas?" Her eyebrows rose, and he cut her off. "Don't say it. Keep those X-rated thoughts to yourself." He grinned. "At least for a couple of hours."

She snickered and rolled off of the bed in one fluid movement, smiling as she walked toward him with all that dark, wet hair, the towel skimming those enticing thighs, the devilish gleam in her eyes tempting him to . . .

Groaning, he sidestepped her and slid on his wristwatch. "Hands off, woman."

Now she was giggling. "Geesh, what happened to my fantasy fulfilling superhero?"

Christ, she was adorable. "His powers need recharging."

His cell phone rang.

"Saved by the bell." She sighed and then turned and slid open his top drawer.

"Hello? Yes, this is Jake Blaine." He listened to some woman from the SCC introduce herself and watched in amazement as Afia folded his underwear. Women. His mother had folded underwear. Joni folded underwear. What was the point? "We did? Great. When and where?"

He moved in beside her, opened the middle drawer, and yanked out a pair of sweats and a tee. "Got it," he told the woman. "Thanks." He powered off then nudged Afia. "Get your hands off of my briefs."

"But—"

"We won the painting we bid on last night," he said, giving her something else to do by shoving the pants and shirt in her hands.

Her face lit up like a Christmas tree. "We did?"

He wanted to wrap around her like a garland. He turned away and sat in a chair to tug on a pair of boots. "The prize chairperson—"

"Sally Clarkson," she said, pulling on the faded blue T-shirt.

"Yup. Said we could pick up the painting anytime this week."

She stepped into the navy sweats and tugged the drawstring tight. "I can't believe we won! That painting was beautiful. Surely several people wanted it. How was it that we had the highest bid?"

He tied off his work boot. "Lucky, I guess."

They looked at each other at the same time.

"My luck does seem to be changing for the better," she said, wide-eyed. "Since I met you."

Jake poked his tongue in his cheek and digested that statement. The last thing he wanted was to become her lucky talisman. He wanted her to be with him out of love, not because she thought he could magically ward off misfortune. "You know what I think?" He braced his arms on his knees and regarded her intently. "We make our own luck. It's all in the mind. Positive thought over negative."

She divided her wet hair evenly over her shoulders and weaved the mass into two long braids. "You sound like Rudy."

He raised a brow. "A friend wouldn't steer another friend wrong, right?"

She cocked her head, studied him for a moment, and then padded over in her bare feet. "You really are my friend, aren't you?"

He took her hand and pulled her down onto his lap, humbled by the trusting look in her eyes. "I don't care if you're young or old, rich or poor, if you live next door or across the country. I sure as hell don't care that you were born on Friday the thirteenth. I will always be your friend, Afia."

She clasped her hands in her lap, her voice stilted and breathy. "I think that's the kindest thing anyone has ever said to me."

He wrapped his hand around hers and squeezed. He ached to say much more. He wanted to be her lover, her husband, but he wasn't sure if she was ready to hear that just now. Although he was fairly certain she'd fallen in love with him, she'd neatly avoided last night's sleepy confession. Something was holding her back, and he didn't want to make things worse, ultimately scaring her off. Still, he had to say something, make some play to set their future in motion. "Yeah, well, that part about you living next door or across the country . . . Gotta be honest, baby, I'd like it a hell of a lot better if you lived here."

She toyed with the end of one braid and glanced away.

"I've been thinking about it, and it makes sense," he plowed on. "Gallow's townhouse is cramped. He's already got a roommate. You're sleeping on the couch, cluttering his dining room with your boxes and racks of clothes."

She shot him a worried look. "Did he say something to you?"

"No. I'm just observant. Things are tight there. I have this big house to myself. Well, except for the cats, and you seem to get on well enough with them. There are two extra bedrooms. You can take one of those if you like. I want you to share my bed, but I don't want to pressure you into something you're not ready for."

Her leg started to bounce.

"You said you had a flair for decorating. I could use some help around here. And," he added lamely, "we could ride into work together."

"I would want to pay my share," she said, "you know, like a boarder. It would only be fair."

He didn't want her money, but he knew it was a matter of pride. Hold on. "I can take it out of your salary. Say you forfeit a hundred a week for room and board." That solved both of their problems.

She shrugged. "Okay."

His heart pounded. "Okay, what?"

She quirked a nervous smile. "Okay, I'll think about it."

"Good." Wasn't the answer he wanted, but then again it wasn't "no." "Still want those waffles?"

She nodded.

"Thank God, because I'm starving." He patted her backside to get her going. Otherwise he'd kiss her, they'd wind up back in bed, and he wouldn't have the strength to peel a damned banana let alone do some record checking on Rivelli.

"I'm really pleased that we won that painting," she said, hopping off of his lap and returning the conversation to safer ground. It's going to look stunning on the office wall. I forget. What was the artist's name? Noah something? I'd like to send him a thank you card."

"I don't remember. I think it's listed on the program." He reached into the inner pocket of the tux jacket he'd draped over the chair. "Here you go." He handed her the gala program he'd tucked away last night, caressed her cheek, and then headed for the door. He wanted to give her a bit of space, some time to think over his offer. "I'm going to check out the closet in the guest room. I think Joni may have left a pair of sneakers in there, and you're about the same size. I'll meet you downstairs." Hopefully, she'd have her mind made up by then and put him out of his misery.

As soon as Jake cleared the threshold, Afia sank down on the chair, her knees as wobbly as her emotions. He wanted her to move in! Her heart cried, yes, but her head screamed, no.

Actually, it was her mother screaming, but she had been listening to that voice for a very long time, and old habits die hard. Especially when there was some truth to what that phantom voice chanted. She was jinxed. A target for bad luck. Men who loved her perished.

She wasn't sure if Jake loved her, but without a doubt he cared. His eyes betrayed the passion and affection in his heart, as did his endearments and gentle touch. He was a compassionate, honest, chivalrous man, and he set her sheltered world on fire.

She knew for a fact that *she'd* fallen in love. Real love. Passionate, giddy love. Cupid had shot her with a million drugged arrows. She was loopy with *amour*. It felt wondrous and natural, and unlike anything she'd ever experienced. It was as if she'd been in love with him, and only him, forever.

I love you.

She'd said it in her dreams, and yet this morning the words had lodged in her throat. She fretted that by confessing her feelings she'd put Jake in danger. A hundred scenarios flashed through her mind, one freak accident after another. With her luck . . .

"We make our own luck. It's all in the mind. Positive thought over negative." Jake's voice bellowed over her mother's, and when the superstitious woman tried to interrupt, Rudy stepped in. *"When the odds are against you, trust your heart and seize the day."*

Afia breathed deeply, allowing a strange sense of peace and determination to envelop her, and suddenly she was surging with the power of free will.

Beth Ciotta

"With my luck," she said, rebelling against living another moment in fear, "we'll get married, have three healthy children, and live happily ever after."

Affirmations are powerful.

She chanted her heart's desire three times and then glanced down at the program in her hand, wondering how she was going to break it to her mother that she was taking control of her own fate. That's when she noticed the listing of beneficiaries of last night's gala. The name of one social service, in particular, was missing. She wasn't naïve enough to believe it was a mistake. She wasn't willing to let it slide to avoid a nasty confrontation.

This was unforgivable.

Seize the day! Crushing the program in her hands, she stood and marched out of the room and down the stairs, chanting the words over and over like a mantra. *Seize the day! Seize the day!* By the time she reached the kitchen her face burned and her temples pulsed. "Are those for me?" she asked, pointing to a pair of navy-blue high-tops.

Jake set down a carton of milk, glanced over his shoulder, and nodded. "They're a six-and-a-half."

"Close enough." She plopped down in a wicker chair and slipped her size-six feet into the shoes, double-knotting the overly long laces.

"Are you all right?"

She looked up. He was stirring a bowl of batter and studying her with a furrowed brow. She couldn't address his concern. If she opened the dam, she'd burst. "Where's the closest bus stop?" she asked, rolling the baggy sweatpants to above her

252

ankles. The jitneys didn't run to Northfield. She'd have to take a bus from here to Margate. She didn't know which one, but she'd figure it out.

He abandoned his mixing bowl and turned to face her. "What's going on, Afia?"

She ignored his stern tone. "I need to go somewhere, to do something, and I need to do it now."

"I'll drive you."

"It's personal."

"Then take my car."

She shook her head. "I can't drive. I mean, I can. I have a license, but I'm a lousy driver. Randy hired Rudy because I'd been involved in so many fender benders. That's how we met. Rudy and I. He was my chauffeur." She was rambling now. Her blood boiled, and she felt dangerously close to overheating. She stood, the program clutched in her hand. "Just point me to the bus stop. Please," she added, trying not to take her anger out on him.

"I'll drive you." Frowning, he flicked off the coffeemaker, put the mixing bowl in the refrigerator, and breezed passed her. "Let's roll."

She caught up to him in the foyer, just as he snatched his keys and opened the front door. "Okay," she said. "But you'll have to stay in the car." She didn't want him fighting this battle for her. *Seize the day!*

He didn't say another word until they were buckled in and backing out of the drive. "Where are we going?"

She gave him the address and stared down at the crumpled program. "How can she be so cruel?"

"Are you going to tell me what this is about?" Jake asked as he navigated Saturday morning traffic. "Or make me guess?"

"I can't talk about it." She was thinking some very unkind thoughts, thoughts that shouldn't be voiced. Except maybe to the witch who'd summoned them.

Jake glanced sideways, grunted his exasperation, and then focused back on the road.

"She thinks she's hurting me, but she's really hurting the children and their families."

"Who? Dora? Frances? I'm guessing here, because you can't talk about it."

"Dora," she growled. "She has the ultimate word. I mean the board votes, of course, but she wields a lot of influence." Oh, she could hear her now. *We've been giving money to The Sea Serpent for years now. They can apply for a state grant, solicit private donations. Let's focus our energy on needier organizations.* "Ooh!"

Jake passed two slowpokes and picked up speed. "Does this have to do with the daycare center?"

"Haven't you been listening to me?" Afia squealed, her adrenaline pumping harder as they crossed the Margate Bridge. She waved the program in the air. "It's not on the list. The Sea Serpent won't get a dime from last night's gala. Mrs. Kelly planned to put that money toward new educational playground equipment. Now the children will have to go without. And why? Because Dora Simmons is a petty, jealous shrew. It's not fair!"

"No, it's not," Jake said calmly. "So what are you going to do about it?"

She balled her fists in her lap. "I'm not sure. The money's already been delegated. Every social service is deserving. I can't very well ask the SCC to pull funds from where they've been promised."

"Weren't funds promised to The Sea Serpent?"

"No. It was more like tradition. My dad co-founded that daycare center. He also served on the SCC board for several years."

Jake shot her a meaningful glance. "Generous man."

Her heart skipped. "Yes, he was." And she'd put his humanitarian efforts at risk by resigning from the SCC and enabling Dora and Frances to act selfishly. What a wimp! Two minutes later she spied Dora Simmons' beach block mansion, and her pulse accelerated. "There it is!" She barely waited for the car to roll to a complete stop before throwing open the door. She was halfway to the cobblestone porch when she realized Jake was following her. "You agreed to stay in the car."

He shook his head. "I didn't agree to anything."

She didn't have the energy to fight him *and* Dora. "All right, but please don't interrupt."

"I won't say a word."

Satisfied, she rapped on the crimson red door with the gleaming brass knocker. Dora's husband answered, dressed in creased white shorts and a blue designer polo shirt.

"Afia." Shock then pleasure registered on his tanned face. "What a nice surprise." Then his wolfish gaze ate up her frumpy attire and spit it out with a flicker of disapproval.

She braced her hands on her hips. "That's right, Bernard. I just got out of the shower and put on the first thing I could find.

This is me without makeup, without brushing my hair, without visible curves. The real me." She thrust back her shoulders and angled her chin. "How would you like to wake up to this every morning?"

Bernard sputtered.

Jake groaned.

She ignored them both and pushed her way into the foyer. "Dora!" She moved swiftly through the house. She'd been here for various meetings and parties. She knew the way to the dining room.

Dora sat swilling her morning tea, perfectly made up and dressed in preppy boating attire. Eyes wide, she clanged her china cup into the matching saucer. "Afia? What in the world?"

She smacked the program on the polished mahogany table. "The Sea Serpent isn't on the beneficiary list."

"Oh." Dora sat back in her chair, crossed her arms, and smiled. "No, it's not."

Afia braced her hands on the table and leaned forward. "I'll make this quick."

She smirked. "Please do."

"You are a fake. You pretend to care about the underprivileged and the disadvantaged. But all you really care about is the attention that comes with organizing and advancing the social events that ultimately help those in need. You're a petty, insecure snob on a power trip. This coming year I am going to do whatever I can to make sure you are not reelected to the board."

Dora's eye twitched as she dismissed Afia with a wave of her bejeweled hand. "As if anyone would listen to a jinxed, fortune-hunting air head."

Unruffled, she pushed off the table and glanced at Bernard who was standing in the archway alongside Jake. The two men couldn't be more different. Bernard represented everything she'd had, and Jake everything she wanted. She turned her back on the wicked witch and headed toward her enchanting prince. "For the record, Dora, I wouldn't want to be in your shoes for all the diamonds in Tiffany's."

Dora snorted. "You can't *afford* my shoes, dear."

Afia flipped her off and kept walking. "I'm sorry you had to witness that," she told Jake as they cleared the front door.

Chuckling, he clasped her hand and squeezed. "I'm not."

His touch warmed her soul, melted her anger, and steadied her erratic pulse. She glanced up at him, swallowing hard at the admiration glittering in those beguiling eyes. "I've never given anyone the finger before."

"If anyone deserved it, she did." He winked. "Bet it felt good."

She grinned. "It did." They reached the car, and her satisfaction ebbed. "Not that it helped The Sea Serpent." She fell back against the passenger door with a groan. "Why wasn't I smarter about managing my money? If it weren't for my mindless shopping and Glick fiasco, I could have bought that playground equipment myself."

Jake nabbed her chin and chided her with a mild frown. "You worry too much. Stop obsessing on what you should have done and focus on what you can do."

What could she do?

He kissed her scrunched brow and then opened the car door

and helped her inside. "You're a smart woman. You'll figure it out."

By the time he rounded the car and slid behind the wheel, she had the answer. "I can put my years of experience with the SCC to work," she said with a smile. "I can organize an event to specifically benefit The Sea Serpent. Find out how much that playground equipment costs and make that figure our goal."

Jake grinned and keyed the ignition. "Can we have our waffles now?"

He sounded so desperate. "Sure," she said, buckling in, and suppressing a giggle. "Right after we swing by Rudy's."

* * *

They were sitting at the table having breakfast and discussing the revival of one of their favorite musicals when Rudy heard the front door open and two sets of footsteps ascending the stairs. His laughter died in his throat, and he dropped his fork to his plate with a clang.

Jean-Pierre reached under the table and squeezed his thigh. "You worry too much. Relax."

Afia walked into the dining room with Jake on her heels, took one look at the scene and froze.

Instead of sitting at the opposite end of the table, as was his habit, this morning Rudy had elected to sit *beside* Jean-Pierre. He knew she must have heard them laughing, and even though she couldn't see Frenchie's hand on his leg, damn him, they were still sitting unusually close. At least they'd already showered and dressed. *Don't think about that shower.* Rudy sat stock still, but his insides squirmed with guilt.

Jake cleared his throat.

Jean-Pierre rose from the table and moved swiftly to kiss both of Afia's cheeks. "*Bonjour, Chou à la crème.*" He tugged at her braids, the hem of her baggy T-shirt, and grinned. "You look cute. Like a *petite fille.*"

Rudy disagreed. She didn't look like a little girl. She looked like a ravished woman. It wasn't just the fact that she obviously wore Jake's clothes. Her skin glowed and her eyes sparkled. She oozed sexuality and . . . confidence.

"You must be Jean-Pierre," Jake said, thrusting out his hand.

"*Oui,*" he said, with a firm grasp. "And you are Jake. *Bonjour.* Would you like a cup of *café*?"

"God, yes." The P.I. glanced at the table, but his eyes were on the food, not Rudy. "Are those fresh croissants?"

Jean-Pierre laughed and rapped their guest's shoulder. "Come with me into the kitchen, and we will fix you a plate."

As soon as the two men were out of earshot, Afia streaked across the room and wiggled into Rudy's lap. She wrapped her arms around his neck and hugged. "You're in love," she whispered in his ear. "I knew Jean-Pierre was the one. I just knew it!"

He rolled his eyes and returned the hug. "How could you possibly know? Nothing happened until last night."

She snorted, pushed back, and smirked. "Sparks have been flying for weeks. Jean-Pierre adores you. He hangs on your every word. Every time he looks at you his eyes soften. You were too busy taking exception to his smart-aleck comments and renegade straight pins to notice."

Even though he was settling into the idea of a long-term relationship, it still felt too good to be true. Jean-Pierre was a creative genius, vibrant, and surprisingly wise for his age. "He's hot for my body."

She shook her head and placed her hand over his heart. "He's hot for what's inside this body. Stop resisting. The more you get to know each other the better it will be."

He raised an eyebrow. "Is that what you're doing with Jake? Getting to know him?"

A sweet flush bloomed on her cheeks. "It's not what it looks like. Well, it is, but it's more." She clasped her hands to her chest. "He asked me to move in with him."

Rudy patted her knee, carefully choosing his words. He didn't want to burst his friend's bubble, but he didn't want her living in one either. "You've only known each other for a week."

She shrugged. "Like you said. Cupid's a quick shot."

He was torn between panic and euphoria. "Are you telling me that you're in love with, Jake?"

She grinned ear to ear. "It's like nothing I've ever felt before. Like being zapped over and over by a live wire. Electrifying. And yet I feel at peace at the same time. Calm. Content. *Happy*." She rolled her eyes. "Sounds crazy, huh?"

He shook his head. "Sounds familiar."

"Then you understand and you won't be upset if I move out?"

"No, I won't be upset." He hated throwing a negative thought into the universe, but he knew things that Afia didn't. For one,

Harmon was trying to get back her money. Jake struck him as a proud man. How would he feel if Afia's bank account overshadowed his by a million or so? And how would Afia feel if she found out Harmon had engineered her job with Jake? Rudy's stomach churned at his own role in the charade. "Just know that our door is always open in case things don't work out."

"You worry too much. Jake and I are going to get married, have three kids, and live happily ever after." She quirked a lopsided grin. "That's my new affirmation."

He expected her to rub her wishbone charm to back up that thought, but, amazingly, she wasn't wearing her bracelet. Interesting. He started to ask her why, but then he caught sight of Jean-Pierre and Jake rounding the corner.

"About what I told you, about being in love," she whispered. "I haven't told Jake yet. I don't want to scare him off."

"He doesn't strike me as the skittish type." Rudy glanced over his shoulder at the imposing P.I. Afia was sitting in another man's lap, but instead of jealousy he only registered pure affection in Jake's assessing gaze. Of course, it probably helped that the man she hugged was her gay best friend.

Jake placed his plate on the table, sat in the chair opposite Rudy, and slathered his croissant with strawberry jam. They traded knowing looks. *We need to talk.*

"We made you an omelet, *Chou à la crème*." Jean-Pierre glanced at Rudy while setting her plate on the table.

Rudy winked, assuring him that everything was fine.

Jean-Pierre smiled.

"Thank you," she said, hopping off of Rudy's lap, "but we don't have time to eat."

Jake set aside his knife and glanced longingly at his spinach omelet. "We don't?"

Afia rounded the table, wrapped her arms around him from behind, and whispered something in his ear.

Rudy watched Jake's eyes and warmed at the genuine affection that burned in their depths.

"Excuse us, gentlemen," he said, pushing out of his chair. "We have some boxes to pack."

Chapter Nineteen

Hands braced on either side of the door, Jake stared at the twenty boxes stacked along the wall of his largest guest room. He'd only been able to fit five into his car. They'd loaded the remaining cargo into Rudy's stretch limo. He and Jean-Pierre had been more than happy to drive over Afia's belongings and to tote them inside in order to get a peek into her new home. She was giving them the grand tour now.

Jake was obsessing over the future.

He'd never known a woman, strike that, anyone, with such a vast wardrobe. She could probably wear a different outfit every day for a year and never wear the same thing twice. An exaggeration maybe, but not by much. The problem was that the bulk of her coats, blouses, pants, skirts, dresses, sweaters, shoes, and purses suited her old lifestyle. They were a harsh reminder of what he couldn't give her. How long would she be content in discount clothing? What if she got the itch to indulge in a designer shopping spree? Would she be satisfied with popcorn and a movie when she was used to caviar and the opera?

Then there was the flipside. What if Kilmore found her money? If she could afford to live in luxury, would she be happy living with Jake? Would she resent his modest income? Would he resent her seven-figure bank account?

Each of those damned boxes represented a doubt, and he couldn't stop staring at them.

"Is anything wrong?"

He looked over his shoulder and saw his princess schlepping up the hall in pauper sweats. He'd been so distracted he hadn't even heard her scale the stairs. "Just thinking," he said, shooting for nonchalant.

She paused a few inches away, wrapped her arms around her middle, a telling, insecure gesture. At least she wasn't stroking her bracelet. She wasn't even wearing her bracelet. He wanted to believe that it had been a conscious choice. *Positive thought over negative.* "Are you sorry you asked me to move in?" she asked.

"No, I'm not." Amazing, in light of the mini-meltdown he'd just experienced, but true.

"Are you sure? You don't look very happy. In fact, you look miserable."

He pushed off of the jambs and met her troubled gaze. His pulse tripped as he fought to get a grip on reality. The truth of the matter was that it didn't matter if she wore designer suits or hand-me-downs. Clothes did not make the woman. Nor did the bank account or lack there of. All that mattered was her heart. If he possessed her heart, then nothing and no one would come between them.

He cocked a playful brow hoping to ease the tension. "I was just wondering if you plan on utilizing this room for anything other than a walk-in closet?"

Her shoulders relaxed, and her lips curved into a coy smile. "Do you mean do I intend to sleep in there?"

"Mmm."

"I'd rather sleep with you."

"Good answer." He crooked a beckoning finger. She moved swiftly into his arms and all of his worries magically receded.

"Have you ever lived with anyone before?" she asked, her arms wrapped tightly around his neck.

"No."

"Are you nervous?"

"A little." No doubt a partial reason for the meltdown. "You?"

"A lot. But it feels right."

"Yes, it does." Cupping the sides of her face, he swept his tongue inside of her sweet mouth, his mind racing with visions of their future. *"We make our own luck. Positive thought over negative."*

He pinned her against the wall, his hands roaming possessively over her curves, the kiss intensifying with each emphatic declaration. *This woman will be my wife. This woman will bear my children. I waited my entire life for this woman.*

He eased back, gazed deeply into her eyes, his heart bursting with tenderness and torrid affection. "Afia, I—"

"Don't say it!" Eyes wide with panic, she pressed her fingertips over his mouth. "Please. Don't. I . . ." She glanced toward the stairs.

Frowning, he kissed her fingers then nudged them aside. "Are Rudy and Jean-Pierre still down there?"

"Yes. They . . . they felt bad that you didn't get to finish your omelet, so . . . well, I showed them your waffle batter."

He dropped his forehead to hers and groaned. "They're making us breakfast?"

"Brunch." She balled her fists in his shirt. "I just . . . can we pick this up later? When we're alone?"

His stomach twisted with pent-up feelings. "I'll ask them to leave."

She shook her head. "That would be rude."

"Then we'll eat fast."

"Not too fast. I don't want them to think we're trying to get rid of them."

"The hell with that." He nabbed her hand and practically dragged her down the stairs. He was going to declare his love, and she was going to answer, "I love you, too." He wasn't willing to wait another two hours to hear the words. He needed to know that what he suspected was dead-on true. That Afia loved him.

He wasn't all that worried about rushing the boys out of his house as he suspected they had their own issues to work out. Gallow had insisted that he and Jean-Pierre weren't sleeping together, but something sure as hell was going on. When it came to sexual tension, straight or gay, it was all the same.

Afia squealed as Roscoe and Barney, the wrestling-wonders, rolled directly in their path. He swept her up and over the cats and kept walking. They were midway through the living room when his cell phone rang. "Shit." He paused to check the number, cursed again when he saw it was Joni. "Go on in," he said, giving her a gentle nudge. "I'll be there in a minute. And start eating!"

Afia waggled her fingers over her shoulder at Jake and chanted, "Oh, my God. Oh, my God," all the way through the living room, parlor, and dining room. He loved her. She'd seen it in his eyes. The words had been on the tip of his tongue. She'd almost been forced to say, "I love you, too." The mere thought made her ill. It would start their relationship off on the same foot as Randy and hers. As Frank and hers. Doomed relationships. Not because she was jinxed, but because she hadn't loved them body and soul.

She had to say it first.

I LOVE YOU.

Rudy and Jean-Pierre had to go.

She marched into the kitchen intending to ask them politely to go home. All she had to do was find the proper words.

Rudy sat at the table pouring four cups of coffee. "What took you so long?"

"Where is Jake?" Jean-Pierre asked, setting down two plates of waffles and then taking a seat on the opposite side. "I want to ask him where he found those antique demi cups and saucers."

Afia pushed her bangs off of her forehead. Oh, boy.

Jake blew into the kitchen before she could say a word. "I have to go. Joni has an emergency, and Carson isn't there."

Her pulse quickened. "Is it the baby?"

He shook his head. "Something to do with an unwanted

guest." He attached his holster to his belt, making sure it was hidden beneath his loose fitting shirt. "She sounded panicked, and she hung up on me. I have to go."

Rudy shoved out of his chair. "I'll come with you."

"Thanks, but, if it wasn't something I couldn't handle alone, she would've called the cops." He nodded to the men and then kissed Afia on the cheek before blowing out of the room.

"Call me!" she shouted. Heart racing, she slumped into the wicker chair next to Rudy.

"Was that a gun?" Jean-Pierre rolled his tongue and growled like a tiger. "Sexy."

"It's an implement of death," Afia snapped. "It is not sexy."

"When someone as tasty as Jake is carrying, it's sexy," Rudy said. "Very alpha."

She smacked a palm to her brow. "Men."

"Eat your waffle before it gets cold, *Chou à la crème*."

"I'm not hungry." What if the unwanted guest was someone like Marty Ashe? A big bully with a bigger gun? "How can you two be so calm?"

Jean-Pierre shrugged. "Jake did not seem concerned."

"He said he could handle it," Rudy said, sipping his coffee.

"Cute muscles and a cocked weapon. All he needed was a cape and tights." Jean-Pierre looked at Rudy, excitement dancing in his eyes. "Do you think Superdick will break the intruder's legs or shoot him?"

Afia groaned.

"We have an idea for your benefit," Rudy said, winking at his partner-in-crime and then leaning back in his chair.

She frowned. "You're just trying to take my mind off of Jake and Joni."

"Who is this Joni?" Jean-Pierre asked, stirring cream and sugar into his mug.

"Jake's sister. She's pregnant."

He gave a disgusted snort.

Afia bristled. "You don't like children?"

Rudy patted her hand. "He likes children. He's just miffed because one of the dancers is pregnant and that entails some progressive alterations. The vice president asked the show's producer to keep her on as long as possible."

She perked up. "One of the dancers in the show is pregnant? Which one? Who's the father?" Could this have anything with Rivelli devoting the weekend to Angela? Was it his baby? Was he going to break the news?

"Selena," Jean-Pierre said with a sneer. "Her boyfriend lives in New York. I have never met him, but I do not like him."

"Stop whining," Rudy said. "So you have to get creative. Look at it as a challenge. I think it's commendable that the casino's going to keep her on." He took another sip of coffee and then focused on Afia. "So about your benefit."

Velma rubbed up against her leg and purred, quieting Afia's nerves with her mere presence. She sighed, thinking fleetingly that cats must be psychic, and then placed her napkin in her lap and reached for the maple syrup. "All right. What's your idea?" If Jake didn't call her in the next half hour, she was calling the police.

"A drag show."

"Excuse me?"

"The gay community will come out full force in support of the queens and the kids. Then there are the fag hags and stags, and that small circle of social elite who simply think it's chic to support gay causes. Between ticket sales, a silent auction, and raffles, that playground equipment is as good as bought."

All ears, Afia nodded while pouring syrup over her waffle. She'd been to several drag shows over the years. All of them well-attended. All of them wildly successful.

"Karl will probably let us use the club as the venue. I'll talk to a few of the girls, but I know without even asking that we can count on Sucha Diva, Miss Trudy, Carmen Chameleon, and Sofonda Menn."

"Think cabaret performance slash fashion show," Jean-Pierre said. "I have some fabulous ideas for costuming."

"Some fresh talent would be nice," Rudy said. "Or a blast from the past. I wish we could get Iva Dream. She was hysterical and, honey, did she have some creative moves." He nudged Afia. "You saw her perform once. *The Flashdance* parody. Remember?"

She smiled. "Flashpants . . . What a Feeling. I remember. Vaguely. Gosh, that was, what, six years ago?"

Jean-Pierre shoved his longish hair off of his face. "So contact her."

Rudy shook his head. "Wouldn't know where to find her. Haven't seen or heard of her in years."

"I love it," Afia said, her mind spinning with ideas. The drag queens took their performances very seriously and would put heart, imagination, and passion into the show, making it unlike anything the SCC had organized in years. This project couldn't lose. She dug into her waffle, energized and suddenly starving. "Let's talk production costs."

* * *

"This is your emergency?"

"Get rid of him, Jake. I can't breathe. I can't function with that horrid creature in my house."

"It's just a spider."

"It's a tarantula." Pale and sweaty, Joni pressed deeper into the corner of her couch, staring wide-eyed at a king-sized arachnid sunning itself on her living room wall.

"They don't have tarantulas in Jersey." Hands on hips, he studied the garden spider that had paralyzed his tough-as-nails sister. "Although he is a hairy bugger."

"Jake!"

Her terrified plea sent shivers up his spine. "Relax, honey. I'll take care of it." Thirty seconds later he'd released the spider into the woods, fetched a cool cloth, and now he sat beside Joni mopping her clammy brow. "I didn't know you had arachnophobia."

"Neither did I. Then again I've never seen a spider that big. I was afraid to move. What if I scared it, what if it ran . . . and hid? What if I opened a drawer or pulled back my bedspread and there it was!" She took the washcloth from him, pressed it to her cheeks and took a deep breath. "Maybe it's hormones. This is so embarrassing. All I had to do was squash it with a shoe."

Jake smiled and patted her leg. "Phobias don't have to make any sense." He thought about Giselle's irrational fear of Friday the thirteenth. He thought about Afia. He'd called her on his cell while releasing the *horrid creature* into the wilds. She'd been ecstatic that he was safe and made him promise not to leave Joni until she'd calmed completely. Panic attacks, she'd said, are horrible. "How are you feeling?"

"Better." She tucked her hair behind her ears. "Actually, I feel like an idiot. I'm sorry I called you over."

"I'm not. I'm glad I could help. Do you expect Carson soon? I'd like to congratulate him on his new job."

"He drove all the way to Hammonton to buy me a particular homemade pie that I'm fond of." She grinned. "I had a craving."

Jake rubbed the back of his neck. "He's a good man."

"Yes, he is."

"You love each other rain or shine. You're in this together, forever."

Her smile faded. "What's going on with you?"

He jammed a hand through his hair. His timing wasn't the best, although, knowing how Joni felt about Afia's track record with men, hell would freeze over before there would be a good time. He didn't need his sister's approval but, damn, a little support would be nice. Whereas he was a novice, she'd spent two years navigating the unpredictable waters of a serious relationship. "Are you sure you're feeling better? I don't want to upset you."

She crossed her arms over her plump breasts. "Spill."

He cleared his throat. "You know your concern regarding my getting romantically involved with Afia?"

Her face crumpled. "I knew it. You're dating her."

"I asked her to move in with me."

"You're insane!" She blinked at him, cocked her head and groaned. "It's worse. You're in love." She threw up her hands. "Oh, Jake, of all people. Aside from the obvious, there are all kinds of possible complications. Have you thought this through? Of course you have. The great puzzle solver. You think you've got it all figured out."

"Rain or shine," he said, giving her knee a reassuring squeeze. "Right?"

She sighed, placed her hand over his and nodded. "Rain or shine."

❋ ❋ ❋

She was on fire. Rudy and Jean-Pierre's suggestion had sparked an inferno of ideas regarding the benefit. After an hour of brainstorming, they'd said their goodbyes. She'd made a few business calls, washed the dishes, and then she'd sprinted upstairs to unpack her toiletries and some essential clothing, hoping to spruce up before Jake got home. She wanted to look her best when she confessed her feelings. She sang the hook of an old Donna Summer hit as she slipped her feet into a pair of pink brocade slippers. *"I . . . love to love you, baby! I . . . love to love you, baby!"*

Shimmying into a pink-silk camisole and a matching Prada skirt, she hustled out of the guest room and into the main bathroom to apply a touch of makeup. Spying a small radio on the corner of the vanity, she flipped it on and dialed up a classic disco channel. Abba's *Dancing Queen* blared from the tiny speakers causing her to smile as she lined her eyes with a muted brown shadow. Images of a strutting Miss Trudy wearing her lime green beehive, gold spandex pants and a glittering tube top floated through her head as Afia tapped her slippered feet in time with the music. Then the song ended and another began. *Flashdance*. Geesh. Talk about coincidence. She rooted through her makeup bag while envisioning Iva Dream and all her practiced moves. Those legs, those feet. So precise. Sequined legwarmers, black fishnets and an off-the-shoulder stretch velvet shirt . . .

She slicked pink gloss across her lips as a more recent memory intruded.

Oh, my God.

Gasping, she dropped the lip-gloss into the makeup bag, scrambled out of the bathroom and down the stairs, nearly plowing over Jake as he breezed in through the front door.

"Whoa," he said, nabbing her by the shoulders. "Where's the fire?"

"Rivelli's apartment."

His brow furrowed. "What?"

"Where there's smoke, there's fire. The proof you need, I'm betting it's in his apartment. Can you get us in?"

He pushed his aviator sunglasses up on top of his head. "You want me to break into Rivelli's apartment?"

"Can you do it?"

He raised an eyebrow as if to say "how can you doubt me?"

and then said, "Just out of curiosity why would I want to take the risk?"

"I think I know who the other woman is."

"Who?"

"Iva Dream."

* * *

Getting burned for B&E wasn't Jake's idea of fun, so he'd convinced Afia to change out of her sexy little dress and into a subtle disguise. They stepped out of the high-rise's elevator wearing black jeans, black baseball caps and forest green T-shirts reading "Fresh As A Daisy Cleaning Service." He'd pulled this ruse more than once. Toting buckets of cleaning supplies, he and Afia had breezed through the apartment building's lobby without raising an eyebrow.

Next step: getting inside Rivelli's condominium.

Piece of cake.

Especially when he had a key.

He nudged Afia inside, closed the door behind him, punched the access code into the security keypad and set his bucket on the floor.

Afia blinked at him. "Where did you get that key? How did you know his code?"

"Angela overnighted a package. It came this morning while you were upstairs. With all that happened today, I didn't get a chance to tell you."

She set her bucket beside his. "You could have told me on the ride over here."

275

"I couldn't get a word in edgewise." She'd spent the entire twenty minutes explaining the difference between transvestites, transsexuals, cross-dressers, and drag artists. Even though he knew the basics, he'd let her ramble on because her overall theory, though a stretch, was damned intriguing. His mouth twitched into a smile. "You're disappointed, aren't you? Thought I was going to pick the lock."

She tugged at the brim of her cap and shrugged. "It's so exciting in the movies."

"It's not as easy as they make it look."

"Could you have done it?"

"Sure. It's a standard pin tumbler lock. The security system, however, would have posed a problem."

She grinned. "I bet you would have figured out something."

"Maybe." He chuckled. "That turns you on doesn't it? You've got a streak of daredevil in you, baby."

She blushed. "I guess I take after my dad. He was a thrill seeker."

And look what it got him, Jake thought. A rhino horn through the back. If they searched Rivelli's apartment without getting burned, at least it would help to put her jinxed stigma to rest. He pulled two pairs of latex gloves out of the bucket and handed her a pair. "Put these on. If you move anything, be sure to put it back where you found it. Understand?"

She nodded. "Why did Angela send you the means to break in?"

"She's hoping I'll find an address book, a note, pictures, something that will ID the other woman. Figured since she had

Rivelli over the weekend, now was the perfect time for me to search this place. Obviously, she's desperate to know his secret."

Afia sighed as she snapped on the gloves. "And he's desperate to keep his secret. Now that we're here, I'm feeling guilty."

"Too late for that." He jerked his head toward the hall. "You take the bathroom. I'll take the bedroom. Touch as little as possible and don't make any loud noises to alert the neighbors."

She gave a cocky salute and tiptoed ahead of him, disappearing into a room on the right.

Jake gave the entire place a once over before beginning his search. Rivelli's apartment was as clean and structured as his apparent life. Everything in its place. It took him fifteen minutes to find what he was looking for, and he didn't find it in the bedroom. The man had stashed his goods behind an ingenious bookshelf that doubled as a closet.

Sequined gowns, velvet jumpsuits, corsets, and body stockings. Feather boas and rhinestone jewelry. Wigs. A supply of bust enhancers and hosiery, including fishnet pantyhose.

Afia came into the room carrying a fishing tackle box. "Bingo," she said. "Eye shadow, false eyelashes, lipstick, nail tips, rouge . . . beard concealer."

Jake jerked his head to the secret closet. "Six-inch platform shoes and thigh high boots, size fifteen. You were right," he said with a proud smile. "Rivelli *is* the other woman."

Chapter Twenty

"You can't tell Angela."

Jake gripped the steering wheel and clenched his jaw. "That's the third time you've said that, Afia. We've been through this. Angela Brannigan is my client. She hired me to find out if her fiancé is cheating on her. I have to report my findings."

She wasn't sure if he was irritated with her or the heavy Saturday evening traffic, but he sounded as cranky as she felt. The thrill of solving a mystery had been short-lived. Now she felt like a traitor. "Can't you just tell her, no, he's not seeing another woman? That wouldn't be lying."

"She wouldn't believe me. She's like a dog with a bone. She'd just hire another investigator."

Sighing, she swept off her cap and brushed her bangs off of her forehead. "Do you have to show her the pictures? The wigs? The bust enhancers?" She'd nearly died when he'd whipped out a camera and started clicking away.

"She wanted visual proof. It's not the kind she's expecting, but it will put her mind at rest. She's engaged to this guy. Don't you think she has a right to know what she's getting into?"

"But it's so personal, Jake." She clasped her hands in her lap, her body surging with indignation. "It should come from Rivelli, not from you. He's not gay. He might not even be bisexual. There's an entire faction of transvestites who are heterosexual, married with kids. You investigated him. Anthony Rivelli is an upstanding, hard working man."

"Who likes to dress up in women's clothes."

She glanced sideways, miffed because she couldn't see his eyes. Was he mocking Rivelli, or merely stating a fact? How could he be so unfeeling about this? "He's an entertainer at heart," she said with conviction. "Role reversal dates back to Shakespearian times. Milton Berle was a drag queen, for goodness sake. It's a form of expression, a kind of escape. I bet the only reason Rivelli keeps it a secret is because the bulk of society doesn't approve. Do you think he'd be the vice president of a casino if his peers knew that he likes to perform in drag?"

Jake scraped his hand along his jaw and massaged the back of his neck. "Afia, I'm not judging the guy."

"But you're prepared to ruin his life?"

"For Christ's—"

"I'm just saying that he should at least be given the opportunity to come clean with Angela. Can't you talk to him first? Give him a heads up?"

"And betray Angela's confidence by letting him know that she hired me to investigate him? That she mailed me a key to his apartment so that I could snoop in his closets? Yeah, that'll give their relationship a shot in the arm."

"Oh." Feeling a little foolish, she thunked her head back against the seat as he turned onto a side street. "Hmm."

"You have to consider all of the angles. You're not giving Angela any credit. She's going to be damned relieved that her fiancé isn't cheating on her. Will she be shocked that he's a cross-dresser? Probably. Will she desert him because of it? Maybe, maybe not. What if she approaches Rivelli with an open mind and heart? What if she wants to understand and to work things out? Maybe he'll be able to come out of the closet, so to speak, at least with her. Wouldn't that be a relief for Rivelli?"

"I'm sure it would." She massaged her temples. "This is very confusing."

He reached over and squeezed her thigh as he swung the car into his driveway. "Listen, we can't do anything about it until Angela contacts me and that won't be until Monday. Let the matter rest for now. Case solved. As soon as we walk through that front door we're done talking business. Agreed?"

"Agreed," she said, suddenly exhausted.

He smiled, took off his sunglasses and tossed them on the dash and then climbed out and rounded the car to open her door.

Afia groaned as she stepped out into his arms. This had been an emotionally charged day, and it wasn't over. She'd yet to tell him her news. Maybe she should wait until tomorrow. "I'm tired. Are you tired?"

"I'm hungry." He whipped around his baseball cap so that

it sat backwards and dropped his forehead to hers. "How about if I make us something to eat, and we curl up on the sofa and watch an old movie?"

She couldn't think of anything she'd rather do. Except . . . "Can I take a bubble bath first?"

He smiled. "Have I told you *my* number one fantasy?"

✻ ✻ ✻

Jake relaxed against the back of the claw-footed tub and soaped up Afia's long hair with her jasmine shampoo. She sat with her back to him, cradled between his legs, sipping champagne amongst a cloud of sudsy bath bubbles. "I like the smell of your shampoo," he said.

"I like the taste of your champagne." She took another long sip, before setting the fluted crystal next to his on the wicker table he'd pulled alongside the tub. Scented candles flickered all around the wainscoted room. The sensual beat of a salsa tune drifted from the radio on the vanity. She moaned with pleasure as he eased back her head and rinsed her hair with cup after cup of warm water. "I think we got our fantasies mixed up," she whispered.

He pulled her flush against him and kissed the top of her ear. "I think we got it just right." Enjoying the feel of her slick, naked body, he smoothed a washcloth over her shoulders, across her collarbone then over her perfect breasts. His pole hardened just thinking about what he was going to do to her later in bed. She was sexy, beautiful, kind, and clever, and he was goddamned dizzy in love.

She'd impressed him by solving the Rivelli mystery, and though she'd irritated the hell out of him with her views on the outcome, he respected her opinions and the fact that she'd fought to get her way. Six days ago she would have avoided the heated exchange. He found it hard to believe that a person could change so fiercely in so little time, which led him to believe that the tigress had always been lurking. She'd just needed someone to lure her out into the jungle of life.

She sighed as he smoothed the washcloth over her ribs and across her taut stomach. Her limbs grew heavy, her breathing shallow. He half expected her to fall asleep in his arms. But then she surprised him by sitting up and swiveling around to face him.

Not so bad. Now he had a prime view of those perfect breasts.

"I never got to ask my questions." She swiped water from her thick lashes and cocked her head. "You know, the interview game."

"Ah." He forced his gaze from her rosy buds to her sable eyes.

"Don't look so worried. I only have two questions." She grinned. "For now anyway."

Okay, she'd piqued his curiosity. He raked back his wet hair and took a bracing drink of champagne. "Fire away."

She traced a finger along the small, jagged scar on his cheekbone. "How'd you get this?"

His skin sizzled beneath her gentle touch. "It's not very glamorous. Bar fight. I was young, drunk, and—"

"In love?" Her eyes rounded to the size of chocolate

medallions. "Were you defending your girlfriend's honor or something?"

He smiled. "I was going to say hotheaded. I've never been in love."

Now she looked stricken.

Hell. He'd meant he'd never been in love before *now.* "I meant to say—"

"Don't say anything!" she squealed, covering his mouth with her hand.

Why the hell did she keep doing that? He raised his eyebrows, and she removed her hand.

"Question number two." She polished off her champagne. "Why did you leave the police force?"

Fair question that deserved an answer, but he wasn't in the mood just now to get into a grim discussion about the lowlifes of the world and the shit they sometimes get away with because of the system. "Let's just say that I don't always like to play by the rules."

She hugged her knees to her chest and shivered. "You mean you saw bad people do bad things, but you didn't always see justice served."

Beautiful and intuitive. "That about sums it up." He reached past her and turned on the faucet, giving the cooling water a hot blast.

She nodded. "I understand. Believe me, I've heard lots of horror stories. I've been surrounded by judges and lawyers my whole life. My godfather's a lawyer."

Dammit. He cranked off the faucet and refilled their champagne glasses. "Harmon Reece."

Her eyes lit up. "You know him?" She tipped the flute to her lips.

"I've done some work for him." Dammit to hell, he did not want to have this discussion here. Now. He leaned forward and stroked his finger along her sudsy jaw. "Listen, Afia. I need to tell you something."

"Wait!" She set down her glass. "I have to tell you first. Before you say it. Before you think it's the liquor and not me." She framed his face in her hands, regarded him intently.

He waited . . . and waited. His heart hammered against his chest as he waited for the words that would make him the happiest man on this freaking earth.

"I love you."

Thank you, Jesus.

She smiled and continued to caress his face as the candles flickered and the music played. As his entire world tilted. "I want you to know that I've never said that to anyone before. That is, I've never been the first to say it. And it wasn't like this. It's never been like this.

"I'm in love with you, Jake. I love you so much it hurts." She leaned forward and pressed a kiss to his lips, a tender kiss that wrapped around his soul and made his heart sing. "I didn't scare you, did I?"

He smiled, gazing at her with the love of a thousand Romeos. "You just made me very happy." He pulled her to her feet, wrapped her in a fluffy towel, and carried her to his bed. Laying her on the mattress, he sealed their love with a kiss and a vow. "Nothing and no one will ever come between us."

Chapter Twenty-One

Sunday waffled into a blur. A beautiful, magical, romantic blur.

Afia had awoken in erotic bliss with Jake inside of her murmuring promises of the day, the night, and a lifetime beyond. By the time he was through with her she'd barely been able to crawl out of bed. And he called *her* insatiable.

She'd retaliated by making and serving him breakfast. Naked.

Up to the challenge, he'd duly nailed her on the kitchen table. It was the stuff of her X-rated dreams. Only there wasn't anything raunchy or tawdry about it. She was in love, and as corny as it sounded, all was right with the world.

Of course, her world would shift slightly the moment her mother returned. Giselle St. John-Tate considered money, status, and power to be extremely important. It was the reason she'd married the bonbon baron, and the reason she'd hate Jake.

Afia had never understood her mother's motives. Giselle

believed that her daughter was doomed to a life of misfortune. There had never, *ever*, been any doubt of that, and yet she continually manipulated Afia into relationships that she swore would bring *good* fortune. Maybe it was just the fortune part that mattered. Maybe Giselle truly thought that money could buy happiness.

It occurred to her in the midst of searching E-bay for Victorian furniture with Jake that she hadn't seriously thought about retrieving her inheritance in days. It was almost as if Henry Glick had done her a favor. By stealing her money he'd given her life. She'd never been happier, never felt stronger.

It was so hard to believe that she had existed before this past week. Who was that person who'd shrunk at the slightest cross-eyed look? *I haven't done anything wrong.* As if she deserved scrutinizing simply for being born on Friday the thirteenth. The notion filled her with disgust. Her mother filled her with disgust. Only now did Afia recognize the woman's superstitious harping for what it was—emotional abuse. Giselle had molded her into a frightened, insecure target for mishap.

She wanted to forget that person. To wipe her from her memory. Jinxed—goodbye. Black widow—goodbye.

She was simply Afia.

In a bid for independence, she'd slipped her charm bracelet into a velvet pouch and tucked it and her fears away.

She'd said yes when Jake had asked her if she'd like to spend the day lounging at the beach. Yes, when he'd asked her to dinner at a steakhouse, and yes to a movie. Yes, to life!

She'd been genuinely sorry to see Sunday come and go.

Except for the fact that she'd gotten to sleep in Jake's arms.

Monday brought a heady dose of reality.

Nancy Ashe stood her up.

"I can't believe she's not coming." Afia dropped her cell phone in her leather bag and fell back against the outer wall of the Women's Center with a groan.

Jake pushed his sunglasses on top of his head and regarded her with a frown. "What did she say?"

"Just that she changed her mind. That she doesn't want anything to do with counselors. That her problems are private." Disappointment flooded through her, followed by a wave of anxiety. "Do you think that Marty got to her?"

His tender gaze flicked from her wringing hands to her wide eyes. "I think she's caught up in a pattern. Old ways die hard."

She realized suddenly that she was clasping her naked wrist, stroking charms that weren't there. Was he talking about Nancy or her? His observance pertained to both of them. In moments of distress, fighting her jinxed mentality proved difficult. Was Nancy's struggle any less of a challenge? She pushed off of the wall with a burst of determination. "I'm not giving up on her."

"I'm glad to hear it." He smiled and pulled her into his arms for a quick hug. "Now stop looking so glum. Today's not a total bust. At least things went better at the daycare center."

"I suppose," she said as he ushered her into the car. "At least no one bit me."

He laughed and rounded the car to the driver's side.

Afia smiled. Actually, as a result of creating a few boundaries two of the children had even hugged her, and that had been glorious. Mrs. Kelly had been a boost to her confidence as well, expressing her delight over the benefit Afia was planning. The older woman had seen a performance of *La Cage Aux Folles* and had loved it. She'd especially liked that song *I Am What I Am*. "Do you know someone who could do that song justice, dear?" she'd asked.

Afia fidgeted in her seat as she envisioned Iva Dream. Her stomach churned with guilt and apprehension. "What time did Angela say she'd come to the office?"

"Three o-clock." He turned onto Atlantic Avenue and then glanced sideways. "You all right with this?"

He was going to reveal Rivelli's secret. He was going to show Angela those pictures and quite possibly ruin the man's future happiness. "No, I'm not all right with it, but I can't come up with a reasonable alternative."

"Everything happens for a reason, baby. Sometimes you have to forgive the process, knowing that the outcome is for the best."

The softness of his voice, the hint of pleading, turned her head. Why did she feel as if this wasn't totally about Rivelli?

"I'm going to let you off at the Bizby," he said, before she could question him. "I've got an appointment. I should be back in an hour or so." He pulled up to the curb, turned to her, and cradled the back of her head, striking her woozy with a deep, tender kiss.

A shiver coursed through her and not the good kind. She eased back and slid off his sunglasses to peer into his eyes. All she read was affection and desire. Still, her body hummed with a sickening sense of foreboding. "I love you, Jake."

"I love you, too, baby." He winked. "Don't reorganize my desk"

❋ ❋ ❋

Jake had taught her how to do a basic background search. She could access various public records from the Internet. If there was any dirt on Angela Brannigan, and her gut told her there was, she'd find it. Afia's fingers trembled as she keyed in the information.

In a matter of minutes she'd learned that Brannigan was a married name and that her maiden name was Falcone. Angela Falcone, daughter of Vincent Falcone. Anyone who read the newspapers, or who'd spent as much time as Afia had around local lawyers, knew the reputation of that man.

Searching through newspaper archives, she found an article on the death of Angela's first husband, Michael Brannigan. Construction mogul and his mistress found dead in the Delaware River, suspected foul play, never proven.

Heart pounding, she shut down the computer and scanned the phone book for the number to the Carnevale. She had to warn Rivelli. Whether or not he knew that his future father-in-law had mob ties was irrelevant. If his fiancée flipped out when she found out about "the other woman" he could be in danger. Men who wronged Angela Falcone died.

Afia shivered. It was like meeting her evil alter-ego.

She dialed the number, calmed her voice. "Anthony Rivelli, please. Yes, I'll wait."

Jake would understand, wouldn't he? Maybe she should have called him first. Then again, he was in an appointment, and it would be rude to interrupt.

"Anthony Rivelli's office. This is his secretary. May I ask who's calling?"

Seize the day! "Afia St. John. I'm . . . I'm with the Seashore Charity Committee. I need to speak to him about last Friday's gala. It's urgent."

"One moment, please."

Her stomach clenched as her mind considered alternate ramifications. What if Angela freaked out when Jake showed her the pictures? What if she pulled a gun out of her purse and shot him, wanting her fiancé's dirty little secret to die with him? She blew out a steadying breath. Jake was right. She'd been watching too much bad television.

"Anthony Rivelli. Good afternoon, Ms. St. John. What can I do for you and the SCC?"

He sounded so . . . *nice.* "I lied," she blurted. "I'm not with the SCC. At least not anymore."

"I don't understand."

"I need to speak with you in person, in private. It could be a matter of life and death."

"Ms. St. John . . ." he started in a patient, but skeptical tone.

"It's about Iva Dream."

Pause.

"And your fiancée."

"I have an apartment in Ventnor. Let me give you the address."

"I know it. I'll meet you there in twenty minutes." She

hung up, grabbed her purse, and raced out the door. God, she hoped she didn't take the wrong jitney.

✳ ✳ ✳

Jake left Harmon's office with a sick sense of dread in the pit of his stomach.

Kilmore had located Glick. It looked as if they were going to recover at least half of Afia's money. His damsel was an heiress once more.

He wasn't concerned that she'd ditch him in order to pursue her old life. She hated her old life, and he had faith in her love.

What worried him is that their relationship was built on a lie. Though Harmon had been adamant, neither he, nor Gallow, who'd also been present for the meeting, were convinced that this was the best way to proceed. In order to spare Afia hurt feelings, Harmon had pleaded that they keep the initial ruse a secret. He'd never hired Jake as her babysitter. He'd never asked Rudy to drive her to the office on the false pretense of hearing about the "job" from the boys at the club.

It was one hell of a lie, and there was a glitch. Giselle knew the whole story. She'd called to check in with Harmon two nights ago, and he'd spilled the beans. *"Don't worry,"* he'd told Jake and Gallow, *"I'll call her as soon as you two leave. I'll handle it."*

But hadn't he also been the one to intimate that Giselle was not a woman easily handled?

Jake rolled back his shoulders, slid on his sunglasses, and keyed the ignition. This had disaster written all over it. He should have come clean with Afia yesterday, but she'd been so thrilled with their day-long date that he hadn't had the heart.

His cell phone rang. He noted the caller and cursed. Speaking of potential disasters . . . "Hello, Angela. What can I—"

"I've decided I don't want to see the pictures," came a slurred voice. "Whatever you found in Anthony's apartment, I . . . I want to see it with my own eyes."

Had she been drinking? Was she driving? Shit. "Are you okay?"

"No, I'm not okay!" she shouted. "The man I love is seeing another woman."

He flexed his fingers on the steering wheel. "I didn't say that."

"You said you found proof!"

Christ, she sounded sloshed. "I said—"

"I'm here now."

"In Rivelli's apartment?" Hell.

"He's at work. Now is the perfect time. Please hurry." She hung up.

Freaking hell.

✳ ✳ ✳

She got into the elevator at the same time as he did. "Mr. Rivelli?"

"Ms. St. John, I presume." He shook her proffered hand. The door slid closed. He hitched back his designer suit jacket and slid his hands into the pockets of his creased brown trousers. "So you know Iva Dream?"

Afia smiled up at him. He was a good-looking man, though not nearly as striking as Jake. Jake. She tamped down a flutter of guilt for going behind his back. "I'm a fan, actually. I saw her cabaret act a few years ago." She leaned in and whispered. "You were fabulous."

He cleared his throat and massaged his brow. "This is a little awkward, Ms. St. John."

"Please call me Afia."

He blew out a breath, glanced at the ceiling, and then studied her with wary eyes. "Afia, I made a conscious decision to pull out of the drag scene six years ago for the sake of my career. I prefer to keep Iva in the closet."

But you don't want to give her up completely. That's why you keep this apartment. He probably spent whole nights trying on Iva Dream's costumes and polishing her dance moves. Observing Anthony Rivelli from afar and interacting with him one on one were two different stories. Though painfully polite, the man radiated a ferocious remoteness that caused Afia's skin to prickle. More than ever she felt as if she'd stuck her nose where it didn't belong. She'd told Jake that he wasn't gay, but how did she know that for sure? Maybe he was in denial, or cocooned in a thick cloak of secrecy. Maybe Angela was merely an unwitting beard.

Wringing her hands, Afia glanced up at a security camera. What if there was audio, or what if, upon reviewing tapes, someone read their lips? If Rivelli was gay, she didn't want to be responsible for outing him. She'd feel much better discussing this inside his apartment, away from prying eyes and videotapes. "Given your professional status, I understand your wish to keep Iva Dream a secret," she said, turning her back to the camera. "If you'd explain your fascination with . . . Iva to your fiancée, perhaps she'd understand as well. The news should come from you, don't you think?"

He narrowed his eyes. "What are you driving at, and how do you know Angela?"

She ignored the question. "Do you know who her father is?"

"Of course. I try my best to maintain a discreet distance, but it isn't always easy. I love Angela, and she loves her father."

The elevator doors opened, and they immediately fell into silence as they walked down the hall. Two doors down from his apartment her heel caught in the plush carpet, slipped sideways, and she wrenched her ankle. "Ow."

Rivelli caught her by her forearm, otherwise she would have fallen. "Are you okay?"

She took a step, winced, and stumbled. "No." Her ankle throbbed. "I think it's twisted. *Darn.*" Of all days to wear heels. "I'm so sorry."

"Don't apologize." He put his arm around her shoulder. "Lean into me. We'll get you inside and put some ice on it."

She felt like an idiot as she hobbled forward, her arm clutched around Anthony Rivelli's waist. White-hot pain lanced through her ankle with every step. A cry slipped out as she tried to shift her weight.

He unlocked the door, punched his code in the keypad, and swept her into his arms and into the living room.

There was nothing intimate about his touch. She didn't feel

awkward or at risk being disabled and alone with him in his apartment. No sexual awareness at all. Maybe he was gay, not that it mattered. Except, if that were the case, it didn't bode well for his union with Angela. They would both be settling, and Afia knew from experience that a union born out of anything less than one hundred percent pulse-pounding, soul-searing, passionate love was a sad, pitiful crime.

Placing her on the couch, Rivelli bent down on one knee, took off her shoe, and ran his hands over her bare foot and ankle, examining the swelling. "About Angela," he said.

She bit her lower lip to keep from crying out as he prodded her injury, breathing deep to stem the tears. That's when she smelled the perfume. *Opium.*

"I really don't want her to know about this," he continued, even though Afia was squeezing his shoulder in a bid for attention.

"Sorry. Secret's out." Angela Falcone-Brannigan weaved into the living room, a glass of liquor in one hand, and her purse in the other. She slammed the drink on an end table. "I knew she'd be young! I just knew it!"

Afia started, her gaze trained on that purse, her heart ramming against her ribs.

Rivelli released her foot and slowly stood. "Honey, it's not what you think."

"Don't you 'honey' me." Angela's bloodshot eyes brimmed with tears. "How could you be so stupid, Tony? Do you have any idea what Daddy will do to you if he finds out you cheated on me?"

"I didn't cheat." His face twisted with desperation. "I've been telling you that for weeks. I didn't . . . we didn't . . ." He gestured to Afia. "She twisted her ankle, for chrissake."

"Oh, spare me! That's almost as lame as the lipstick excuse." She stumbled back a step, her long, wavy blond hair flopping over one side of her contorted face. "I know you." She waggled her purse at Afia. "You're that snooty slut who made me break my mirror. You jinxed me, stole my man. But that's nothing compared to what I'm going to do to you." She glared long and hard, envy sparking in her gaze. Envy . . . Envy . . .

The evil eye.

For a moment Afia was paralyzed. Her mouth went dry, and her stomach heaved as one of her greatest fears disoriented her with the ferocity of a cyclone. She could feel her life's juices being sucked out of her, her dreams of bearing children evaporating as the other woman cursed her with a wicked, white-hot glare.

Angela pulled a little silver revolver out of her purse, and the buzzing in Afia's ears grew to a deafening roar.

Rivelli held out his hand as he inched closer. "Give me the gun, honey."

Out of the corner of her eye, Afia saw Jake moving carefully into the room, and her heart shattered into a million pieces as her jinxed past hit her with a full force body slam. No!

Matching Angela's hateful glare she forced herself to her feet, intending to command the woman's attention. Her ankle gave out and she pitched forward, just as Jake and Rivelli sprang forth and the gun went off.

✳ ✳ ✳

This was a warped-ass version of hell. Joni stood on his right bitching to Carson about how love had struck her brother careless. Gallow and Jean-Pierre stood to his left admiring and discussing his six-pack abs. The foursome had been going on like this for a good five minutes, and Jake had had his fill. Where was Afia?

A nurse had whisked her into another room to examine her swollen ankle, but they should have been done by now. He wanted to see her, to touch her, and to know that she was healthy and calm. With all of the chaos he still didn't fully understand what she'd been doing in Rivelli's apartment in the first place. When he'd walked in on the volatile scene, he'd had to shut down emotionally and focus solely on Angela and the weapon. His stomach still lurched at the thought of Afia being on the losing end of that gun.

"And another thing," Joni said, wagging her finger at him. He rolled his eyes, blocked out her nagging, and tested his bandaged shoulder. Sore but mobile. The bullet had just grazed. He turned pleading eyes on his brother-in-law. "Will you please take her home?"

Carson put his arm around Joni and tugged her toward the examining room door. "Come on, sweetheart. You heard the doctor. He'll live."

"Amazingly. He's lucky that bullet didn't go through his heart! A few inches south and . . ."

Carson frowned at Jake as he urged his wife into the hall. "You realize I'll be hearing about this all night."

Jake just waved. "I'll call you tomorrow." Joni was right. He'd been damned lucky. Lucky the bullet had hit him and not

Afia. His breath had stalled in his lungs when she'd stood up to divert Angela's attention. Brave, but stupid, and as soon as he gave her a thorough kiss, he'd give her hell.

He smirked at Gallow and Jean-Pierre. "Don't you two have somewhere to go? Other abs to ogle?"

"We could go to the club," Jean-Pierre said, shooting a hopeful look at his partner.

"I could definitely use a drink," Gallow said. He rapped the slighter man on the shoulder. "You go ahead. I'll meet you there."

The Frenchman sashayed out, Gallow stabbed his hand nervously through his hair, and Jake lost his grip on his patience. "Where the hell's Afia? You said her ankle wasn't busted, just sprained. Are they still wrapping it?"

Gallow rubbed the back of his neck. "We have a problem."

Jake's stomach dropped.

"Giselle's here."

"What the fu—"

"She flew back early, tracked down Afia on her cell and, well, she's here, and it's not good."

Jake tried to slide off of the examining table, but Gallow-the-caretaker frowned and pressed strong hands to his thighs, anchoring him to his spot. As if he were going to pass out from a damned flesh wound. "Where's Harmon?"

"He's still down at the police station fielding questions from reporters. They're booking the Brannigan woman for assault." Rudy grunted. "Freaking assault. They should nail that crazy bitch for attempted murder."

"They might try. It depends on if the prosecuting attorney

can make the case." Familiar with the complicated state statutes, Jake could well imagine the upcoming trial. "No doubt her lawyer's banking on the heat of passion angle. Also, the fact that she was drunk complicates matters." With her daddy's connections he wouldn't be surprised if Angela got off with a minimum sentence.

"Yeah, well, Harmon's trying his best to downplay Afia's role." Rudy sighed. "Apparently it's a media circus."

"I'll bet." A shooting involving a mob boss's daughter and a casino executive. Talk about a scandal. Even worse, if Rivelli's secret hit the newspapers Afia would never forgive him. Although with Giselle here that was probably the least of his worries. He shooed Gallow back, hopped off the table and winced.

"The doctor asked you to stay here until he returned."

"Screw that. Which room is Afia in?"

Shaking his head, the big man followed him into the bustling hall. "Three doors down on the left."

Heart pounding, Jake blew over the appropriate threshold ready to do battle with Giselle, but the only person in the room was Afia. Dressed in her sleeveless, baby-pink dress, her ankle wrapped with a thick bandage, she sat on the edge of the stark examining table looking small, fragile, and shell-shocked.

She met his gaze, and the room instantly buzzed with unspoken hostility.

Temples pulsing, he paused two feet away, unsure as to what her mother had told her. He ached to rush forward and pull her into his arms, but the aloof look in her eye told him to keep his distance. "Where's Giselle?"

"Downstairs, signing my discharge papers."

He worked his jaw. "Why? Is she taking you home with her?"

She didn't answer, just stared at him with those cool, cool eyes.

"How's your ankle?"

"It's just a sprain." She swiped a hunk of hair off her pale face and nodded toward his bandaged shoulder. "You could have been killed."

"It's nothing. A flesh wound." Her chilly demeanor sent shivers down his spine. He could feel her pulling away. Had Giselle made things even worse by getting her worked up with that jinxed shit? "You know you had nothing to do with this, right? Not in a superstitious way."

She scraped her teeth nervously over her lower lip. "I'm doing my best to believe that."

"You didn't know I was going to be there. Hell, *I* didn't know until ten minutes before. It was crazy coincidence, that's all."

She nodded.

Frustrated, he raked his good hand though his hair. "Can I come over there?"

"I'd rather you didn't."

Goddammit. Years of dealing with emotional, distraught women hadn't prepared him for this heartbreaking moment. Dredging up any sort of professional distance proved impossible. Because this was personal, and because he was the one who'd inflicted the pain. In this moment he was every bastard he'd ever cursed.

"I should have listened to you when you wanted us to investigate Angela," he said lamely, looking for a way to warm her up. He'd been stunned and angry with himself when Afia had told him the woman was a Falcone. He'd been suckered by a flimsy my-man-done-me-wrong song and a river of crocodile tears. "I should have conducted a background search. I should have trusted your instincts. They've been dead on all along."

"I disagree. I didn't suspect a thing where you were concerned." She started to stroke her wrist, the imaginary charms, and stopped herself. "The other night, you said you'd done some work for my godfather." She met his gaze—direct, steady, *cool*. "Was I one of those jobs?"

His heart pounded. Christ, how was he going to make this right? *Tell her the truth.* "It started out that way, yes."

"You manipulated me."

"Afia—"

"I thought you believed in me."

Her voice cracked and so did his heart. "I do believe in you."

"You claimed to be my friend."

"I *am* your friend. I will *always* be your friend." The next words scraped his throat raw. "No matter what."

She dropped her chin and shook her head. Her long hair tumbled forward, making Jake ache to smooth it from her troubled face. "You said friends don't steer friends wrong, yet you sure took me for a bum ride," she croaked. "Harmon paid you to look after me, to . . . to keep me out of trouble for two weeks."

"I gave the money back." He inched closer. "Quit the assignment days ago."

"I was an assignment?" Her head snapped up, eyes over-flowing. "Were you going to fire me at the end of next week, send me home to my mother? Was I a burden? An amusement? A fun lay while it lasted?"

His throat constricted. "How can you even ask me that, Afia?"

"How can I not?" A jerky swipe of the hand smeared tears and mascara across her cheeks. "How can I believe that anything we had was real?"

"Don't doubt us, baby." Close enough to touch her now, he cupped her face and dropped his mouth to hers. The kiss begged forgiveness with all the love in his heart. Easing back he gazed earnestly into her eyes. "This is as real as it gets."

She pushed him away. "I won't be coming back to your house tonight," she said with an icy politeness that set his teeth on edge.

He swallowed hard and backed toward the door, feeling as though he'd been dismissed, knowing he should go or risk making the situation worse. "Will you be coming back home at all?"

A piece of his world fell away with her whispered reply. "I don't know."

Chapter Twenty-Two

Taking control was one of the hardest things Afia had ever done in her life. Taking control meant having to push away the man she loved. It meant having to stand on her own two feet. No well-meaning guardians. No good luck talismans. Just herself and an army of positive affirmations.

When the odds are against you, trust your heart and seize the day.

Her heart told her that Jake's love was sincere. He was an honest, caring man who'd gotten tripped up by another well-meaning man, Harmon. *"Everything happens for a reason, baby. Sometimes you have to forgive the process, knowing that the outcome is for the best."* He'd been telling her that, though they'd met under unfortunate circumstances, they'd ultimately fallen in love. *"This is as real as it gets."* But that didn't change the fact that he and Harmon had manipulated her. Even Rudy had felt the need to maneuver life so that it didn't smack her in the face.

What they didn't understand is that she'd been surviving hard knocks since the day she was born, and she was ready to battle and conquer life's demons. She had to be happy on her own before she could be happy within a relationship.

So she'd let Jake walk out the door. She'd absorbed the hurt in order to draw strength.

In contrast, breaking off with her mother had been surprisingly easy. When Giselle had first stormed into her hospital room, Afia had allowed herself the brief illusion that she'd cut her honeymoon short because she was concerned about her daughter's well-being. But then Giselle had launched into a tirade about Glick and the missing fortune, and the truth had blasted Afia with the force of a ruinous hurricane. Her mother was a shallow, abusive, superstitious woman who wreaked havoc on her life. There was no making sense of her, and Afia no longer wanted to try. When Giselle had started to expound on the consequences of being born on Friday the thirteenth, Afia had simply tuned her out.

Power had surged through her veins when she'd asked her mother and her new, obnoxiously pompous husband to drop her at a hotel. "We make our own luck," she'd said as she'd hobbled out of the car on sheer will and crutches. "It's all in the mind, Mother. Positive thought over negative. I am currently removing all negative aspects from my life, and that includes you."

In the coming days, Afia focused on herself. She rented a small apartment and spent hours reading self-help books that Rudy had been more than happy to lend her. She adopted a kitten, enlisted in a driving school, and devoted more and more time to the daycare center. At night she dreamed of Jake and took solace in knowing, that someday, when the time was right, they'd be together.

She healed. She grew. She lived. And the weeks flew by . . .

* * *

Every hour seemed like a day. Every day like a week. Letting go was the hardest thing Jake had ever done in his life.

The bitch of it was in knowing that Afia didn't need him. She wasn't jinxed. She wasn't inept. She was a strong, intelligent woman, and she was doing just fine on her own.

They'd spoken on the phone. She'd called him the day after they'd parted at the hospital to resign from her job. "You were right," she'd said. "I don't have what it takes to be a private investigator." At first, he feared that she doubted her ability to learn the more specific ins and outs, but then he realized that what she lacked was the much-needed emotional distance that got him through most of his cases. She wasn't willing to become a detached cynic, and he loved her all the more for it.

Subsequent phone discussions had been like pouring alcohol on a gaping wound, but he'd endured because he was her friend. It hurt like hell because he wanted to be so much more, but he'd take what he could get. Afia was a uniquely special person, and he was blessed to have her in his life at all.

He knew through Gallow that she'd given half of her fortune away to charity while investing the rest for her future. She was tooling around in a compact car and working thirty hours a week at The Sea Serpent. Her drag show benefit had been a huge success. He'd attended, and his heart had pounded like a sonuvabitch as he'd hugged her and congratulated her at the after-show party. Resisting the urge to kiss her, to beg her to come home with him had been the limit of his endurance.

That had been two weeks ago, and he hadn't seen or talked to her since. He goddamned couldn't bear it.

He stared across the room at the landscape painting hanging on his office wall. The painting he and Afia had bid on and won. For a while he'd been able to draw comfort from the artist's colorful vision—a majestic sunrise casting warmth and rays of a promising new day over fertile farmland. A new day. A new beginning. But lately, the painting only conjured loneliness and pain.

Aside from Angela Falcone-Brannigan, who awaited trial and assured jail time, Jake seemed to be the only one suffering from the initial lie that had brought them all together. Afia had forgiven Harmon and Rudy. Rudy and Jean-Pierre were happily "attached." Afia was happily single. Giselle, the bitch, was free and clear of her "jinxed" daughter. Even Anthony Rivelli had attained a semi-happy ending. He'd escaped marriage to a violently jealous woman with his job and secret in tact. Jake and Afia had promised to forget about Iva Dream, and most everyone had skipped merrily into the sunset.

Zippety-freaking-do-dah.

The phone rang, jerking him out of a bout of self-pity. He rolled back his stiff shoulder, shoved aside a case report, and leaned across his desk to snatch the receiver. "Leeds Investigations."

"Get your ass over to the hospital now, big brother. I'm in labor."

✳ ✳ ✳

Joni's phone call took Afia by complete surprise. She'd been under the impression that the woman blamed her for Jake getting shot. Knowing her pregnancy to be a delicate one, she'd steered clear of the mother-to-be these past weeks, not wanting to be the cause of any undo agitation. That Joni wanted her there for the birth of her baby was astounding . . . and nerve-racking.

Jake would be there.

She hadn't seen him in two weeks—the longest, most miserable two weeks of her life. Though he'd kept his distance as of late, he'd proven to be a genuine friend, supportive and not at all controlling. But she ached for so much more. Why hadn't she been more aggressive? She'd waited for the right moment, and now it seemed as if she'd missed the boat. Apparently, he'd moved on. It was a bitter pill to swallow, but she told herself she wouldn't crumble when she saw him. She wouldn't make a scene by asking him why in the heck he'd given up so easily.

I am willing to be Jake's friend and nothing more. I am happy in my solitude.

Bull. She'd be happier with Jake.

Her heart pounded as she entered the hospital. The same hospital where she and Jake had parted ways. When she asked at the desk, the nurse told her that Mrs. McNichols had already given birth, and that she could proceed directly to the maternity ward.

A place of new beginnings.

Jake stood at the nursery window with his hand pressed

against the glass.

Afia's palms grew moist and heart fluttered. *Go to him. Say something, and for God's sake don't ramble or cry.* "Congratulations, Uncle," she said, coming up behind him, her pulse racing a billion miles a minute. *Do not crumble.* "Niece or nephew?"

"Niece. God help me." He clasped her hand and pulled her in beside him. "Kylie McNichols. Second one to the left. Isn't she cute?"

His touch ignited a firestorm in her heart. "Adorable," she said, past the huge lump in her throat. Kylie was tiny, pink, and sweet. Afia longed to have a baby just like her. With Jake. She glanced up at him, her heart swelling at the adoring expression on his face as he smiled down at his niece. *Be aggressive.* "I hope you don't mind that I'm here. Joni called me."

He squeezed her hand. "I'm glad that you're here. I think Joni probably called you because she's tired of hearing me bitch."

She swallowed hard. *Think positive.* "About?"

He turned to her then, traced a finger along her jaw. "About how much I miss you. These last two weeks have been hell." He quirked a pathetic smile. "And I let my sister know it."

Dizzy with relief, she placed her palm over his chest, reveling in the frantic beating of his heart. How could she have ever doubted the strength of their love? She connected with this man. "I missed you, too."

He swallowed hard. "You did?"

She nodded. "Very much." *Trust your heart, trust your heart . . .* "Jake?"

He tucked her hair behind her ears, his tender touch igniting a thousand dreams and desires. "What, baby?"

"You know that thing about us being friends, no matter if we live next door or across the country . . . I have to be honest. I'd like it a hell of a lot better if we lived together."

He dropped his forehead to hers and let out a slow, shaky breath. "I'm going to marry you, Afia."

"I know." She moistened her bottom lip, relished in the zap of the live wire, the zing of cupid's arrow. "And we're going to have three children. I didn't just scare you, did I?"

He smiled, those mesmerizing emerald eyes glassy with bone-deep affection. "You just made me very happy."

"Nothing and no one will ever come between us." She tunneled her fingers through his hair and sealed their love with a kiss.

She was the luckiest girl on the planet.

Charmed by Beth Ciotta

Coming December 2004

The Princess is in danger . . .

Beloved storyteller to hundreds of children, Lulu Ross champions non-violence. Just her luck, she is tiara over glass slippers for a man who carries a gun. Professional bodyguard Colin Murphy is s-e-x-y. Too bad he's delusional. Who would want to hurt Princess Charmingóa low-profile, goody-two-shoes who performs as a storybook character at children's birthday parties? Surely the sexy gifts from a secret admirer are meant for her sister, a bombshell wannabe action-star. Or are they?

Murphy is determined to protect Lulu . . .

whether she likes it or not. Perpetually cheerful and absurdly trusting, the locally famous kiddy-heroine refuses to believe she's in danger. Tipped off by the FBI, Murphy knows otherwise, but convincing Lulu that she's the fantasy target of a mobster's fixation is like trying to hang shades on the sun. Contending with a woman who favors bubblegum lip gloss and a pink poodle purse becomes an exercise in fascination and frustration for the world-weary protection specialist; almost as frustrating as resisting her whimsical charm.

N 093281504X Paranormal Vampire Fiction

Coming April 2004

Heart of Vengeance

A Historical Romance from Tracy Cooper-Posey

A woman in hiding.

In order to find her father's killer,
Helena of York is forced to play the most dangerous game of her
life. The Saxon noblewoman, now an outlaw, must adopt a false
identity and pose as a Norman in the courts and great halls of
Richard I's England. Should she be unmasked, her life will be forfeit. But Helena is willing to pay any price for her revenge.

A man shunned.

Stephen, Count of Dinan, once Richard's greatest friend
and most able knight, finds himself an outcast from the court
for reasons shrouded in mystery.
Now known as the "Black Baron," he finds himself
a friendless outcast in a glittering world he has come to despise.

Two dangerous destinies.

The only goal in Stephen's life is to restore his honor and once again
serve his king. The only desire in Helena's life is to kill the man
who destroyed her father and her future. Then the "Black Baron's"
suspicions draw him into Helena's web of deceit and, together, they
find themselves entangled in a greater conspiracy that threatens the
throne of England itself, and two embattled hearts that
have allowed themselves to be touched by love.

Available where you favorite books are sold.
ISBN 0-9743639-7-9